THE DEVIL'S KEY

KEVAN DALE

GET SORCERY OF THE STONY HEART
FOR FREE

To instantly receive the free novella *Sorcery of the Stony Heart* and the exclusive novelette *A Spark of Will* (unavailable anywhere else) sign up for Kevan's free Readers Club at kevandale.com

1
___

IN FLAMES AND STEAM

Gloucester, Massachusetts
July 1862

The lonesome road hooked down to rocks where the ocean pushed in, and there she was, the *Jack Ketch*, clear in the moonlight. The ship huddled sideways up against the shore, her masts tilted out towards the sea. She rode the swells, dark and silent, looking as lifeless as the scores of dead Irish who lined the beach not a mile off, washed up and plucked from the restless gray Atlantic. I hadn't found my blockhead of a brother nor my younger sisters among the rows of sodden corpses lined up on the sands of Gloucester, so I put my hopes on the ship itself as I made my way down the tide-slicked incline, all the while worrying how I would tell the rest of my family—especially my ma—that my great idea of bringing them over had been the death of them.

Every time the waves curled over and crashed in, the rocks echoed with the mournful sound of timbers scraping and heaving. A dozen men stood close by, devising a strategy for securing her, and half that again searching up and down the rocks with lanterns and torches. Pair of fellas hurried up towards the main circle of men, grunting under the weight of something draped across their shoulders.

"Good work, lads," one man with a lantern said. "Now get it up over the edge."

It was a cargo net, with coils of rope and hooks. They moved in up to their thighs in the water and swung those hooks around their heads, letting them go at the right moment to send them up onto the rail of the ship. By the time the lads shimmied to the top, they were little more than moonlit edges and silhouette as they pulled up the ropes tied to the big cargo net. The half circle of men moved forward, a few carrying lanterns out into the water.

I pulled the front of my cap low and made like I was just another one of the gang, waded in and climbed up that shifting net right behind a big bearded fella. The ship rocked back and forth, sometimes dangling the net back out over water and rocks, sometimes slamming it forward into the slick wood. It was a trick at the top to swing up and over the gunny, but not breaking my neck on the rocks below seemed a fine idea, so I managed it. Then I was up on the deck of her, the very deck where all those dead folks had trod their final weeks and days, my family included—and right away I knew there weren't nobody alive on board save me and the men who'd scrambled up the side. The stillness reached out and wrapped a cold hand on my heart as I walked the deck. Rails and ropes, black doorways and hatches, all deathly as a forsaken graveyard.

Everything was dry and neat—whatever else had happened, she hadn't foundered or capsized. Some of the men went to the starboard and looked down, only to come back shaking their heads. I looked up and could see her masts rising against the clutter of bright stars. The fellas with the lanterns headed to the back of the ship. I followed. As I passed the netting where we'd climbed up, a shadow reached out and took hold of my arm.

"And who are you, lad?" His voice was salt and sea spray, his shoulders hunched.

"Just having a look."

"You ain't with Paulie."

"And I'm betting that Paulie don't own her," I said.

"Does right now."

There was a fast whisper of steel and seven inches of blade caught the moonlight on its edge. He held it up with the tip pointing at my chest.

"I'm looking for my family," I said.

"Piss off, unless you want me to gut you right—" he said.

I didn't let him finish. I swung my left hand up and knocked the knife away. Quick as you'd like, I clocked his knife hand with a downward cut of my other fist, and came right back onto his face with my cocked elbow. The knife flew from his hand and clanged onto the deck. He staggered from the gunny, his nose busted good, blood pattering down in fat dollops. Didn't want him coming back at me, so I grimaced and punched him right in the back of the skull, sweeping his feet out from under him. He was out cold before he hit the deck. I looked around to see if anyone had noticed, but the rest of the men had already started down into the ship. I dragged him off behind the wheelhouse. Took a minute to scrounge up rope, then had him tied and gagged. My fingers shook, and the knuckles throbbed. Was never keen on using my fists, but I'd learned how to when it counted—and I wasn't quitting that ship until I'd put my eyes on every inch, Paulie or no Paulie.

I found the doorway leading down into the guts of her, the below decks, light and the muffle of low voices ahead. The 'tween deck stairs were narrow and steep and shadowed from even the faint shine from the moon. I reached the bottom. Behind me, the passageway ran back farther, heading into a little room with three pairs of portholes, a pair to a wall. The captain's cabin, and Paulie and his crew had already been through it. The small desk was shoved aside, drawers pulled out, papers spilled out over everything. I turned and moved along the narrow gangway towards the quarterdeck. I slowed down as I neared the lantern light.

"I don't like it, and I don't think we will," a voice said.

The next voice spoke with a rumble of anger. "You'll do it because I says so, and that's what we're here for. Keep moving."

"But Paulie," another voice, higher, said, "this doesn't make no sense."

"Do what I said."

"But it's in our way."

"Then move it, you lazy wharf rat."

Nice bunch of gentlemen. I hung back. Boots scuffled. Heard a scraping, something large being pushed across the rough flooring. Something of it gave me a chill. The lanterns shifted, and the light fell off and moved farther into the ship. Dipped my head through a low doorway and stepped into a hold. Some crates loaded with musty clothes had been pried open. Beyond them stood four coffins lined up next to each other. Remembered that morbid detail from my crossing: they were for those who died close in to shore; if you died farther out, all you got was a wrap of canvas and some rope, and into the drink you went, food for the sharks that followed the ship. The air held a stink of corpse, so I guessed that at least one coffin was occupied.

Closer to the other side of the hold, I found what the men had been shoving. It was big and made of stone—a rectangular box, standing waist high. Wide canvas straps tangled underneath it. Nearer to the wall of the hold, a cover of stone was on the floor. A wooden box sat inside the stone one. I pulled back. It stunk to high heaven like a rotten bog, with the bite of sulfur. I wrinkled up my nose and peered in. It was a coffin like the others, but longer. In the dim light, I could make out marks on the underside of it. Deep, long scratch marks, thousands of them, dug out near all the way through the wood of the lid. I wanted to step away from it, like I'd want to step away from a rotted body crawling with maggots. I yanked my hands from the edge of the stone box and wiped my hands on my pants. The rocking of the ship, the long wooden coffin with the scratches, the groaning of the timbers—my mouth went dry and my palms slick.

Crossed the rest of the hold, peering up the next passageway. Paulie and his crew were up that way, lantern light jerking this way and that, voices arguing, hatches banged open. Thought I'd have better luck looking for another way down belowdecks, into the berths meant for the frightened and seasick families, and away from that band of thieves. Turned and hurried out, staying in the shadows. As I neared the 'tween deck stairs, footsteps pounded across the hold. One of Paulie's men. Got ready to fight him, but he shoved into me, scrambling past into the dark passageway.

The ship listed more to the ocean side, a deep shudder rattling the hold. A sudden flash lit up the passageway on the far side, a split-moment before a gunshot. Two more followed, quick. Shouts burst out. The ruckus got louder up ahead, and I made the light of a fire, bigger than a lone lantern. Against that orange glow, a fella came tearing along the passageway.

I blocked his way. "What'd you find?"

"It got Bennie!" he said, his voice high and thick with a seacoast accent. "Come right out of the shadows and got him, took his head clean off. Its eyes smoldered."

It happened fast, a heavy clank of chains and a waft of foul air. A shadow rose behind the fella. That horrid bog stench hit me full-on. In a quick second, the fella was yanked back. His scream hit a high note only to be cut short with a thick snapping sound. For a heartbeat, the shadow turned and the feel of it was like nothing I'd ever held in my worst night terror.

"Come here."

The words hung in the air, low and somehow musical. Just hearing it was like having my ears rubbed with velvet. Maybe the inside of my skull, too. Gunshots sounded and a slug of lead ripped through the air a hand-width from my head to splinter the wooden wall behind me. The shape in front of me spun and charged the shooter, blocking out the light of the fire with a form that reached the top of the passage and still hunched, doubled over. I spotted the broken body on the floor, the one who I'd stopped.

I staggered back and bolted.

Reached the 'tween decks stairs and tore up them three at a time. On deck, I took in a heave of the night ocean air, wanting to get the putrid smell out of my nose. Another scream broke out where I'd come from, a voice high and wavery like a woman's. Now, I'd seen men fight like wild dogs, seen some knifed in the belly, seen fellas shot in the legs, the neck, the chest. But I'd never heard men scream like they screamed on the *Jack Ketch*. I sprinted across the dark deck and heaved myself over the gunny. Two men burst out of the gangway and tossed themselves over after me.

"What is it?" I said, not slowing even a notch.

Neither one spoke. Got to the bottom and splashed a few steps in the water as the ship towered over me, a black cliff. I got out of the surf and away from the ship. The other fellas fled into the darkness. Tall flames climbed up the back end of the *Jack Ketch* and the smoke from the burning timbers filled the wind. In the burning, the deck of her was plain to see. Something moved up there, a slouching figure backlit by the flames.

Lanterns came to the beach, strung out in the darkness from town, the news of the wreck having spread. I kept back, making my way up a rise that gave me a better view. From up there I could see the top of the ship. Fire leapt out of the stern and the quarter decks in the middle, taking every rope and bit of rigging. One mast was soon on fire and the sail rippled and tossed off bright orange embers on the wind. The men from the town got close, but couldn't do much but watch as the flames stretched high into the night sky, lighting up the beach and waves as the ship rocked on the surf. The two back masts came crashing down in a fiery tumble and something let go on the ocean side of her. She rolled off sideways, making a terrible hiss as the blazing deck slid into the ocean. In flames and steam, the sea took her. Not another soul came off. Not Paulie, not a one of his men. Not the hulking shadow who'd spoken.

Not my family.

2

———

THE FACES OF THE DEAD

Reached the center of Gloucester a short time later. People milled about on the gaslit streets, talk of the wreck and her burning passing quickly on to those who hadn't been there. The first of the big drays from the beach where the victims of the *Jack Ketch* had washed up passed by in a clatter of hooves, bodies stacked in it, shadows from the street-lamps draped across the faces of the dead. I watched as it faded down the dark street. Lanterns moved along the stony beach where the bodies were being loaded. Heard one fella say they were taking them to one of the city's ice-houses, adding that if they could keep a few dozen tons of cod and swordfish and halibut fresh each day of the year, then one hundred and twenty-one bodies would be a snap. I turned away, haunted by the images of bodies weighted down with tattered clothes, skin blanched by the chill Atlantic.

I was about to fetch my wagon and team and start the heart-broken ride back to Lawrence when a commotion down the street caught my ear. A crowd gathered outside a sea-washed box of a tavern called Pickett House. Lads ran to and fro, and one of them called to his mates about survivors. I pushed through the crowd. The Pickett House's door was open and light and noise spilled out. Front room had a low ceiling, smoke hanging in a fog over a crowd of fishermen, men with dark eyes and wind-burnished skin, faces red with drink. In the center of the big room, a group of people huddled around the hearth, shivering in spite of the heat. Maybe a dozen of them, looking miserable for the wear, some holding tin bowls of stew, others masonry jugs. I scanned their faces—and my heart leapt a turn and a half: a lass sat on a crate, her arms wrapped around two younger girls, all three of them barefoot, their clothing damp. The young ones were Careys at a glance, my sisters—hair shot through with copper, skin pale as the inside of a wheel of cheese, freckles scattered across their faces and arms, bright hazel eyes that didn't miss a thing. The despair I'd wound up—a spring brought to snapping—loosened and relief washed in.

"Nell! Rose!" I called out. I shouldered my way between folks until I reached them. Eyes all around watched us, taking in the rare sight of death being cheated out of his latest black strike. I swept the girls up into my arms. Nell was so young as to have had no real memory of the last time she saw me in Ireland; Rose hadn't even been born yet—but they grabbed me anyways, and I felt the life of them in their skin. Held onto them like a drowning man.

"Finn Carey?" the lass said. She had a familiar look, but I couldn't place her. She stood. "I'm Maggie. Maggie Lane. From Kildalkey."

Now, I remembered the Lanes from the village I came from, deep in County Meath. Big family. Couple of them were smiths; lot of women, too.

"You saved them?" I said.

"Best I could, yes."

"Jesus, thank God. How'd you do it?"

"I swam, kept swimming. Held them tight until I thought I couldn't. Skiff plucked us out."

"What about my brother Liam?"

She shook her head.

"You're sure?"

"He stayed—him and a few others. My brother Arthur. They tried to stop it. None of them made it off the ship."

People started in on her, pressing in on us, hurling questions at Maggie and the other survivors. Rose looked around and started bawling. Maggie reached over and lifted the five-year-old from my arms, went to work soothing her.

"Come on," I said, grabbing Nell by the hand. "Let's get the girls out of here."

I led them through the tavern, suggesting none too politely to people to let us pass. We pushed through the doors and into the night. Sea air filled our noses as I took the lasses to the stable yard I'd hitched the wagon and team in for two bits. Moonlight skimmed the cobbles, shone off the windows of the captains' houses that dotted the heights. The horses nickered.

"They're yours?" Maggie said.

"Aye," I said. "And they're greedy ones, too. Working to eat me out of hearth and home. Such as I have."

Nell and Rose looked at the horses. I lifted them both up onto the wagon, then turned to Maggie.

"Well," I said. "Welcome to America, Miss Lane. Seems as though no one from Kildalkey can get here any way but the hard way—and then there's what you did. I don't know how I can thank you. You saved what's closest to my heart when you saved these gals."

"Didn't think we'd live to see it."

"You've family waiting for you? I'll drive you there myself. A thousand miles wouldn't be too far after what you've done—and I'll still owe you."

She glanced out to the dark street, then back at me. Took a deep breath that might've had tears trying to break it up. She sniffed them away, rubbed her nose, and put a tight smile on her mouth. "Was just Arthur and me," she said. "He was handling everything. Had the money. We don't have family here."

"None?"

"None."

I nodded. "Well then—it's as good as if you do, with us. I've room enough. I can get you good work at a decent wage. And speaking as someone who set foot in America without knowing a soul or having even a penny to his name—though I'll admit to not swimming the last mile, as you did—I'd be more than glad to spare you the troubles I went through getting settled."

"Stay with us," Nell said, from the back of the wagon. She and Rose had their hands on the sideboards, watching.

"Stay," Rose echoed.

"I don't want to be a hardship," Maggie said.

"Hardship and I have had more than a few tussles over the years," I said. "But we've come to an understanding—and hardship has grudgingly come to live with the fact that I'm stubborn enough to win out every time. You come with us. Couldn't think of a better way to thank you, Miss Lane."

She hesitated.

"Come on," I said, holding out a hand to help her up into the wagon. "You more than did right by yourself. And the girls. Let me return the favor—one Kildalkian to another."

"I won't be a bother?"

"Course you won't," I said. She nodded and took my hand. I helped her up, then went around the far side, checked the harnesses, and climbed up onto the driver's bench. Reined the horses out of the stable. Even with the moon up, the air pressed in, thick and humid. Got the team out onto the street and headed south, the harbor a dark void off to our left, the murmur of the surf drifting up. None of them said anything and I let them keep their silence. We cleared the edge of the town, leaving the lights behind us and nothing but moonlight to show me the road, and the turn that would bring us to Lawrence come morning. Fields passed. Stands of maple and elm. The clink and steps of the team filled our ears.

"Some dry blankets in the back," I said. "You can rest."

"I'm fine."

She shifted and tugged at her dress. Looking at her, her face rang a bell—though of her, or of the Lanes in general, I couldn't say. If I'd seen her back in Kildalkey, she'd still have been young; ten, maybe twelve years old. And now she stood taller and had filled out well in the chest, not that I sat there staring at them.

"I'll dry off," she said, "and never so much as dip a toe in the bloody ocean, ever again. Don't think I'll even look kindly at a puddle."

I held my questions back. Having grown up around Irish women, I never knew one that could make way for silence overly long. When Maggie spoke soon after, it was with a quiet voice.

"Something was wrong with that ship, from the first, and that's the truth," she said. "I felt it as soon as I saw the masts from the quay—but I feel things like that, always have. Wasn't just me though. I don't think there was a soul aboard who didn't feel it soon as Ireland slipped out past view, and it only got worse the farther we got."

I believed that in a way I wouldn't have before setting foot on the *Jack Ketch*.

"Talk got on about it being a cursed ship. An old slaver, spirits of the stolen prowling the holds and galleys. Tale made the rounds that the haunts of all the sailors that'd drowned had gotten jealous of us and wanted to drag us all down into the deep, keep us for new company."

"Boat full of Irish is a boat full of tales," I said.

"Thought so, at first. But there was something wrong. A chill for no reason. Darkness comes, or belowdeck, the shadows moving strange. Even the sounds of the waves rushing along the hull took on a forlorn tone. People were having trouble sleeping, plenty of them waking up screaming. Nightmares."

She looked off toward the dark ocean.

"Didn't sleep more than an hour a night. It was terrible. Kept my thoughts to myself, even with Arthur on me about what was wrong. He knew something was bothering me. And then when we were two days out, all the rats came up from the holds. Caused mayhem, that—until they hurled themselves through the scuppers and into the ocean. Hundreds of them. Left a trail behind the ship until they drowned."

We passed in and out of moonlight and tree shadows. She fanned the front of her dress, trying to work the damp out.

"And don't you think I'm nothing but a hysterical girl. I know what I felt—and you should've seen the men on the ship. Setting guard. Looking around belowdecks. Turning themselves into a regular little army."

"The crew had nothing to say about it?" I said.

"A dozen of the oldest or drunkest sailors on the Atlantic. Wasn't much of a ship. Only one passenger didn't seem to mind. In fact, he seemed pleased with the whole affair, smiling like a big old tomcat watching a bird with a broken wing trying to hop away. Older fella, bald, taller'n you by a good head."

I stood a touch over six feet.

"Slav, or a Pole. Flashed a smile that tightened my guts. His eyes were worse. Like coal—except coal that wanted to see your skin peeled off. Moment I saw him, I felt a touch of the grave on my heart. And about a week ago, your brother spotted him leaning over, talking with the girls. Ran over in a heartbeat, chest puffed out, rolling up his sleeves to start throwing fists, telling this fella that if he so much as looked at the girls again, he'd be swimming the rest of the way and wondering how deep all his teeth had sunk."

"Sounds like Liam."

"Right thing to do. And don't forget, weeks went by on that rotten ship, everyone more and more convinced that we'd never see America, nor anywhere else, ever again. But it didn't matter to the fella. He just nodded his head, as if Liam had just commented on how lovely the ocean looked. Turned away.

"But Liam hadn't been far off, even though he never laid a finger on him, and no matter how much that fella smiled. That night a storm blew up. Shrieking wind tearing off the tops of waves, the ship crashing down from one trough to another, masts creaking. Waves higher than hills. Don't think there was one of us who didn't try making our peace with Jesus and Mary as we got ready to drown. Word was—later—that he'd been going through the galleys and holds, asking around after the girls."

"In the middle of a gale?" I said.

"That's right. Soaking wet, pushing his way right through knots of the praying and the sick. Got sent up out of one by a group of men who wouldn't put up with him. Last any of the passengers saw him. Crewman next morn said he'd seen him get swept overboard by a wave that swamped half the deck under four feet. Pulled right into the dark sea."

"Why the girls?"

"Don't know. Don't want to know. We'd spent a fair amount of time together, being the only ones from Kildalkey, and me knowing them since they were both in nappies. I kept them distracted from everything about that black crossing, much as I could. They're both lovely."

We crossed a lone bridge, the planks knocking beneath the horses, the sound of it echoing up from the river passing black beneath. I twisted and looked at the girls, curled up and sleeping in a blanketed tangle.

"The storm died off the next afternoon," Maggie went on. "The edges of it tattering away behind us, the sun going down ahead of us. We'd made it, so we thought—because beneath the sunset was our first glimpse of America, the light skimming the tops of trees, stretching all up and down the horizon. Captain and crew were abuzz, figuring out how far the storm'd blown us off course from Boston."

The moon matched our pace through the pine.

"But soon as the day faded, it started," she said. "Air around us changed, like that. The promise we'd held at the sight of America soured, along with the hope that we'd made it. Malice, strong as smoke, came from belowdeck. No one knew what to make of it. Then, pounding. Screams. Something tore the ship apart.

"Folks were getting killed. Couple of them came sprinting up out from below, hurled themselves right over the rails into the ocean. That set everyone to panicking even more. Some started for the two lifeboats, but one of them broke off and hung from one line."

"What'd Liam do?" I said.

"He and Arthur put me and the girls near the end of the ship, then gathered a dozen of the strongest men they'd met on the crossing, fashioned what weapons they could, and they went down belowdeck. Neither would listen—I was telling them, begging them, not to do it."

"Not much of a listener when he gets his blood up," I said.

"And Arthur was cut from the same cloth. Last I saw of them, Finn. Once they got down below, it was a ruckus like I'd never heard."

"The crew?"

"Took the other lifeboat, they did, fighting people off with oars and guns. We watched them go and then were left on the ship. Well over a hundred of us, on that deck. Shouted curses after the crew, but then grew quiet. Noises from below'd stopped. Came from up near the back of the ship—a shape."

"Stop talking. Don't ever talk!" Nell shouted, right between our shoulders. I nearly had to add "need clean trousers" to my list of worries at that.

"Nell, she was just—"

"I know what she was doing. She shouldn't. Can't. I don't never want to hear about it again. Not for a hunnerd years!" Nell shouted. Lass shook, she was so worked up. Held on to the lip of the wagon like she'd probably hung on to the rail of the ship.

"It's all right," I said. "We won't talk about it anymore."

"And not later. Not ever."

Maggie shushed her and told her not to wake Rose. In truth, I put the pieces together well enough, having seen what I had.

"Fair enough," I said. "We're done, and it's behind us. The whole sorry mess. You get some sleep, Nell. You're safe, I'll see to that."

Nell seemed satisfied enough by my word, though she gave us both a pointed look before turning back into the wagon and curling off to sleep again. Maggie rode along in silence for another half hour. When she nodded off, I urged her to sleep, so she climbed over the bench to where the girls were, patting my shoulder without a word. Left me with my thoughts as the moon rode the whirl of starry sky through the rest of that long night. My mind kept prodding and poking at the death of the *Jack Ketch*: the coffin with the scratches, the shape that'd loomed up, stinking of bog-rot. The brightest stars hung low to the east, over the dark expanse of ocean disappearing behind us.

3
———

CANTUS DE DAMNABILIS I

Puhitse Abbey, Latvia
Nine years earlier
The prisoner, exiled, watched from the edge of the forest as daylight retreated to embers. Stone walls, wooden lintels, masonry roof fading into shadow, the deepening sunlight climbing until it brightened only the highest stone of the chimneys. Then night.

A cold wind stirred the trees and twisted off the wood-smoke from the chimneys. The prisoner raised his head. He left the shadows of the wood and crept to the walls. From window to window he went. Candlelight. Spare benches. He found a doorway that led through a small goat yard. The animals bleated and trampled one another to get away. He waved a hand and they dropped over, dead.

He entered the main building through an archway. Up ahead, he heard the sounds of life, of prayers sung in grotesque voices. He ignored them. Down. He needed to go down. He sensed it—a pull that drew him. At the end of a flagstone corridor, he stopped. The doorway was narrow. On either side, wards that shone to him with a hateful light that made his bones cry out. He set his jaw and took them down, ignoring the lightning that pulsed up his arms at their touch, ignoring the sizzle of flesh. With a hardness borne of his imprisonment, he withstood the pain and snapped them to pieces, then tossed them to the floor.

Stone steps brought him into the dank cellars where a chill came off of the walls. Low arches, barrels, crates of stored goods. An oil lamp with decades of soot printed on the wall over its glass burned weak. Beyond, another stone passage with light at the end.

The prisoner slowed. He felt the thrumming of blood, the sweet contractions of a living heart; behind it, the air of his home that hung ever so faintly in the spark that kept it moving. He peered around the corner. His eyes danced.

A holy woman in a chair by another oil lamp. Asleep. Her foolish mouth hung open, her wrinkled face stretched in a repose not unlike a corpse. Behind where she sat, three alcoves, one large, two small.

The prisoner gaped.

He approached the alcoves. In the dim light, he saw that the largest of the openings was lined with symbols, row upon row of crosses intermingled with drawings of pathetic saints with glowing halos behind their heads. But the bones drew his eye. Dull-lustered by centuries, they were stacked in such a manner as to resemble the hated cross itself. The longest of the bones was half as long as the woman whose snores filled the chamber.

He looked up to the alcove above, his thoughts blackening. In the weak lantern light, in shadow, sat the skull of the one he'd admired more than heaven itself. Grime and mold befouled it. The prisoner reached a thin hand out, touched the front, placing his palm on the forehead of his friend. After all he'd been through, it was still as bright in his mind as his first days. He lifted the skull from the opening, ignoring the images that burned his eyes, that shook his starved muscles. He held the skull and faced it.

"My brother."

At the sound of his voice, the holy woman closed her mouth and worked her lips, opening her eyes. For a moment, she stared at him quizzically—wondering whether she was dreaming, perhaps. He looked at her.

"A dream, young sister. Yes. Every moment you slept or woke or prayed near my magnificent brother. A dream."

Her eyes widened. Her mouth opened, but before she could yell out he smashed the skull against her head with both hands. The force was great enough to both shatter the front of her own skull and the chair beneath her. Not enough. He swung the skull by one twisted horn, driving the other horn deep into the holy woman's neck. Speared such, her blood spilled in ribbons.

"Now sleep," he said in his ancient tongue.

He shoved her into the alcove that had held the skull, yanking the horn from her. He cradled the skull, then kissed it and placed it with the bones before turning to the third alcove. This one had a door of lead panes and brass. He drove his fist through the glass, then ripped the brass free, sending it to clang on the stones.

On a dusty pillow, laced beneath cobwebs, was the key.

The prisoner's anguish, the exhaustion, the fury, the despair—all of it evaporated. He reached in. Lifted it. The weight of it filled his hand. From up above, carrying down the stairs to the cellars, the peal of bells began. The sound of them brought a smile to his face.

Let them ring, he thought. This was his moment. He turned once more to the remains of his brother and bowed. Then, off to the stairs.

The bells continued to peal as the slaughter began.

4

———

MISTER CAREY

"Now just be sure to stay busy," I said. "You run out of something, ask for more. Don't be gabbing much, either. First couple of months is when you'll earn—or lose—the most respect, and what you get'll follow you around a long time. So make it good."

Lawrence was waking as I led Maggie and Nell through the streets to their first day of work. I'd gotten them both jobs as spare hands at the Everett Mill. Around us, the city stirred: icemen getting a start on the heat, night-pails emptied, smell of bread frying in grease riding the breeze, men setting up carts with apples and beer and sausage. Clothing hung from ropes between tenements, from between row houses, from the company housing, all of it catching the soot that hung in the air six days a week.

Nell and Maggie half-listened, both taken away by the scene. Soon enough, the Everett rose before us, the rising sun on ninety windows, each pane holding a glint. I pointed out the clock on the side.

"The bells will ring at seven. Be inside before it does, every day. You do that much, and trust me—you'll stand out."

Dropped Nell off first, sorting scraps on the second floor, among the rag and burr pickers. She looked nervous. I spoke a few words to the floor boss, then knelt before her.

"You'll do fine. Mr. Hambry here runs a nice crew. And you're a Carey, so you'll fit right in. You're good?"

Nell nodded.

"Then I'll see you at lunch," I said.

"Thank you, Mr. Carey," Hambry said.

"And you, Mr. Hambry."

Looked back a couple of times as Maggie and I headed to the stairs. Nell followed Hambry and a few other young girls as he brought them around the dozens of bins, and the stacks of fabric piled up. We reached the stairs and started up. Folks were still coming in the doors from outside, it being seven.

"Mister Carey?" Maggie said.

"That's right."

"Ain't that something."

"Fitting, is what it is."

"I'm impressed."

"That would make you one of many, Miss Lane—if you don't mind the bold truth. It's how I got to be the city's first Irish assistant floor boss."

She swatted me on the shoulder, easy. "You aren't."

"Oh, I am. And soon, I'll be the city's first Irish floor boss. And after that, the city's first Irish mill foreman."

She looked me over as we climbed the stairs and saw that people all said good morning to me.

Had a job for her on the fourth, starting as a spare hand among the looms and jennies that handled the worsting, doubling, and spinning for the trousers and blue jackets for the Union Army. Windows looked out over the city. Billy Devon was the floor boss, and decent enough to the Irish who worked for him. I left Maggie with him and took the stairs—hot already, a heat I knew as well as I knew every creak and worn groove on the wide maple stair runners—to the fifth, which I ran.

Did a quick walk around, checking in with the men who turned leather into shoes, the machinists who kept the gear running, the runners, the department heads. Once I sorted the issues of the morn, I headed to the half-office near the stairs.

Young Theo McCarty worked the bench next to it, a wiry lad who couldn't keep still for half a minute, nor keep a thought from passing his lips. Lot of the men up on the fifth couldn't put up with his stream of chatter that started at seven and went near straight through to the other seven, which is why I'd finally moved his bench over to where I was, away from the others. Busy as I was six days of the week, I came to learn every last thing about: his ma and sisters; the Everett's foreman Mac, who was (to Theo's pure horror) sweet on his widowed ma; the dozen or so lasses he fancied; his thinking on the war, the mill, the river, the church, the family that owned the mill, the sky, his feet, his old village of Devonvale, General MacClellan, and darned near anything else under the sun he'd ever clapped his eyes on. I rarely minded—while he more than not acted half of his eighteen years, he could also drop a joke or a wicked imitation of someone I'd still laugh about a month later.

Theo had his face pinched tight.

"You need to use the privy?" I said.

He stepped aside and pointed at his work bench. Bunch of leather for mid-soles was cut up and great gouges marred the wood of the bench. Someone had taken a knife to his work area, hacking away at anything he'd left out. Couple of letters scratched into the wood read: m-o-n-y. I looked around at the nearby benches. Men settled in for the day, jawing and sharpening their tools. Didn't see no one giving Theo the evil eye.

"Fitzgerald do this?" I said.

Theo'd been tussling with a certain Tommy Fitzgerald and

his brothers, nasty pieces of work who thought the world owed them notably more than they deserved.

"Keeps saying old Avery owed him a hundred dollars before he skipped out on my ma last spring."

"Theo, you know we won't stand for no feud. Especially not when property of the company gets into it."

"I know it. Not like I did it myself."

"Fair enough," I said. "Clean it up and do what you can to make sure it don't happen again."

"Not going to let anyone kick me around."

"And that's half your problem right there. Those Fitzgerald boys are about as lazy as they are dumb, and they're twice as mean as both put together—so you'd best be careful."

I rapped my knuckles onto his bench and he nodded, then I got drawn to a problem with one of the big standing presses that two company mechanics gathered around, grease already smearing their sleeves and the day just started.

COUPLE OF HOURS later I had to go to the first floor to find out why we'd run short of uppers. As I left the stairs, I spotted Theo's friend Tommy Fitzgerald. His right eye was nasty swollen and the white part was angry red. He wore a stained leather apron. Tried to sidestep me after giving me a snotty look—I didn't let him, stepped right in front of him, bringing him up short.

"Morning, Tommy," I said.

"What's this?" Jutted his chin out at me like it was his mill, looking at me with lids half-closed.

"This is the floor boss of the fifth telling you that I get wind of you up there getting careless with company property again, you'll be out of work alongside the rest of your family."

"Got no proof."

"Proof of what, Tommy?"

Nodded his head, nasty smile on his face. "That's right. You think you're so much better'n the rest of us."

"I only work harder. In addition to being a handsome gentleman."

"You go ahead and lord it up all you want—but you ain't always here, are you?"

"A cleverer man than myself might think that's a threat you're making," I said.

"Fancy house in the Plains, little horse team. Well, you ain't the mayor yet. Fact, you ain't nothing but another Irishman on the make."

"Wonder what that makes you." I took a step closer, our noses almost touching. "You lay a finger on Theo, you set foot on the fifth, you so much as look at the Plains, and I'll see you tossed out of here."

"You wouldn't want to make that mistake."

"So you'd care to find out?"

"I don't work for you."

"And I can get you fired, just the same."

"Got work to do."

He tried to walk by me. I didn't budge. He knocked into me with his shoulder, then swung his arms wide, letting me get a good look at the knife he wore inside his leather apron. Tannery knife, sharp enough to skin a deer. Held his apron aside for my benefit.

"What—this? This here's property of the company of the same type you're on about, Mr. Carey?" He pulled the knife out and stepped in close at me. "Try to be safe, but there are accidents."

"Put it away. Now."

"Sharp as hell, too."

I had to step back to avoid getting nicked. He smiled. That was a mistake. I reached out before he was expecting it and grabbed the knife hand, right on the wrist, in a grip tight as I could manage, which held the strength of seven years hard mill work. Twisted, hard, and stepped to the side, which pulled his arm straight and locked it cruelly. The knife dropped to the floor and stuck in, blade-first. He cried out—but I didn't let him go far with that before I rolled his arm hard, pinning it up between his shoulder blades and running him forward into the wall. He grunted. His breath stank of tobacco, onions, and decaying teeth.

"You just cost yourself your job," I said, not letting him budge. "And if you even spare a second thought about Theo or me again, you'll cost yourself and your family jobs at any mill in the city. I'll see to that. You understand?"

He tried to wrestle free, but I leaned in onto his arm until he had no choice but to give in, the tendons of his arm stretched to tearing. I hadn't been raised a fighting Carey for nothing.

Was that moment that Mac Harriman, foreman of the entire Everett, happened around the corner, leading a group of men not in the dress of mill workers. Collars, waistcoats, beards and thick sideburns. Knew who they were: scientists and engineers hired by Mr. Abbot Winthrop to improve the workings of the mill. Spending half a month looking at every step in our process. Mac's eyes landed on the knife and swept over me and my friend Tommy Fitzgerald. I let Fitzgerald go, leaving him to flex the wrist and elbow of his knife hand where I'd pinned him.

"Whose is that?" Mac said. Couple of the scientists exchanged glances and frowned. More footsteps followed, and the Honorable Hiram F. Oliver—Mayor of Lawrence—came into the hallway, red in the face, wiping sweat with a kerchief, talking with a tall fellow in a long coat. He took the scene in within a pair of seconds and called the scientists over to observe something outside the big windows. Mac broke off and came over.

"Assigned to this fine gentleman right here, Mac," I said. "Offered to show me just how sharp it is."

"Oh, he did?" Mac said. Fitzgerald said nothing, nor did he

move to gather up the knife. He straightened up and pretended like his arm didn't hurt. It hurt plenty though.

"Sharp enough. Problem is—he's clumsy with it. Waves it at assistant floor bosses. Cuts up company property with it."

"That's a dirty lie." Fitzgerald said.

"And I'm afraid we're going to have to let him go," I said.

Mac nodded. I turned back to Fitzgerald.

"You're through here; give me that apron."

Fitzgerald glared at me and Mac, but he took off his apron anyhow, let it drop to the ground, ignoring my outstretched hand. Mac and I walked him to the door. The scientists watched it as though it were part of some exhibit. Mayor raised his voice and led the company off to the stairs. We watched Fitzgerald start off across the mill yard, spitting and cursing.

"Have to be careful with that one," Mac said.

"He's nothing but a thug."

"From a family of them, and very much the reason Mr. Winthrop is still not sure that hiring so many Irish is good business. Talk about something like that won't make that any easier."

"One bad egg. It's over."

"Better be. You all right?"

"All right now."

We stood there until Fitzgerald crossed onto the bridge that spanned the north canal. Last time anyone at the Everett saw him alive.

5
____

THE IRISH IN ME

"You think these fine folks have to wrestle their young ones clean?" Maggie said.

Nell and Rose wore patched dresses, scrubbed up clean and none too happy for it. We walked across the great lawn of Mr. Abbot Winthrop's house, an enormous affair with a high gambrel roof and eaves, a widow's walk on the top, a house built from the fortunes of the mills, bigger than any building—including the church—back in Kildalkey where we'd grown up. The sun shone on the windows and rails and on a weathered brass arrow that pointed into the wind. Men and women in Sunday dress finer than ours talked in small groups between the high hedges that bordered the property. Children played about, hair neat, hems and cuffs without a fray on them.

"I'd imagine that they leave most of their wrestling to the servants," I said.

"That's our problem," she said. She pushed a lock of her hair back with an exaggerated sweep and pursed her lips. "Not enough domestic help."

Struck me I was looking at a perfect picture of what America was, to us: a lifetime of living in crowded rooms in sad little villages across the ocean, and one fine day you might find your-self on the grounds of a lovely mansion. Long tables with linen cloths stretched along a cobbled patio, piled high with a feast of roasted meats, pies, fancy bits of cake, and any number of nibbles. Glasses of wine stood in parade like General Halleck's Army of the Potomac. Nell bolted over and shoved candied breads into her mouth as though she hadn't eaten in a month.

"Nell."

She looked over at me and crammed another bit into her mouth.

"Want some," Rose said.

"Get a bite for your sister, do it neatly, use your fingers—not your entire hand—and try not to act like a heathen," I said.

"Carey. There you are," a voice from behind said.

Mac Harriman came over. Wore a hard felt derby hat and a suit with a collar. I'd never seen him in anything but his work clothes and suspenders. I told Maggie to keep an eye on the girls and went off with Mac.

"Don't have a suit, Mac," I said.

"It's fine. Neat enough."

"Didn't realize there'd be so many rich folk."

"Say hello to him and his missus, then you can enjoy yourself."

"What should I say?"

"Just don't talk about work. He hates it when folk do that on a Sunday."

"Do I introduce him to my family?"

"Not unless he asks."

We strolled over to a white gazebo that stood ringed with fragrant rose bushes. Bees lumbered from bloom to bloom in the warm air. Cigar smoke drifted. There stood Mr. Abbot Winthrop, the richest man in Lawrence, one of the richest in all of Massachusetts, and a man who sent my pulse to racing with admiration. He chuckled with two other men, one of whom I recognized as being part of the mayor's office. Mac brought me to stand next to him while he waited for a decent break in their conversation. I noticed that Winthrop's kerchief had the letters ALW embroidered into the corner. He turned to Mac.

"Mr. Harriman. I see you've made it."

"Kind of you to invite me, sir," Mac said and nodded in my direction. "You remember Mr. Carey, floor boss on the fifth."

Winthrop turned to me. He waddled forward—no small man was he—his red face shining bright beneath his white brows and whiskers, and extended his hand.

"Carey," he said. "Of course. Welcome."

I shook his hand. I couldn't read from his eyes if he actually remembered me or not, having only been introduced to me once in passing.

"Thank you, Mr. Winthrop. You've a fine house."

"Make yourself at home. Did you bring your family?"

"I did, sir. Sisters. And their nanny. Arrived from Ireland last week, sir."

As the words tumbled out of my mouth, I noticed that I'd turned Maggie into a nanny without her knowing it—thinking Winthrop wouldn't think well of an unmarried young man living with an unmarried young lady, regardless of circumstance. My accent sounded heavy in my ears.

"Married?"

"Unshackled, sir."

"Well, cherish your freedom before they measure your wrists, lad." The men laughed. Winthrop turned to the others and cocked his thumb at me. "My first Irish assistant floor boss. Anywhere in the city. How many years have you been with us, Mr. Carey?"

"Seven and a half, sir."

"Seven and a half. Tell them how much I paid you at first."

He remembered me.

"That would be nothing but an opportunity, sir. For which I'm still grateful."

Winthrop smiled. "Worked for nothing for half a year. Told Mac here that he'd do it for free, and if he didn't convince him he wasn't the best worker in the mill, not a cent would he earn for it. That right?"

The men watched me.

"To a word, sir."

Mac clapped me on the shoulder. "Nothing but a skinny lad, not much more than twelve years old, but he carried boxes of shoe leather up and down the stairs from the first to the fifth, twelve hours a day—and a bloody hot spring and summer it was."

"So that's the secret to not getting fat," Winthrop said to more laughter.

"But never once did he complain," Mac continued, "and always asked for more. Now, he's my right hand. Knows the mill top to bottom—there isn't a spindle, mule, loom, card grinder, warping mill, spooler, winder, or reel he hasn't spent time on."

Winthrop opened his jacket and pulled out a cigar. He snipped off the end and handed it to me. "Carey. Now that's an English name."

I nodded. "From some time back, sir. As the family lore has it, the Careys were from England, but left for Ireland at about the time that various other Careys were having their heads rather unfortunately removed from their necks in the wars for the crown."

"Well, that English certainly runs strong in you, Mr. Carey. Now, please enjoy yourself this afternoon."

I thanked him for the cigar, and headed off, glad for not having made a blundering fool of myself, and honored that Mr. Winthrop felt confident that the English in me was strong enough to make sure that the Irish in me wouldn't get drunk and throw up into his fancy crystal punchbowl.

. . .

REST of the day went fair enough. Caught Nell trying to lift a couple of silver spoons and a pewter napkin holder and got them back before anyone noticed. The lass gave me a blue storm of excuses. Told her to zip it and to behave as though she were having tea with the Queen of England. Child needed civilizing, that much was clear.

Later that evening, I sat out in the carriage house's loft door that looked out over the back alleyway and sniffed at the cigar that Mr. Winthrop had given me. Lantern light shone in the nearby houses and the gas streetlamp glow traced the cornices and ledges of the mills ten blocks on. The smell of the river was thick in the air. I flipped a wooden match against a rough board and cupped the flame, drawing it into the leaf, filling my nose with the aroma of it. I puffed on the cigar, seeing it all before me. Winthrop'd made a fortune. No reason I couldn't make one, too —and then he, along with everyone else, would see it wasn't just English running strong in me.

6

I KNOW KILLERS

Next morn, we headed to the mill. Sunlight was heavy and cut angles into the thick air over the canals. Everywhere you looked, it was brick: the mills, the chimneys, the sidewalks; all ruddy in the summer light, reflecting into the air itself. Nell was quiet and polite, both states sitting unnatural on her. Maggie wore her hair back in a long auburn braid. Waiting for some drays to pass along Essex Street, Nell turned.

"I want to talk with Liam," she said.

Couldn't do nothing but put an arm around her narrow shoulders. "I know you do. We all miss him."

"But I want to talk with him."

"Well, that's not how it works, Nell. Once a person is gone, they're not available for talking."

"Beyond the grave. Like Maggie does."

I looked over at Maggie. She shook her head at Nell.

"Sorry," she said. "I meant nothing to come out like that."

"A séance. And peep-stones. Or ghost-writing," Nell said. "I want to try all of it."

We crossed the street, joining the crowds headed to the mills. Maggie held Nell's hand until we reached the other side.

"They're things my mother taught me," Maggie said.

"Are you serious, now?" I said.

"My grandmother, women all the way back in my family have it. It's a second sight. Sometimes we can feel the dead. See them. Talk to them."

"Don't imagine they'd be much in the way of conversationalists," I said. "Being dead and all."

Touch of blush rose up from her collar onto her throat. "They're not always. But sometimes they'll surprise you. Mostly, it's good for simple things—finding water, lost things, telling the sex of a baby before it's born. Divining rods and peep-stones. Like that."

"I want to ask Liam what being dead is like," Nell said. "And can he float around and watch people? Move through walls? Move things around, or even take things?"

"Interesting line of questions," I said.

"Not just that," she said, quickly. "The other stuff Maggie said. Respects, and all."

"Respects?"

The blush reached Maggie's cheeks. "To give a spirit final thoughts and goodbyes. It's what they need."

"The spirits, or the living?" I said.

"Well, both, I suppose. But it's more for the spirits. When their end is tragic, they'll haunt the world until they can be put to rest, released to move on beyond the world's curtains."

"A very generous offer, Maggie," I said, "but I think it might be best if we keep our thoughts on the here-and-now. Especially those of us with more imagination than common sense."

Maggie nodded, understanding what I was getting at. Nell walked ahead of us. Maggie turned and mouthed the word "sorry". I winked at her.

The city rang as the various mill clocks tolled seven. A crowd gathered outside the Canal Street entrance, just past the storage end of the mill. Usually, the yard had cleared well out by that time of the morn, the last stragglers hurrying inside. My first thought was that there'd been an accident with a machine. Happened often enough, and meant clearing out part of one floor until we cleaned things up and got it running again, being careful not to let too many of the workers see the hand or patch of scalp or arm pried from the gears or spindles or rods of the machine in question. I'd carried a few of those bits out in a scrap of burlap myself, as a matter of fact.

Got closer, saw what everyone was looking at: a body hung from the iron lantern to the left of the doorway, and quite a mess it was. What I first took for soggy hemp rope that the body dangled by was in fact guts. Blood streaked up against the bricks near the door, a lot of it. The fella's arms were askew as though he were halfway through a fancy back-flip into a swimming hole. His eyes had been gouged out, some of his teeth pounded from his mouth. My pulse hammered.

"You girls go in the other way," I said.

Maggie hauled Nell down to the next doors, not letting her get a view of the body. I pushed through the crowd to the body—and recognized him right away. My pal Tommy Fitzgerald, never to pull a knife on me nor anyone else, ever again. Was his thick nose and dark eyebrow, no mistaking. Up on the edge of the building that housed the blacksmith and carpenter shop, a line of crows dotted the slate, looking as though they had it in their beady minds they'd come across the best meal they'd get all summer. A few ladies over by the side of the crowd relieved themselves of their breakfasts.

"All right," Mac Harriman said. He stood at the top of the steps, waved his arm off to the other set of doors. Everyone looked at him. "Staring at this won't get shoes made, nor let the police here do what they need to. Move it off. That's right."

The crowd slipped to the other doors and Mac and I hurried them along. By the time we'd cleared most of the folks off, the police were pulling at the body, trying to get it down. The innards stretched and a wet sound came from the body. It put in mind my great-uncle, who used to spend days making mutton sausage back in Kildalkey before the hungry years; gut casing could stretch, it could.

Mac came over and whispered, "The hell is this?"

His gaze didn't leave mine. I glanced once over to the body just as something let go deep inside the cavity and it fell. The police tried to catch it, but the head hit the stone steps with a thunk and a clack of teeth. The guts slapped down upon the steps. Thick-necked copper with a big mustache who'd yanked him down shrugged a loop of guts off of his shoulders.

"Not a bloody idea."

"It's Fitzgerald."

"I see who it is."

He looked hard at me.

"All I did was fire him, Mac. You were there. I only hoped to never put eyes on his ugly face again."

"Well, someone wasn't happy with him."

I looked over at the steps and then up at the light fixture where the body'd hung. "Then someone did us a favor we didn't ask for."

We both stepped aside as the police carried the body past us, laid him out on the ground. One of them went to their horse, getting a blanket, while the one with the mustache worked to gather up the guts, pushing them into a pile using the toe of his boot. A cruel gash ran from his privates to his ribs, the blood still glistening and fresh.

"All right. Get folks to work," Mac said. "And tell Theo to keep his voice down if he's going to go on about this all day."

"Right."

I nodded and turned to go, ended up walking right into a big policeman.

"Wait a minute," he said, putting one of his meaty hands onto my arm. I could have thrown all my muscle in any direction and he'd have kept me in that spot. So wide across in the shoulders that I marveled that they had uniforms that fit him. Only came up to my chin, but he likely tipped the scales at three times my weight.

"You know him?" he said, smiling. Smile seemed real enough —though what exactly there was to smile about seeing a man strung up by his own guts was hazy. His eyes didn't smile, though, dark and on the clever side.

"He worked here," I said. "'Til I fired him day before yesterday."

"What'd he do?"

"Pulled a knife. That'll get you fired."

The copper looked me over, still with that smile on his face. I spotted a wet stain on the shoulder of his uniform where Fitzgerald's guts had landed on him. "And it was you he pulled the knife on?"

"Trying to muscle one of my crew for some money. I explained to him we don't stand for such nonsense. He gave me a bit more."

"What's your name?"

"But he was fine when he left."

"Not what I asked."

"Finn Carey."

He nodded toward the body. "And his?"

Mac walked over to us. "Tommy Fitzgerald."

"One of old Douglas's brood?" the cop said.

"He was. Worked here two years."

"Thought no one in that family worked."

"He wasn't that good at it," Mac said.

"None of them are."

The copper turned back to me. "You in the company housing?"

"Got a place down in the Plains," I said.

"How'd you manage that?"

"I'm a floor boss."

"Oh, well in that case. What street?"

"Over the end of Currier."

Half a dozen flies circled the air over the body. Noticed gore on the copper's shoe from where he'd pushed around the guts.

"You see him again after you fired him?"

"Not 'til I came around the corner five minutes ago."

"Fitzgeralds are a nasty bunch. Must've figured he might come after you."

"Thought crossed my mind," I said.

"Killing him would solve that problem."

"And so would staying clear of him. You think someone would gut him and then stroll on into work to admire his handiwork?"

"A killer might."

"You must know more than me, then."

"I know killers."

Police wagon showed up, and they went about getting the body onto it. The horses were skittish at the scent of the blood.

"Can I get up to work then?"

"Am I done asking you questions? Let me see your hands."

I put my arms out. He grabbed each hand by the wrist, looked close at it, flipped it over. Wasn't gentle about it.

"Roll up your sleeves."

I did it and he looked at both the fronts and backs of my forearms, all the way to my elbows. Glanced up and saw faces peering down from nearly every window of the mill near where we stood. If anyone hadn't known of my trouble with Fitzgerald before— well, that was done with.

"Turn," the copper said. Grabbed my shoulder and spun me. Pulled at my collar, looking at the skin on my neck, around my shoulders.

"When did you bathe last?"

"Don't know. Couple of days back, maybe."

He stopped looking at me as I turned back around.

"They work in the same shop?" he asked Mac.

"No. Fitzgerald was a tannery man. Carey runs a different floor."

"He told it straight?"

"He did."

"Look like he would come after him?"

"Who, Fitzgerald?" Mac said.

"Either."

"Fitzgerald, maybe. Carey, never. One of my best men."

The copper stroked his mustache for a half a minute, looking at the mess where the body had been hung.

"Can I get him up to work?" Mac said.

The copper nodded. I started off to the stairs.

"Hey," he yelled.

I stopped.

"Two R's or one?"

"What?"

"In Carey. Two R's or one."

"One."

"Now go."

7

THE DEVIL COMES TO LAWRENCE

The lovely thing about work for us lucky ones with the fire in the belly was that it never ended. That's how I came to be standing with my friend Conlin Nagle before his forge later that night. Nagle had built up his blacksmith shop around the same time I bought the team of horses, and was a good man, hardworking. After my twelve hours at the mill, I'd made two deliveries with the wagon, and one of my horses had thrown a shoe. By the glow of the hot coals, we chatted as he worked my horse's hoof with pincers and his hoof knife, getting it ready for the new shoe. That horse was a sonofabitch, but Nagle kept him calm.

"You could shoe the Devil himself," I said.

"And I fervently hope that I never find out if I'm the next St. Dunstan or no. Sounds a dangerous business," he said. Keeping the foot between his legs, he reached over and took up a rasp, smoothing the hoof with it. I patted my horse's flank to keep him calm. I looked into the shadows thrown by a sudden wavering of the heat from the forge and a sliver of unease took hold, as though a corpse had raised its hand and lightly touched the back of my neck with its finger. A dread fell across me, and just like that I stopped listening to Nagle talk. Could hardly breathe for it, certain as I was of being watched. Looked out the smithy's big door, but the small patch of street beyond was empty. Most windows that part of the city were dark, some of them lit with pale moonlight. At the turn of the narrow alleyway, a shadow moved.

First wondered if it were one of Fitzgerald's clan, marked me on the streets and followed me. I got a glimpse of a pale face with thick sideburns when a thin flash of lightning lit the cityscape and the hills beyond. The sound of distant thunder floated up from out west of the city.

It was my brother Liam, no mistaking him. His face twisted up, and he vanished back into the shadows behind him.

"I'll be back, Nagle," I said. I darted across the street.

Nearly garroted myself on a laundry line, getting by it with a curse. I sped between the buildings, cutting around wooden bins and loose bricks until I came out a street over. Looked empty. I searched a little in both directions, passing through pools of gas lamp light and shadow, by darkened storefronts and open taverns, catching snippets of drunken talk and laughter. Spotted a figure duck into a narrow alley. I went after him. The rank, sweet garbage pushed ahead of my shoes.

"Liam! Bloody stop!" I yelled.

I was out of the next alley when a sound stopped me—it was all around me, a moving river of trash. The ground moved, twists of shadows sliding between where I stood and the canal. Rats, hundreds and hundreds of them. One of them nuzzled up my pant-leg, and I shook him off. Ahead of me, Liam stood on the stone that edged the water. His cheeks were pale and thin; his eyes gleamed from dark sockets. He had the ridiculous sideburns that Maggie told me he'd grown on the crossing. Rats poured around him, throwing themselves into the water, a writhing mass of fur and pink tails. I took a few steps forward.

"I can't make him angry," Liam said, his voice choking the words out, "or he fills me with fire."

He gave me a baleful look before stepping off the edge and into the canal. I shouted his name. Near the edge, I lost my footing on the hard back of a fat rat and landed on top of a dozen more of them. Their filthy fur brushed my face and neck and more scrambled up and over my legs and back. One of them raced across my head, his claws sharp needles in my scalp. I flung them off, pushed them away in a panic, got myself to my knees and my feet. One rat clung to my shirt by his teeth and I had to tug him off. I looked in horror at the water, covered over with drowning and drowned rats, their brown and gray bodies blackened in the water, floating down with the slow current. I didn't see Liam anywhere. Next to me, the last of the rats tumbled in with a screech.

"Liam!"

Searched that roiling surface, looking for a hand, a shoulder, a thrash of him. The water stunk like a cross between a soiled nappy and a rusty pale of water. Nothing. Something pale caught my eye amidst the ratty frothing. Got myself half out over the water and swirled my hand around in it, knocking rats aside, looking to get a grip on what I saw.

Liam's hand clamped around my wrist—and before I could so much as scoot back to pull him out, he yanked me straight into the water. Oily darkness muffled the world, cold water reaching its fingers into every nook of my clothes, jamming its way up my nose and into my mouth. Opened my eyes and saw the pale oval of my brother's face in front of me in the ghastly shadowed world of the canal. Must've screamed, since a wall of bubbles came up between us. I thrashed and pulled and tried to work myself free, pure panic. The filthy water let my wrist slip free and I burst the surface. Rats scratched at my face, trying to keep themselves from drowning. A hand grabbed my ankle, but before I let him pull me under again,

I stretched and got a hold of a piling that lined the canal. Used my other foot to get my shoe right onto his face and kicked as hard as I could. Kept kicking until he had no choice but to let my ankle go.

I was up over the edge and onto my feet, curtains of water sloshing down from my soaked clothes. Soon as I was a pace away, I glanced back. The rats had by this time spread downstream.

"Finn."

The whisper came up from the water. Liam dragged himself up. He lurched after me, his clothes sopping wet, his face lost behind his hair. I backed off, leaving the towpath and heading into the long grass that grew up behind the buildings. All the while, Liam's damp footsteps got closer.

"Come here," he said.

"Jesus Christ almighty," I said. "Where've you been, what's happened?"

His eyes rolled back in his head for a moment before focusing on me again. He kept walking, as did I. "You kept it from him."

"What are you talking about?"

"And you're next. Then the others, the young ones. You shouldn't have touched it."

"We're getting you to a doctor, someone that can fix you up. You ain't right."

Not watching where I was going, I backed right into a brick corner of one of the warehouses that lined that stretch of the north canal. Liam blocked me. His hand came out and touched my collarbone, right where it met my throat, that tender spot. His hand was cold, like something brought up from the deep sea. He opened his mouth, and a stream of water rolled out over his lips. Terrible smile cracked his face in two and his hand tightened on my throat. Tried to bat his arm away, but he clamped down tighter. Shoved myself forward. He didn't budge. I choked, trying to gasp, not being able to get in even a thin stream of air.

A woman's voice shouted in a tongue I'd never heard.

Liam's grip relaxed enough for me to get in a lungful of blessed air. The woman stood at the end of the alleyway I'd come down. Again, a shout. Liam barked at her, guttural yell. He let me go. I slid down the brick wall, rubbing my throat and gasping to not black out. She came out of the shadows of the alleyway. Not tall, hair cropped close, dark clothes. She held her hand before her, palm facing out. Something hung from it.

"*Muusu teevs debesiis*," she said. Her voice was rough.

A shudder ran through Liam, head to toe. He leaned forward and arched his back. His tongue stuck out and a roar came out of him.

"*Sveetiits lai top tavs vaards!*"

He flew back as though a horse had galloped straight into him. He landed at the edge of the canal and a bellow of rage came from him. When he tried to get up, the woman walked toward him, holding both her hands up now.

"*Lai naak tava valstiiba, tavs praats lai notiek.*"

Liam writhed, slamming his head. He leaped up, ungainly and awkward, like he was play-acting being a marionette.

"*Kaa debesiis taa arii virs zemes*," he spat out. His tone was mocking—even though I didn't understand a word of it, I didn't miss that. Now, Liam'd barely mastered the Queen's English, so where he'd picked up that strange-sounding tongue was yet another mystery.

The woman shook her head. She lifted her hands and whispered: "*Valstiiba. Valstiiba.*"

With that, Liam laughed—only there weren't no mirth to it. He cried out and charged her. A half-dozen strides from her, he stopped, held back by nothing I could see. A terrible yell came from him. Lightning flashed and the buildings and ground caught the roll of thunder that followed. Still yelling, he turned and leaped toward me. The woman sidestepped, putting herself between the two of us. Liam cried out. He spun and in a pair of strides was at the lip of the canal where he leaped into the water, hitting the surface with his arms pinwheeling. He disappeared. The sky opened up, hard rain erasing any sign of him from the water.

The woman approached me. She stood slight of build, dressed like a priest—black cossack, white collar. Stranger still, her hair was cut short, in the style of a man. A silver rosary hung around her neck and another wound around her right hand; she fingered the beads with her thumb as she approached. Nearer, I made her out to be younger than I'd thought, around my age. She knelt down next to me.

"You are all right?" She placed a hand on my shoulder.

"Just relaxing after a quiet dip in the canal," I said. "What'd you do to him?"

"Sent him back. With a message."

"Back where?"

"To his master."

Her English was halting, thick with some accent I couldn't place, but her tone was commanding. She helped me to my feet. The canal was loud, the rain making riot of the surface. Nowhere did I see a shape in it, nor climbing from it, and could barely pick out the bodies of rats, clumped as they were against the stone edges.

"He's my brother," I said.

"Your brother."

"He was on the ship. The *Jack Ketch*."

She nodded, as if something came clear to her that she'd suspected.

"Come," she said. We made our way around the bits of trash that littered the towpath that ran alongside the boisterous canal. Soon, the path veered off as the canal ran underneath an iron bridge that held up a run of train tracks. Rain made rivers in the gutters and the street lamps flitted, their glass housings running with water.

"You've seen him since?" she said.

"Thought he'd died with the others."

She said nothing, running the beads between her fingers as we walked. We crossed out onto Canal Street. She turned toward the river.

"Because of the ship, isn't it?" I said.

"In a manner."

"Well, I was on it, after it washed up. Saw what was belowdecks. Giant coffin. And something else was there."

She stopped and turned. Her eyes were pale, carrying a weight behind them. "Yes. You feel it, the city feels it. Something has crept in that makes the dusk worse. Takes away from the daylight, from the sunshine, from easy feelings. Makes the shadows stronger, the night. No?"

"I'll note you don't quite have the wild-eyed look of terror on your face I did on that ship."

"Wild eyes?"

"You don't sound surprised."

"No surprise. Veln."

Didn't recognize it, but her voice was light on the word, as though she wanted the very sound of it off of her tongue as quick as possible.

"The serpent, the dark ones," she said. "Fallen. *Maceklis, izpaligs.*"

"Beg pardon?"

She turned and started off again, staying to the side of the road, her gaze tracing the rooftops against the storm, peering into alleys and down dark lanes. She didn't slow. "You think I'm a madwoman?"

"It's midnight, and I just climbed out of a dirty canal that my dead brother dragged me into, along with a few hundred of his vermin friends," I said. "I'm more open-minded than I otherwise might be."

"You haven't heard the rest of my story."

"Try me."

"The veln are the cursed—rebels against God," she said. "For their defiance, they were thrown down from glory and imprisoned below the ground, chained in rock and soil, passing centuries so. Thousands of years."

I didn't say a word.

"Am I mad yet?" she said.

"Getting closer. Go on."

"And this one—this deadly, wily, thieving darkness—is on the verge of what he thinks is his time of renown, when he can at long last stab at the eye of God."

"Not something I hear every day, I'll give you that."

We neared the westernmost bridge that spanned the Merrimack, the water running broad in the rain below. Lightning showed the surface currents as deep gouges racing by. We were both good and drenched.

"As I told you," she said.

"You're talking about angels—fallen angels?"

She gripped the iron rail and paused. Thunder echoed among the hills and city. "They are the veln."

"I thought they went to Hell. With the Devil."

"The Devil was their captain. First to escape his bonds. Five centuries ago, he made his way from his prison in the Far East into the heart of Europe. For one hundred and fifty years, he brought death to village and city, to forest and burg, farmland, lonely crossroads, distant hamlets. All the while he searched for his brethren, releasing them when he found them."

"He escaped?"

"Sadly, he was not watched over. Nearly forgotten."

"By people."

"No. People have nothing to do with this. Forgotten by the angels."

"Seems too noteworthy to forget. That aside, one would figure that God'd remind them."

"One would—save that the mind of God is as dark to us as the space between the stars."

"I don't seem to recall that particular sermon in church, begging your pardon," I said.

"The church lost its way."

"You're not with the church."

"I'm with the true church. I haven't grown blind."

A clap of thunder shook the bridge beneath us, the strike of lightning coming down at the top of Gale's Hill off to our right.

"So you're saying the Devil's come to Lawrence?"

"No."

"But you—"

"The Devil was killed in 1498, in the forests along the eastern shores of the Baltic Sea. Trapped in a river valley and destroyed in the middle of the most terrifying storm ever seen."

"Missed that sermon, too," I said. "So who's here, then?"

"There are four hundred and thirteen still bound. The fallen. And one escaped. Somehow. And he's been running, working to release the others, one at a time." She watched the water, frowning. "For a decade now, he finds them, unbinds and strengthens them. In desolate forests, empty wastes. Weak, at first. Vulnerable."

She glanced around at the lamplight that dotted the dark city, at the brick and slate that ran with rain as the blue-white flashes of the storm danced overhead. The iron of the bridge hummed with the gusting winds and downpour.

"He brings them what they need, then moves on, searching for the next."

"What do they need?"

"Souls."

"Like my brother's."

She shook her head.

"Different. Your brother is his servant, a verg. A slave."

"Liam'd never put up with that."

"He's in the thrall of the veln. Once he's under the influence of the veln, his own will is destroyed. The veln controls his soul."

I wiped the rain off my brow.

"You never met Liam," I said.

"You never met veln."

She walked across the bridge. I followed.

"So what do I need to do to rescue him?" I said.

"You're not listening."

"Heard every word."

"The veln will see him dead before releasing him. His mind would break, your brother, his soul ripped from him, leaving only a shred. A torment worse than death."

Before I'd come to America, hardly a day had gone by when I didn't have to trouble myself with making sure that brother of mine was all right. That he wasn't getting in yet another fight with the village bullies. That he wasn't hiding in the barn out back because our father was on a tear and looking to whip the hide from him. That he knew to watch after our sisters, even when I wasn't around. And I'll tell you one thing I knew as well as I knew that the sun rode the sky, east to west: there was nothing he wouldn't have done for me—as there was nothing I wouldn't do for him.

"Where should I look for this veln?" I said. "There's got to be a way to free him. More ways of killing a cat than choking it with cream."

We reached the other side of the bridge. She paused, looking up the road ahead where it wound between buildings, then back at me.

"Where should I be looking?" I said.

"You shouldn't."

"I'm more hard-headed than that, ma'am. They can be killed —that's what you're after, ain't it?"

"Yes."

"I'll help you. Know this city inside and out."

"What you're asking is more dangerous than you can imagine."

I put out my hand. "I'm Finn Carey. That was my brother Liam."

She looked at my hand. After a moment, she shook it. Her grip was tougher than I expected.

"Sister Ieva," she said.

"Where do we look, Sister Ieva?"

She frowned at me, looked around into the storm and night. "Could be anywhere. Remote is best. Someplace abandoned."

"That's where he finds them?"

"That's where he brings them. They are released from the earth where they were bound."

"He digs them up?"

"Unbinds them. With something he stole. A key."

Lightning threw shadows across the bridge, the river, turned the rain to glass.

"Then I hope he's resting well," I said. "Because things are about to get a lot more difficult for this veln."

"Words are easy, Mr. Carey."

"Words are deeds, when you get them from this Carey. You'll see."

The rain grew heavy as we started off down the street alongside, and as she told me her story.

8

CANTUS DE DAMNABILIS II

uhitse Abbey, Latvia

Nine years earlier

The night grew chill after the sun sank behind the forest around Puhitse: the Holy Hill. Sister Ieva readied her traveling bag by the light of the stars so as not to alert the other Sisters that she was leaving. *Will the Virgin appear? Urge me to stay?* she thought, not for the first time. The thought was worn smooth, past meaning and almost a taunt now. The hope of a vision had held such power to her younger self—a child found wandering in the snow by a traveling tinsmith kind enough to drop her at a convent a days ride away, a child who'd survived a village massacre. A sad story, but not uncommon in those days, in that part of the world.

The Holy Hill, where the Virgin appeared, the claim was.

While Ieva loved the hillside brooks, the deep forests heady with pine resin and earth, the meadows that grew burnished under summer suns, she had never seen nor heard even a hint of the Virgin herself. And now she knew it was past time to leave. The cloistered life wasn't for her, as much as she owed to it. Discipline. Strength. Those she'd learned from the Sisters of Puhitse. Faith—no. Independence—of course not. Life?

Not nearly enough.

Sleep was out of the question. She paced, wrapped herself in a blanket, prepared to wait until after the compline prayers when the abbey would grow silent until the vigils began in the hours before dawn.

So it was that when the bells above the chapel rang, she gasped.

Do they know? she wondered, going to her window. Those bells never rang at night, not in the decade she'd been there. Then the screams began, resounding throughout the stone corridors, across the courtyard.

Her blood seized up inside her. She didn't stride out the door, as she'd planned—she fled out the window, like a five-year-old. Hung down, dropped into the courtyard. The wind dotted the air with dried leaves pulled from the rooftops. She saw one Sister sprawled lifeless in an archway. In terror, she ran the other way. Moving from one bush to another, hugging the trunks of trees, she hid in the courtyard, too frightened to go further.

Yells of the Sisters stopped. She gathered her nerve and—crouching—ran from the courtyard to the side-yard, under a wrought iron archway that led into the cemetery, the final resting spot of three centuries worth of nuns, not quite one hundred graves. She stopped by a worn monument. On the far side of the graveyard, a terrible shape stood, a shadow still in the wind. She tried several times to bolt to an opening, but each time, the figure closed further, blocking her way until she huddled next to a headstone, terrified and furious and frustrated.

And he came then, slouching out from the archway of the convent, with two of the Sisters with him, one in each cursed arm. They struggled, but they had no chance. He walked them over to the cemetery, and when he spoke, his accent was perfect, as though he'd grown up a mile from there in the local village.

"I thought I felt a stronger heat than these," he said, his foul voice rising above the wind.

"Let them go!" Ieva shouted.

"You can help them, child. Come."

Her terror only grew. She looked for a path to escape. The Sisters struggled, and she recognized them then: Mother Beatrise and Sister Aija, who had been so kind to her.

"Let them go and I'll do it," she yelled.

The figure laughed, a revolting sound that conjured rendered flesh. "Your lies shine bright. As does your bravado. Your sweet insolence, no? Step forward now, or one will pay with her life."

Ieva didn't. In fact, she crept backward, hoping the gusts of wind and the leaves that rode them might hide her movement. The figure came closer, dragging the tormented Sisters. "As I thought. Well. You must not yet trust me to keep my word. Pay attention."

With that, he grabbed Sister Aija, a kind woman with one leg shriveled from birth, by the back of her neck and drove her face into the stone corner of a headstone with such force as to crack the stone as well as her skull. Her limbs shot out in a jerk, then she dropped in a shower of bone and blood.

"See? You've murdered her with your cowardice. Poor thing. Shall we continue?"

Ieva bit down on her fear. She stood. The wind tugged at her robes. "You did that. Not me."

Again, cruel laughter.

"And if you close your eyes, this will all go away. Then you can sneak away in the night, an ungrateful whelp slinking off from those who took you in—isn't that right?"

"Let her go. You can take me."

Mother Beatrise shouted at her to run. Ieva ignored her.

"You have courage, child. I knew it. We shall come to enjoy our time together, I think."

"Now."

The figure paused, didn't take his vile gaze from her. He flung Mother Beatrise forward with a cruel shove. She staggered and fell, a dozen paces from Ieva. Ieva rushed forward, helped the frail woman to her feet.

"Now your end of our bargain."

Mother Beatrise gasped for air. She fumbled with her robes, clawing at her throat. "Medallion," she whispered.

"Now, child. I can still ruin her if you entertain thoughts of cheating me."

The older woman wrenched a tarnished medallion from beneath her robes, the leather cord worn. She yanked it hard enough to break the leather and shoved it into Ieva's hand.

"Uriel," she whispered.

Behind her, the shadow rose, the fiendish face leering. "You've just cost her her life—I don't care for waiting, child."

As he reached forward, Ieva leapt at him, holding the medallion aloft and putting herself between Mother Beatrise and the shadow. And she felt it, for the first time: a holy fire. It flared from the medallion of the archangel Uriel, a relic older than the abbey itself. The heat rode her hand, her arm, the length of her spine, swelling her heart, opening her soul to a current she'd never imagined. In the light, the fiend was clear, a thing of horror from the furthest edges of nightmare. He reeled back with a booming yell. His head swung back and forth with a fierce snapping, his legs staggering.

Ieva could barely speak. The waves passing through her touched every muscle, every bone, the hairs on her head, her belly. Aloft, the light grew blinding. "In the name of the Lord, be gone," she said, her own voice strange in her ears. "You have no place here on this hallowed spot."

The figure hurtled backward, flung through the air, smashing against headstones, coming to a stop pressed hard against the iron of the fence. A roar came from him that echoed out over the hilltop and the forest surrounding.

Ieva walked toward him, the light moving with her. Another bellow tore from his throat.

"Your wandering shall be brief, your binding eternal," Ieva said, not knowing where the words came from, nor what they meant.

The side of the figure's face erupted in boils and his scream was agony. He pried himself from the fence, hurled himself sideways and through the gate, and loped off into the darkness, disappearing into the thick forest by the road. Ieva stood as a statue. As the sounds of the night returned to her, she noticed that the light had faded, receding to the faintest glow. Her limbs shook, her breathing slowed. She lowered her arm as one coming to from a daydream. The abbey was silent but for the wind.

She turned and ran to Mother Beatrise, but the life had left her, her weak heart failed. Ieva was the only one alive in the abbey. And by morning, the only one alive in the valley.

9

CURSED BE HIS NAME

Another bawdy song broke out in the Hemlock Street Tavern. Officer Ernst Glockner nodded along, one hand resting on the handle of his nightstick, the other on a tin mug of beer. He kept a smile on his face. Inside, he was disgusted, appalled, and certain he was witnessing the reason the city was going to hell: the Irish. Glad-handing each other and calling out their greetings as though they hadn't gotten swilled together just the evening before. Breathing beery fumes as they yelled into each other's ears, glassy-eyed and flushed with drink. Bumping into each other as they crossed the smoky room, ale and beer sloshing to their ill-fitting shoes, then breaking out into song as though they were all part of some grand society, draining their glasses after the final tuneless note.

"Don't give yourself the vapors, Ernst."

Glockner looked up. At his shoulder, a man with clever eyes, shirt sleeves rolled up and his vest open. He took off his cap and sat next to Glockner.

"I care too much," Glockner said.

"There's your mistake right there. Trust me."

Tom Barley lifted a pair of fingers and the barkeep brought

him over a dram of whiskey. Barley dug a coin out of his pocket and slid it across the bar. He sipped the whiskey.

"I'll trust you not to break into song," Glockner said.

"You can remove that from your list of worries."

Barley's face lit up in the glow of a match as he lit a ready-made cigarette he fished from a heavy paper packet in his vest pocket. He placed the match in an ashtray. "Mayor's none too happy about what they found on the Everett."

"Nor am I," Glockner said.

"Hence your scouring of the streets."

"Know where to look."

"Blood feud?"

"Maybe."

Barley watched the crowd through the smoke. Couple of men argued, raising their voices up over the steady clamor.

"Fist fight, sure," Barley said. "Smashed bottle, jagged glass. Course. Knife, sometimes. Guns now and then. Write those articles month in, month out. But strung up and gutted, out on display—that's new."

"Some killing is for the killing. Some is for the message."

"Who's the message for?"

"Fine question."

"Newsman's instincts," Barley said. He reached up and took down the stub of a pencil tucked behind his ear, pulled out a tattered note-booklet from his other vest pocket. "You mind?"

"Didn't ask you to meet me for the pleasure of your company."

"Oh, the shock."

"Just get the name right."

"Storied and illustrious career can do a lot for an ambitious man in Lawrence."

"As can inside details of confidential police dealings," Glockner said.

Barley finished his whiskey, then rolled the glass on the edge of its bottom, looking at the light through it. He raised it up and the barkeep clinked the bottle against the rim and gave him a refill.

"You've any ideas?" he asked.

"Course I do."

"And would any of those ideas care to pass from behind your mustache?" Barley said, eyeing him over the rims of his glasses. Glockner didn't answer—his gaze had turned elsewhere in the room and fixed there. Barley noted that he hadn't seen him take a single sip of his beer since he'd sat down with him. He turned and followed Glockner's gaze. A man slouched through the crowd, coming to a stop in the shadows by the fire. He gazed around. The conversation drained from the room the longer he stood there. No songs erupted. No laughter broke like a wave. Barley turned back to Glockner with a cynical look, about to tell him he wasn't interested in any stunts—but he could see that Glockner was as wary as he was.

"The *Jack Ketch*."

The figure by the fire spoke in a voice that put the grave into people's minds. That single phrase turned the drunken cheer of the tavern bad as fast as if the stranger had dumped out a bag of severed limbs.

"The ones who lived," he said. "Where are they?"

The man looked around, unwashed and disheveled, with pale skin and auburn hair, red sideburns framing hollow cheeks. He got no takers. A good number of men left their drinks and scurried out. Glockner got off of his bar stool, keeping his hand on his nightstick. A man at a nearby table stood.

"Don't think none of us care for you being in here, lad," he said.

The stranger turned to him. His eyes held a glint of firelight in the shadows. "The girls," he said.

"Suggest you take your leave. Now," the man said.

"You'll tell me."

"You won't get another warning, friend."

Another fellow stood up, the whiskey glow of his cheeks flushing to a red anger, his hands in fists.

"You'll tell me or you'll sleep on the other side," the figure said.

Glockner pushed his way through the thinning crowd. Barley jumped to his feet, his pencil scratching across the open page of his note-booklet even as he did. Before Glockner could get close, the two men rushed at the stranger. With a terrible speed, the stranger's arms shot out and grabbed the two men by the front of their shirts.

"Sleep," he said.

He slammed their heads together with such brutal force that the crunch filled the room, flesh and bone bursting in. Both bodies fell —one shuddering as though struck by lightning, the other limp with a misshapen eyeball hanging from its shattered orbit. Blood and more spilled to the boards. The tavern erupted into a panic, men heaving themselves to the door, tables knocked over. Some of the men tried to clobber him, but the stranger reared back like a feral hound and clawed at their faces. One man grabbed a lantern from its hook on a beam and swung it, clobbering the stranger on the side of his head in a great cracking of glass that sent a bloom of flame across his sideburn and ear and burning lamp oil trickling down his neck.

With no pause, the stranger grabbed the fellow by his throat and crotch and lifted him overhead. The fellow yelled out, swinging the remains of the lantern, smacking him in the back with the flaming end, not doing much more than burning himself before being thrown into the fireplace. His scream ended when his head slammed into the stone edge of the hearth. The stranger looked over the room, backlit by the fire, stone still. Fire climbed over his clothing and his hair smoldered in places.

"Get away from him," Glockner yelled. He had his nightstick out and shouldered men aside. The stranger eyed him.

"Is it your turn to play?"

Glockner pointed the nightstick at him. "You're done. I'm giving you three seconds. Down on your knees, hands behind you."

A twisting smile cracked the stranger's face. "Are we praying together?"

"Now!" Glockner said.

"Our Father, who rots in Heaven, cursed be His name," the stranger said, his voice mocking and graveled. "His kingdom done, His will is none, on Earth as there is no Heaven."

From the shadows along the wall, the barkeep stepped forward with a pistol. A finger of flame leaped from the barrel three times as he emptied the chambers at the stranger from less than ten feet away. The shots punched him hard in the chest and in the stomach, sprays of blood fanning out behind him—but he stood there as though leaning into a strong wind. He took a step forward. At that, the rest of the crowd ran for the door, cutting through overturned chairs and tables.

"Get back from him," Glockner said.

The barkeep took a few steps back, swung open the chamber of his piece, and fumbled around with a pocketful of bullets, trying to load them in. The stranger sprung forward in two steps and clamped his hand on the barkeep's throat, who panicked, trying to pry the fingers off even as he turned a shade of red, then purple.

Glockner closed in and hit the stranger with his nightstick, hard as he could. The man didn't even notice. The barkeep's gun fell to the floor. With a vicious speed, the stranger lifted him and shoved him back, pounding him against the wooden beam where the lantern had hung. The hook went clean into the back of his skull, sending him into a spasm. Barley watched it all from the corner of the bar. He made a mark on his note-booklet for each time Glockner brained the stranger with his nightstick, then scrawled the phrase *better luck to subdue a bronze statue* to use later in his article.

Glockner panted, his hand gone numb from the beating—but the stranger just turned and looked at him, smiled. He darted his arm out and snatched away the nightstick. Glockner ducked back. The stranger took the nightstick and slammed himself over the head with it hard enough to snap the black-painted maple, sending the top two thirds of it skidding across the floor. He tossed the handle back at Glockner, who batted it away as if it were a dead thing.

"We'll play again, you and I," the stranger said. "And have even more fun next time."

Bits of his clothing smoldered as he loped out of the tavern, past Glockner's reach, past the bodies, leaving behind a sweet stench of rotting flesh. Barley stood up from his crouch.

"We can scratch blood feud from our list," he said.

"Bucket," Glockner said, pointing. Barley lifted the bucket of water from the bar and ran over. Glockner took it from him and doused the flames on the floorboards where the burning lantern had spilled. He crouched and lifted the gun that the barkeep had dropped, popped in the four bullets he could find.

"Tell me you're not going after him," Barley said.

"That's exactly what I'm doing."

"You're not that crazy."

"Tell the station, two blocks over. They'll get men out."

He closed the barrel of the gun and ran to the door.

"What about these?" Barley said. He pointed his note-booklet at the bodies of the dead and dying.

"Have them send a doc."

Glockner stepped outside. The night air outside had grown supple, the city wrapped in a humid fog that put a glow around every lit lamppost and window. Bits of the tavern crowd stood in clumps across and down the street.

"Which way?" he shouted.

Patrons pointed up the darker end of the street, heading north. Glockner took off along the street, glancing back once to see the orange tip of Barley's readymade in the darkness. Neighborhood here had lots of lights on in the crowded apartments stacked above grocers, tailors, barbers, feed stores. Following the street north, the housing grew more worn, ending with the tenements that stretched along the south banks of the river above the dam.

He didn't glimpse the stranger, and soon had to slow to a trot, his pulse pounding in his collar, his lungs feeling like undersized bellows. Yelling caught his ear. He stopped. Two women screamed curses out into the darkness, standing beneath a haloed street lantern. Beyond, an iron railing where the land tumbled to the black water of the south canal. The heavy width of the Merrimack lay beyond, a sliding void of darkness that cut the city in half.

Glockner approached them. Prostitutes, he saw.

"Now you show up," one woman said.

"You see anyone come this way?"

The woman had her hand to her mouth, heavily lined eyes wide. The other—Glockner recognized her long red hair, had seen her often enough—tried to slip a knife away before he spotted it. He didn't care.

"Took Fanny, he did," she said.

"Who?"

"Disgusting rapist, that's who. Filthy."

Glockner looked back. He nodded his head. "From there?"

"Didn't see which way he come up. One moment we was just minding ourselves, the next he swipes in and grabs her. By the hair. Drags her off screaming."

The other one shook her head. "Wasn't right. Tell him what he said."

The one with the knife shook her head, frowned.

"Called back to us, he did. From right down there."

"Called back what?"

"Said he'd be back for us soon, so he could sing us a lullaby."

"Pale skin?"

"And sideburns, yeah."

"Stay here."

Glockner climbed over the rail and skidded his way down until he reached the canal edge. A worn path ran along both sides. The stones of the walls above the water stank with silt and scum. Clouds hid the moon and stars, darkness held fast. He stared in both directions and saw no one. It was a sound that drew him, a rasping in the goldenrod and weeds next to the path. As he stepped over, his foot landed on something that moved. He lifted his foot and hopped to the side. More sounds—slapping on the stones, writhing on the dirt of the path, rustling the grass.

He reached into his pocket and pulled out a match. Struck it on the stones and cupped the flame as it lit the ground before him, faint.

Eels.

The color of guts, twisting and gasping. At least a dozen of them. Glockner went to the edge of the canal. Water reflected the flame, streaks of tiny puddles dotted the stone. The vile things had leapt from the water. He stared at the surface of the canal as if he could wring a confession out of it, wondering what had gone into the water that had driven them out.

Around him, the eels slowed their struggles.

10

DOWN INTO THE SILT

The long summer sun slipped beyond the western edge of the city, drawing out shadows. I'd delivered four barrels of printers' ink from a river barge to the building that housed the *Lawrence Tribune*, and had a dozen heavy coils of hemp rope to drop off at a cooper's shop on the other side of town, all the while lost in the tale that Sister Ieva'd told me. A day having passed, it'd taken on the feel of a nightmare: horrible and slow to fade. Maggie sat next to me on the driver's bench, having cajoled me into taking her along for my deliveries. Wagons and drays filled the streets, along with mules pulling a flat canal boat. Wide-necked policemen sweated it out in their ridiculous uniforms, while shopkeeps leaned in their doorways or sat on barrels and benches in the humid twilight. All about, the heavy stench of coal smoke hung, mixed with the sweeter scent of horse droppings flattened in the roads. Maggie looked at the crowds around the saloon doorways, smoke and loud talk whirling around them.

"They'd have loved it," Maggie said.

I looked at her.

"Arthur, and Liam," she said. "Life everywhere, here. They'd have eaten it all up like it were just for them."

Your brother is his servant...the veln controls his soul.

Was all I could think of, poking and prodding the tale that the strange Sister Ieva had told me. We would meet up the next eve and search the city. Told myself that I'd know soon enough whether her devil—the veln—was naught but a figment of madness, or if it was the one terrible explanation for what happened since the *Jack Ketch* had floated in from the darkening sea. I flicked the reins, and the team put a spring in their gate. Water brown as a tarnished penny rolled through the sluices of the dam, and the river downstream was wide and running strong, its surface catching the last colors of sunset, shouldered by the mills that stretched all the way to the bend a mile down.

"If I'm not mistaken," I said, "someone on this wagon could ask them directly."

"I knew you would take it funny."

"I will say I'm a touch more willing to entertain the unusual than I was a month back."

She shifted in the bench, turned. "It's called *sien begeondan.* Sight beyond."

"And it runs in your family?"

"In the women. From way back. Some of them were witches. Or known as witches, anyhow."

"Have you tried?" I said.

"Tried?"

"To reach Arthur. Or Liam."

"Not really. No."

"Why not?" I said.

"It's...not a thing to do lightly. Nell didn't understand."

Around the city, lanterns came to life with the growing dusk.

"Be surprised if that girl sleeps a wink tonight," I said. "Between that and the mess at the mill this morning."

"She didn't see it," Maggie said.

"You're sure?"

"Course, it was all anyone talked about all day, though. And Nell has big ears."

As I'd feared, talk of the murder of Tommy Fitzgerald had spread like fire at the mill. Fully two thirds of the tales had me gutting him and stringing him up myself—a lesson to those who'd think to cross an Irish floor boss. Maggie'd overheard Nell taunting young Rose about the ghost of Tommy Fitzgerald.

"I'll talk to her," I said.

"Her mind seems is a wild horse," Maggie said.

"A bloody herd of them sounds more like it. Good thing no one mentioned anything to her about talking to ghosts."

We rode in silence until we neared the cooper.

"Are you lonely for home?" I said.

"Can't decide what I miss more—the skeletal misery, or the filthy hardships," she said.

Like most of us who'd come over, we spent little time talking about the cold hunger that stole across our old home, leaving towns and villages and families cut through with little to plant besides fresh grave-markers.

"Though I will note we tried to limit our labors to fourteen hours daily," she said.

"Plain lazy."

"Well, you understand that we're only mortals."

"A rather common excuse," I said. "Heard it all before."

"Have to leave time for sleeping."

"Overrated."

"And for courting."

"Nonsense, lass."

"Lass? You're a year older'n me. Talking like you're my father, you are," she said. She stretched her foot over and shoved my leg. "Now why aren't you out courting anyone? Important man like you. Handsome suitor to make the upstanding young ladies of Lawrence swoon."

"Too busy. Probably too Irish, for most of them."

"I doubt most would care."

"Welcome to Lawrence," I said.

"Well, you can't say you aren't swatting away the attentions of half the loom girls, the spare hands, the folders. Noticed how they look at you at the mill, big eyed and batting their eyes."

"I cut a rather impressive figure," I said.

"There's got to be some gal you fancy. Tell me."

"Perhaps you'll need to consult your peepstones to find out."

"Oh, I'll find out. Be sure of that," she said.

I shook my head. Maggie reached over and tilted up the back of my cap, sending the brim down over my eyes.

"You keep yourself too busy," she said with a laugh.

"You said as much, yes," I said. I righted my cap.

"You can have a bit of fun now and then, you know."

"I get the rest of the family over here, I get a stretch of fields and a barn, I get some fine horses—then I'll have all the fun due a self-made man of wealth and honor. Handsome lad like myself."

Evening stole across the sky as we neared the cooper shop.

WITHIN THE HOUR, we were back in the Plains, having already said goodnight. I'd hung the last of the tack on the carriage house wall when a scream cut out into the silence, from the house. I ran out into the yard. Lantern flared to light on the second floor. From the turn of the narrow alleyway out back, I caught the racket of footsteps tearing off, along with laughter. When I reached the corner, they were gone, disappeared out into the far darkness across the street.

I hurried up to the house and pushed in through the back door. "Where the girls?"

Heard Rose crying, loud and unhappy. I hurried to their room, only to find the door open. Rose stood in front of her trundle bed, tears on her frowning face. Maggie rushed in and swooped her into her arms.

"Nell?" I said.

"They took everything!" Nell said. She knelt in the corner before the trunk at the foot of the other bed. The lid was open. Her face was a perfect little picture of Irish fury, complete with tears jittering on her lids. We all talked at once.

"Are they gone?" I said, shouting above the rest to be heard.

"Everything!"

"Everyone stay here," I said. I took a circuit of the house and the yard. The thieves were gone. Even so, it took time to calm everyone down enough to suss out what'd happened: Nell had woken to Rose's cries, brought on by two men ransacking the next room over; the thieves heard her crying, and bust into their room, and rifled through the trunk and drawers, taking not much of anything, near as I could figure.

"Tried to stop them," Nell said. "Punched one of them good, right in his peener."

She flicked a stray tear away with the back of her thumb.

"Nell," Maggie said.

"You don't need such language," I said. "And you shouldn't have been so foolish."

"They was stealing."

"Don't matter. Let them take it. They could've hurt you."

"Knocked me down." She showed us a robin's egg on the back of her head from where she'd hit the floorboards. "And I hope they die."

I tallied up anything missing. Couple of candlesticks and a jar of coins was all we found gone. Nell claimed they took a bag of buttons from her room, which sounded ridiculous. I got the doors locked, and Maggie and I put the girls back to sleep. Nell kept on about different ways she wanted the thieves to meet their bloody ends, even as we shut the door.

"You'll be all right out by yourself?" Maggie said. I'd given her my room, making up a corner of the carriage house for my bed.

"I'll be fine. Just shout if you hear more'n a mouse. Be here in a heartbeat."

"I thought this street was safe."

"Is. Usually."

"You telling the police? This is the Plains, after all."

"And we're still Irish. They won't lift a finger."

"You think it was the one you fired, don't you."

"Happen to. Yes," I said. Second sight or no, she had the right instincts.

"But it was his own fault."

"Not in his mind."

"How much further you think it'll go?"

"I'll see that it ends, don't you worry. Keep the girls from dwelling on it. And maybe keep Nell from punching anyone's johnson."

She nodded. I bid her goodnight and went back to the carriage house, making sure the doors locked behind me. Stood outside in the night for a short time, watching the darkness as the moon rode up above the house, above the city. I watched as the lantern went out in the upstairs rooms. I locked the carriage house door and headed out into the darkness.

The hulking shapes of the mills along the canal were lit by the lanterns. The water smelled different at night, more of silt and rust, less of the tanning waste and dyes that often ran through it while the mills churned.

You have a fancy house in the Plains, little horse team. Well, you ain't the mayor yet. Fact, you ain't nothing but another Irishman on the make.

Looked across the canal, into the shadows of the buildings, in the pools of light from the lamps.

Ain't you something. Better'n the rest of us.

Followed the angle of Franklin Street and came out to the river itself. As I followed upstream, the neighborhoods grew more shabby. Flimsy walls and roofs made of cast-off materials, greasy paper hanging in rough openings for windows, folks moving in and around fires burning in rusted lanterns or buckets, and the ever-present smell of night soil. Soon enough, caught the deep throom of the water spilling over the dam, tasted the vaporous texture on the air. The lane wasn't more than a wide dirt path. Closer I got to the dam, the worse the houses—and you'd be being generous to call them that—got. Still knew my way around, even though I hadn't set foot in the shanties for years. Had to skirt around a couple of skinny hounds fighting before I stopped a pair of dirty young lads running by.

"You know the Fitzgeralds?"

"What if we do?" the taller one said.

"Where do they live?"

"Mansion on the hill. And you smell like a crapper house."

They broke up at that and tore off into the night.

"Thanks for the help, lads," I called after them. Asked a few others and finally got a grandmother to point her gnarled finger off to a shack wedged up in between a couple of mounds of dirt and rock. Like the other houses, oiled paper filled in for windows and a tattered blanket hung in the doorway. From inside, a babe or maybe two were yammering. Walked up to the door and rapped my knuckles against the boards.

Some shouting passed back and forth inside, and a woman pushed aside the blanket. Patch of ground lit up with lantern light as the blanket moved aside. Tall woman, glaring out with one eye aimed off to the side, made it hard to say for sure what she was looking at.

"Evening," I said.

She leaned back from me, squinted her good eye to a cautious slit.

"What you want?"

"Name's Carey. Finn Carey. Tommy around?"

Young girl tried to peer around her and got swatted away. The smell of cooking smoked up the humid air.

"No one's got nothing to say, leave us alone."

She turned and let the blanket fall. I blocked it and ducked inside. Place looked little less muddy than the lane outside. Stretched back under sagging boards, walls tattered and grimed, couple of mismatched lanterns casting smudged light. Half a dozen children watched me, from floor, from cloth-draped box, from torn cushion.

"Hate to barge, ma'am, but I need to see them," I said.

The woman spun on me, jabbed a finger. "Out, sod off! Niall, get out here."

Her yelling started off a number of the children to screaming. Wondered how many were Tommy's. Man looked out from back room. Came out, face flushed.

"Told you not to let no one in," he said. Two scars ran across his ugly nose, suggesting that he was one who didn't have enough sense to get around life reasonably. His voice had a slurry wilt to it.

"Came in. Barging in," the woman said.

"Looking for Tommy," I said.

"Says who?" Scar-Nose said.

"Finn Carey. The one who fired old Tommy. I'm here to tell you and any of the others who aren't here that you've one more chance to stay the hell away from my family. I won't be warning you again."

He swayed on his feet and pulled his lips back, his tongue sliding along the space where teeth had been. "Ain't had enough? Well lads being lads, is all. Knew they couldn't get it bloody done. Couldn't even hide it."

The woman spat. Kneaded her elbows. "Leave us alone."

"Where'd they go?" I said.

"Oh, I knew it," Scar-Nose said, shaking his head. "Beaten and broken, and them so full of steam on it."

He talked to himself. His eyes were bleary and he could barely keep upright. Raised his finger like he'd just remembered something. Stagger-spun and headed back through a tilted doorway. I looked at a muddy toddler, frowning in the corner, and shook my head. Brought my family over from Ireland to make sure they never lived like this again, and the Fitzgeralds couldn't seem to leave it behind.

"They ain't done nothing," the woman said.

"As a matter of fact, they have. And it best not happen again, ma'am."

Scar-Nose came back in, a pistol in his hand. "Now none of them whining pups knows how to keep their sloppy thieving on the up-and-up, so full of piss and vinegar they are."

He pointed the gun at me after a moment of searching. The woman shrieked and bustled the nearest children in to the corner.

"Wondering what the hell they got. Sell it, I tell them. But they want to burnish it with their snotted noses, don't they? Oh, look at this, Niall. Ain't it all that and a cup of whiskey, to boot. Not a toenail worth of loyalty to family. Not a toenail."

He took a pair of uneven steps forward. The barrel of the gun lost me for a moment, but he swung it back.

"Put it down, Niall," I said.

"That's better. Not dumb enough to follow you outside. Dumb, they was. Got all I need to stay out of trouble right here, fella. Don't I?"

"You do. Clearly."

"Singing a different song now, aren't you? Coming into my home. Threatening my family. Knocking heads with my brothers. Where'd you take 'em?"

I let him get closer. He wanted to talk more than he wanted to shoot, I guessed.

"They should've listened to you," I said.

"They should've. Should've," he said, nodding his head. "Right about that, for once. No one bothers, but I ain't lying in a ditch, nor a grave. Still right here."

He waved the gun. The children had scurried off to the hallway.

"Shoot him in the face, Niall," the woman said.

He spun on her.

"Can't you see I got it all under bloody control, woman?" he said. Started to say something else when I grabbed him from behind. Got one arm around his throat and pulled him back off-balance, while I grabbed his gun hand and bent it back. His hand tightened, but I took the gun by the barrel and twisted it right out of his grip. Another step back and I had him leaned back so far that I let go of his neck. He dropped to the dirt floor with a grunt.

"You dirty sonofabitch," he sputtered. His eyes rolled. "Spinning the bloody room, too, ain't you."

I lowered the hammer on the gun. He tried to get up, but I put my boot on his shoulder and sent him gently back to the floor. "Don't worry. I won't shoot. Fact, gonna take the gun with me to make sure that no one does any shooting here. But you'll remember to tell your brothers to stay the hell away, won't you?"

"Dirty trick," Niall muttered before he turned his head sideways and vomited.

"You'll tell them, won't you?"

He nodded his head where he lay, bile strung from his lips. The woman cursed. Another lovely day in the shanties with the Fitzgeralds. I nodded goodnight to them and stepped outside to follow the lane over to the dark river. What folks I passed said nothing, just marked my passing with suspicious eyes, men gathered around a burning barrel, smoking pipes, women emptying pails.

I reached a point near two abandoned hovels crouching by the rocks that lined the shore. I took the bullets out of the pistol, tossed them and the gun out into the black flowing water of the river. The gun made a heavy ploonk sound, a moonlit lick of splash marking it. The river took it.

Watched the moon shine on the current for a minute, then turned and headed back to the Plains.

11

PEEPSTONES

A brief rain at sunset the next day left the city smelling clean for a time. The roofline to the carriage house dripped as I readied the team. Had a night's worth of work ahead of me. Led the team out and locked up the carriage house.

"There you are."

Maggie stood at the edge of the porch. The lamp from the yard pooled her shadows around her feet.

"Got my peepstones," she said. She pulled a small sack from the inside of her dress. She untied it and pulled out a handful of white stones, quartz.

"Forgive me, Maggie," I said, "but I'm already later than I'd like to be."

"A couple of minutes can't hurt," Maggie said. "Said I could show you."

I let go of the handle on the side of the carriage and stepped down.

"So. What are these peepstones then?" I said.

She held them out for me to see. In the yellow light, they didn't look like much.

"They belonged to my great-grandmother, and they focus visions," she said. "Like dreams right in front of my eyes that tell me of things that are normally hidden. Or lost."

"And how do you peep them?"

"Step one is that you take it seriously," she said. She grabbed my right hand. Her hand was soft. "And step two is like this."

She closed her eyes. After a few moments she let go of my hand.

"Give me your cap," she said. I looked at her; she raised an eyebrow. I took off my cap and handed it to her. She took the peepstones and put them into it, then put her face into it, holding it to the sides of her head with both hands.

"Seriously you said," I said.

"Quiet."

Maggie lifted her head, the cap still covering her face, and turned this way and that, angling her head in different directions. I looked at the horses, hoping it wouldn't take long.

"Searching," she said, her voice muffled. "See that clear enough. And anger. Unbelievable anger."

She went quiet for a minute after that. Wind loosened rain from the shingles.

"Not always clear what they'll show," she said. Something in her voice changed.

"What're they showing?" I asked. "Is it Fitzgerald?"

Maggie turned and faced another direction, adjusting the cap over her face again. Stayed silent.

"Someone else? Something else?" I said.

"Flames. Glowing flames." She shook her head. "You can't reach him. And you don't want to."

"Him who? Is it Liam?"

"Black as a grave, that's what I'm seeing. Black as a grave."

"Can you recognize where? The river? Clock tower?"

"No, no, no!" She ripped the cap from her face, shaking her head.

"Jesus. You're crying," I said. The streaks around her eyes caught the lamp light. She wiped them away, still shaking her head.

"That happens. It's nothing."

She handed me back my cap.

"Well?" I said.

"You should stay. Don't go out."

"What'd you see?"

She put the peepstones back into the little bag. Her fingers fumbled.

"I don't know. Didn't make sense—but I don't like it," she said. "Never seen anything like that."

"Like what?"

"You wouldn't understand. It's not clear. It's feelings. Feelings and sights. Can you trust me?"

"It's not about trusting you, Maggie. But I gave my word to someone."

I put my cap back on. Patted the nearest horse on the flank and climbed up onto the carriage, got the reins straightened out.

"It's not a lark, Finn."

"Never said it was."

"Let me come with you. Keep you company."

"Lovely offer, but got to do this one on my own," I said. "You stay here, keep an eye on Nell."

"Hold on," Maggie said. She turned and hurried into the McAllisters kitchen door, came back a moment later, something in her hand. She stepped up onto the runner of the carriage, creaking the springs. One of the horses swished his tail. Maggie handed me a canteen, warm to the touch.

"At least take this. Builder's tea, plenty of sugar. Made it for you. Keep you going," she said. I took the canteen. She stayed on the runner. I turned to thank her when she leaned forward and kissed me. Was a bump, like she'd been going for my cheek, but hit my mouth instead. Her lips were softer than I'd ever thought, warm. After a confused second, the kiss melted into something more than a peck on the cheek.

"Maggie," I said, pulling back.

"Quiet," she said, coming in and kissing me again. She pressed her hand to my own. She leaned in, her lips on mine. Half a minute went by and I broke off. She stepped to the muddy ground, pushing aside a lock of hair that'd gone across her eye.

Fella I'd met once who'd traveled all the way out to the Pacific Ocean and back told me about a summer wildfire he'd seen at the foothills of the great Rockies: storm came down from the mountains, looming black and purple, the top high enough to be lost from sight. Lightning danced inside those towering clouds and sprung to the ground, and everywhere it hit a fire started, whether it was a tree or a bunch of them or a bush or wild grass and heather. They got caught up on the wind and grew and spread, and—he swore the truth of it—within half an hour, the whole valley was aflame. By midnight, the sky glowed a devilish color as far as he could see. No fire wagons, no canals, no one to stop it.

As Maggie looked at me, I wanted to take my gaze away from her lovely face and hair, her smooth lips, her dark eyes, the graceful curve of her throat painted by moonlight. I couldn't.

Some storms get the better of you.

"You keep that in mind, Finn." She smiled. "And don't go falling asleep while you're working. Need you well."

With that, she turned and went to the porch. I flipped the reins, getting the team moving. As I turned out onto the street, I glanced back. Maggie stood on the porch, a shadow, watching me go.

12

AND NOW LAWRENCE

Made my way across the city. Saloons and taverns boomed with voice and song, throwing light out onto the streets, and even at that hour other wagons and their pounding teams cut through the darkness. A breeze carried the stink of the city and sent scraps of cloud speeding in front of the stars and the rising moon. I came to a cross street of squat storefronts. On the corner was a wedge-shaped flophouse, sign painted to its brick side reading KING ST. BOARDING ROOMS. Pulled the team to the edge of the road. A figure stepped out of the shadowed doorway.

"Sister Ieva," I said.

"You're late."

"Apologize for that. Came as soon as I could."

I was about to get down to give her a hand up, but she climbed up next to me on her own. Put a canvas bag at her feet.

"Thought maybe you came to your senses," she said.

"My senses and me have had a falling out, if you must know the truth. Tea?"

I held out the canteen for her. She shook her head. I uncorked it and took a sip. Could've floated a canal barge on the tea I'd already drunk that day, but I didn't see much sleep ahead. I flicked the reins, and the carriage lurched forward.

"You think we'll find him?" I said.

"It won't be easy."

"Remote, you said. Lot of forest past the hills. Thick along the riverbanks far as you'd care to go. He's hiding there, could take a long while to find him."

She watched the city unfold as we rode. Noticed she had her beads out.

"In the past, could have been. I think now is different," she said.

"How's that?"

"The boat. And before he crossed. He's grown more used to population."

"Europe?"

"Morocco. The port of Rabat. Where I last found him."

"How far have you chased him?"

We passed between gas lanterns, the wagon loud on the cobbled roads.

"From Latvia. Always on the outskirts. First small villages, out of the way. Places where it could be weeks before anyone noticed that the homes were empty, the hearths cold. A valley disappeared. A forest silenced. Then, nearer to larger towns and cities. Krakow, Bucharest, Stuttgart. Turin. Saragossa. Cordoba. Into a sand-worn place of ruins in Northern Africa."

"And now Lawrence."

"Yes."

We drove through the midnight, searching.

The river—the very reason for Lawrence—ran through the city west to northeast. Western end held the dam, wide expanse of black water beyond it; downstream, the canals powered the giant mills, one north of the river, one south. Road and rail bridges spanned the steady flow, while streets and lanes came off the spine of the river like ribs, stretching out into the neighborhoods that reached up into the hills.

We slowed as we looked over silent train yards and lonesome barge docks, empty save for the occasional night watchman in a lantern-lit shack. Took us past every bit of the city I could think of that was remote enough to fit Ieva's description of where this thing might have slipped in and made a lair. Each time I brought us to a new spot, Ieva would look around, eyeing the ways in and out, fingering the beads that clicked on her rosary. Was an hour or better past midnight when I pulled the wagon clanking and banging over a rough bit of road that edged the marshland down where the river made her great turn to the left. Horned owl called out from the darkness of the marsh. A low building sat by the river's edge.

"Gristmill," I said. "Got flooded out a couple of years back. Fella works as a boiler man at the mill used to work there, mentioned it a few times."

I stopped the wagon. Night sky filled in the shadows and outlined the rotting sills and collapsed roof of the mill. Ieva watched it.

"If not here, should be," she said.

"How'll we know?"

"There's a feeling that nags and pulls at something—something—don't know English of it. Part of mind that raises fear. For warning."

"Got it. I was on that ship, remember."

"Then you know."

I climbed down and gave her my hand. We found an old path nearly lost beneath cat-brier and blackberry bush, leading to a well that'd gone to rot. We paused. Sound of the river passing by the banks was all we heard.

"And if we find him?" I whispered.

"We leave."

"You said we'd be killing him, unless I heard you wrong."

"Eventually. Not at night though. Most strong then. During daylight, they hide, they are in a stupor."

"Even Liam?"

"No. The verg, the slave, will be driven on, day and night. They may not even be allowed to sleep at all, from what I have seen."

"Sonofabitch."

"Their souls are poisoned. Ruined."

I didn't want to believe her words, not about Liam. We stopped talking and approached the building. Nothing stirred. Ieva sniffed the air and I remembered the stench from the *Jack Ketch*. I smelled nothing but river mud and decaying ferns. Put my hand on a windowsill that'd gone soft with mold. The inside of the building was black broken with stray chinks of moonlight.

"Looks empty."

A breeze blew out of the marsh, clammy and rich. I walked over to the doorway and put my hands on the warped boards of the door. I gave it a pull, and parts of the bottom caught on the sill and I had to give it a good tug. The hinge gave a rusty sigh, and it opened. I braced it with my shoulder.

"What do you think?"

Ieva leaned in past me, searching with her gaze. A falling ceiling hung with cobwebs and leaves that'd come in the torn roof. The base of an old wood stove sat in the corner. Beyond, a wide doorway opened into the mill. Ieva squatted, ran her fingertips along the uneven floorboards.

"Dust," she said. "Not disturbed."

She stood and moved through the falling slices of moonlight. Noticed that she moved with grace, smooth and controlled. Wasn't like Maggie. She stepped to the large doorway. I followed. The mill room had held up better under the crush of New England winters—roof intact, a few panes of glass still in the muntins. Sounds of water came up from where the mill wheel had once extended out.

"Not here," she said.

"What're we looking for?"

"Signs. Tracks, in and out. Disturbance. Bodies."

"Bodies?"

"With new veln, there are bodies brought. To feed on their souls. I've seen as many as a score."

"Alive or dead?"

"Both. Neither."

"I don't follow," I said.

"They're alive when brought. Brought by verg. Then, their souls are taken. Devoured. The bodies remain alive. Breathing, heart beating weak. But they're past this world by then." She turned and cut back through the front room. "We keep looking."

I glanced once more at the darkened mill room and followed her. The humid night air outside was better than the musty air of that crumbled building.

"But we can kill this thing. If we find it in the daylight."

She rattled the bag she carried.

"This isn't my luggage," she said.

We followed the path back to the carriage. She slid the bag up before her, then climbed to the bench. I got up and took the reins. The moon had ridden down to the western hills. Ieva turned.

"We keep looking?"

Nodded my head. "Night is young, and there's still tea left, Sister."

13

———

WATCH OVER US AGAINST THE DEVIL

Dawn was hours away. Father Ralph Flaherty returned to St. Mary's, exhausted. Another family sliced through with cholera, another long vigil after the mother had succumbed to the dry collapse. He walked along the pathway to the rectory with his leather bag at his side and his head down. Fog slid along the walkway with him, ghostly in the lantern light. At the back steps, he paused. The stars blurred in the humid air above Lawrence, deep in the black. Along the cemetery behind the church, the trees were silhouettes, shifting in the wind, leaves whispering.

An unexpected dread touched him. He turned to the door and unlocked it and was just pushing it in when footsteps hurried up the walkway behind him.

"Father Ralph."

Flaherty pushed the door open and waited.

"Miss Constance," he said.

The spinster bustled along the path, cradling something in her arms. She came to a stop before Flaherty, breathing heavily through her small nose, touching a gloved hand to the decorative hat that angled over the braided hair on either side of her head.

"I wondered where you were," she said. "The lights were out."

"I was with the Murphys. Mrs. Murphy passed."

Constance crossed herself and pursed her lips. "I'm sure it was a comfort just having you there. A helping hand up to heaven, Father Ralph."

Flaherty wasn't sure about that—the poor woman had been a lifeless husk after a week of violent diarrhea.

"Well, it is late, Miss Constance."

"And I couldn't live with myself if I didn't see that you had a hot meal after all your sacrifice. I've made you a hearty—"

"White pudding and turnip."

She smiled.

"You and I are peas in a pod, Father Ralph. Finishing each other's thoughts."

She slid past him with a rustle of skirts. Flaherty sighed and followed her inside.

WITHIN THE HOUR, Father Ralph bade Constance goodnight from the side door. She heard the latch slide as she headed off along the path, passing by the cemetery. He'd eaten well, and of course the blessing over the meal had been wonderful, just the two of them. Busy as he'd become of late—masses filled to standing, even the evening ones—she knew her role in his life, and in the life of the church, was different. Unique—that was the word.

And if Father Ralph had to dedicate himself to the Father above, then Constance had no difficulty in dedicating herself to Father Ralph.

What would that poor man do without me? she wondered, not for the first time.

She turned the corner. The street lantern was dark and shadows held fast along the headstones.

"Watch over your servant, Lord," Constance sang-sung. She smiled. A feeling grew on the side of her neck as she walked. She slowed and glanced into the cemetery. The light was still on in Father Ralph's room upstairs in the rectory behind the church. Beyond, the steeple of St. Mary's rose into the sky, blacking out the stars behind it.

"Darling."

Constance stopped. The voice had spoken from the cemetery, clear. She strained to see into the blackness.

"Father Ralph?" she said. Her voice quivered, not entirely with the jolt of being startled. She'd often wondered how it might happen—just as she'd always prayed hard on such filthy thoughts.

Someone stood among the headstones, halfway between the rectory and the sidewalk. Constance smoothed the front of her dress. A heat hummed in her lower belly.

"You frightened me. That's not nice," she called out.

"I'm sorry. Come."

The thrill was so much more powerful than Constance had ever even imagined. It was happening. Images leapt to her mind —their hungry mouths, her dress and petticoats in the grass among the grave markers, his words in her ear, his part finally touching her own. Her breath tightened.

"You're sure?"

"Yes."

She stepped forward, placed a gloved hand on the cast iron edge of the gate and pushed. It opened inward with a screech. Standing twenty yards into the cemetery stood a tall figure, an inky shadow. Still and indistinct, the thought of him filled Constance with a sinful heat. A humid wind gusted. Her eyes jumped back and forth, straining to make out Father Ralph in the deep shadows of the cemetery, halfway between the far side and where Constance had entered.

"Whatever you need, Father Ralph. I have it for you," she said.

"Anything?"

"Anything. Anything at all."

She cut through the weathered headstones, crosses and rectangles, an angel here and there. A shuddering chill brushed the back of her neck. She came out along a row between the graves. He stood next to a marble cherub grasping a twisting pair of musical pipes. He held out a pale hand. Constance stepped forward.

"I won't breathe a word to anyone, this is just between you and me."

She stopped. A sickening smell hit her nose—rot and unclean flesh. Behind the figure, the light inside the rectory of St. Mary's went out.

"Father Ralph?" Constance said. Her insides went watery.

"I'll take you to meet a much better Father."

Cold laughter crawled from the pale face. It wasn't Father Ralph. Glimmering eyes and blanched skin, sideburns. Constance's shoulders and chest went tight. She spun around, ran. Before she got half a dozen strides, a shadow rushed at her from behind an obelisk grave marker. Constance threw her arms up. She got hit hard, flipped onto her back. She grunted in surprise. The figure who'd hit her got to its feet. Constance recoiled when she saw it was a young girl dressed in fouled night-clothes, her hair crusted with grime. The girl limped forward and stood over Constance. Her face was grotesque—wide at the brow, narrow and elongated at the chin, dark nubs sprouting out from her temples. Her arms hung down into the hooked claws of gangly fingers.

"Stay away," Constance said in a desperate voice, holding her hands out in front of her face.

Boot-steps crunched the ground behind her, coming to a stop just behind her head.

"She loves her new Father. You will come to feel the same. Father will enjoy your heat."

Constance screamed. The sound had barely crossed her lips when the girl fell on her. Her struggle was short.

. . .

FATHER RALPH RELAXED as the first pale of dawn filled his room in the rectory. He sat on a hard chair in the corner, a blanket across his lap in spite of the humid night. If he'd slept at all, it had been without realizing it. On the table next to him, a bottle of brandy, the mouth of it sticky. Fumes hung stale in the air. He shoved off the blanket and stood. His knees cracked; his mouth was a down-turned line. The scream that had called his name then trailed off in terror replayed yet again in his mind. Throughout the long night, so had the words of his parishioners from the past weeks.

Peered in my window, it did, Father. White as the underbelly of a fish.

Feet of a goat, prints bigger than my hands.

The Irish filled Masses now, leaving nothing but room to stand. Seeking understanding, seeking answers.

A shadow crept in and took 'em away, Father. Left nothin' but the stench of charred skin and brimstone.

Seeking protection.

The streets are haunted when the sun goes down, they're saying. Curse has come upon us.

Father Ralph looked out the window at the familiar horizon of brick chimneys and hills. Thin clouds to the east wore the light of coming sunrise. He pushed the hair back from his forehead, flattening it into place. He looked at the door to the hallway. Cleared his throat.

Creeps inside, it does. After them as lost their faith, Father Ralph.

He'd heard noises in the night, from inside the rectory. He took his Bible from the bed stand and knelt, bowed his head and muttered the prayers, his hands following their well-worn paths, forehead to chest, shoulder to shoulder.

You'll protect us and watch over us against the Devil, won't you Father?

When he finished, he stood, closed the Bible, and went to the door. The smell hit him as soon as he stepped into the hallway. Feces. The floors were neat, undisturbed. Father Ralph took a pair of steps. The second floor stair landing was still in twilight. He half-expected to see something standing there, obscured in shadow. The stench grew stronger, strong enough to gag him, to make his stomach flip. He paused at the top of the stairs.

"Miss Constance?" he called out.

Your name. She screamed out your name. And you froze. You did nothing.

The sound of his voice died out in the empty rectory. He went down the stairs. The kitchen was lighter than the hallway. When he stepped in, he saw that the door stood open. The vile stink fouled the room. He scanned the floorboards. Nothing. The farther he went, the stronger it got, and the more it worked into his nerves.

The grave, the skulls, empty black holes, the worms, deep water, burning bones, nothing nothing nothing forever.

A fear bleaker than any he'd known took him. He steadied himself on the edge of the table.

"Fresh air," he croaked. He rushed to the door. The sooty bite of Lawrence air had never tasted so clean. For the first moment since leaving the corner of his room, he felt he could get on top of the nameless terror that had choked the sleep from him. After a few moments, he was about to turn back into the rectory when he noticed that something was wrong in the cemetery. He crossed the bricks until he reached the wrought iron fence. Beyond, every headstone marker in the cemetery—every cross, every angel, every plain stone—sat in the grass, knocked flat. Crows dotted the upturned markers, lined the fence. The further Father Ralph looked around, the more of the silent birds he saw. In one sudden moment, the birds—from the roof, the wall, the fence, the trees and markers in the cemetery—rose into the air in a flurry. The mass of them blotted out the sun just breaking the hills, their shadows crawling across the side of the church behind him.

The crows swirled and spun in a black whorl that rose and moved out over the trees out back, disappearing into the morning, the stragglers and outliers dotting the sky. They disappeared over the hills.

Father Ralph wished he'd brought the brandy with him.

14

ONE KNOT OF THIS MYSTERY

There was tired, and there was tired—and I'd gone beyond both on the lanes and roads of the city by the time the sun cleared the mills and set the river ablaze with moving gold, mist still clinging to the banks. Got myself to the mill early and stood with the men by one of the coffee carts. One of my eyelids twitched—and I'd barely even started in on the twenty-seven cups of coffee I expected the workday would require. The talk was of the mill dogs, a couple of fifty-pound terriers that Mac had brought in to keep the vermin busy in the basement. Not a one of them was to be found. Didn't come up for their food scraps, didn't come at a whistle.

"Found naught but a line of crap going down the hall past the boilers," one of them said. "Like one of them thought shittin' while runnin' seemed a fine thing to do."

As the talk turned to other matters, I spotted Maggie and Nell heading into the mill. Maggie's ivory face searched this way and that. I raised a hand. She paused for a moment, but then had to chase after Nell, who never saw a set of stairs she didn't want to barrel up or down at full speed.

I walked in with Mac Harriman. He didn't look much better rested than me.

"You anyone in mind we could use for a night-watchman?" he said.

"New fella quit already?"

"Came by around two this morning to check in on him. Gone. Bottle on the floor of the shack."

"Theo'd love it. Always on about joining the army."

"He's a knack for keeping men away, don't he." Mac rubbed his temple. "But I'd never hear the end of it, from him or his ma. He'd be around during the days and they'd both go crazy."

I headed up the stairs and clapped him on the shoulder.

"I think of anyone, I'll see what I can do," I said. He waved me well with the first two fingers of his right hand and headed to the big office.

BY THE AFTERNOON, the heat broke for a spell. Summer storms came in low over the valley, bringing with them streaming rains. Lightning caught the hills in wicked blue-white jags, thunder shaking the glass in the Everett's windows. Grew dark enough that the lamp crews had to go from floor to floor, lighting the wall lanterns so everyone could work.

One of my crew—a block-headed fella named Paulson with a couple of missing teeth and onion breath that'd hurt your nose from ten paces—wheeled a wooden handcart with the latest two-dozen shoes he'd put together down the far end of the floor, where they'd get their finer stitching before getting polished and boxed up. I spotted a rosary hung up on the side of the creaky cart. Wasn't the only one I'd seen that afternoon.

"What's this?" I asked him, nodding to it.

"All right I have it there, Mr. Carey? Mother made me promise to keep it with me. Talk going around, sir."

He said a mouthful. Thought about all the lonesome spots I'd looked at with Sister Ieva during the night. I nodded to Paulson.

"Don't worry it—just get it out of sight if you see Mr. Winthrop about."

Paulson nodded and started up alongside the machines once again. Took a closer look as I went about my business and saw more stuff hanging up around people's workstations: rosaries, some medals, little leather bags holding who knows what. In two spots, I saw tiny piles of what looked like pigs' teeth. Mr. Winthrop'd have my head if he noticed any of it—his deep affection for the Irish notwithstanding—but I let it go. If half of what Ieva said was true, none of it could hurt.

Came back to my office to find a man sitting in there, drenched from the rain now blowing sideways outside the windows. He wore dark trousers and a traveling jacket and cap. In his hand, a damp note-booklet, smudged with pencil marks.

"Finn Carey?" he said.

"Aye."

He extended a hand. "Tom Barley. Lawrence Tribune. Hoping you'd have a minute or two."

I shook his hand. Didn't have the grip of a working man, that was sure.

"What can I do for you, Mr. Barley?"

"Couple of questions about Tommy Fitzgerald."

"Already spoke with the police about that."

"I know you did," he said. He ran a hand through the thinning hair over his ear and looked at me through the half-height spectacles he had perched on his nose. "Wondered if you know anything about his brothers."

Thought of the ransacking of our rooms, the hovel down by the river. Kept all such thoughts off of my face.

"Hear they're just as useless," I said.

"And a couple are just as dead. Rory and Donal."

Didn't let any surprise show on my face. "Then let me join the thousands in Lawrence who aren't surprised by that, Mr. Barley. Not one of your finer families."

"You haven't heard."

"Should I have?"

"Both of them had their eyes gouged out, their faces clawed and torn. Tongues missing."

"Jesus."

"You were down to the shanties looking for them, as I understand."

"Looking, yeah."

"And why was that?"

I sat at my desk, motioned for Barley to sit. He did. Glanced outside my door where Theo hunched over a set of uppers, muttering to himself and making a face.

"Was having a problem with some of them. You probably know that."

He nodded.

"So I headed down there to give them a message to stay clear of me and mine. And, no—that message didn't involve nothing more than a little bit of floor time for one of them. Niall, it was. Took a rusty pistol from him. Did us all a service."

"You think they were coming for you?"

"Think so. Had a break-in. Pretty sure it was them."

"No police," he said.

"Irish stealing from the Irish. No one in blue cares."

"You're a floor boss."

"That don't wring quite enough of the Irish out of me, far as the police go."

"Suppose not."

He looked at me for half a minute and I held his eye right back.

"We could keep staring at each other," I said. "Or I could get back to work if I've answered your questions."

"They take anything valuable?"

"Not yet. Why I wanted to put a stop to it."

He glanced at his note-booklet and then looked back up at me. "Police think it's a blood feud."

"That what you think?"

"I think something else is going on. Something that started out in Gloucester." He watched me.

"Gloucester," I said.

"You've heard of the wreck of the *Jack Ketch*."

"I'm betting you already know some of my family came over on her."

He flipped over a few soggy pages of his notes. "Sisters. Got them jobs here, right?"

"One of them. And a neighbor from back in Ireland."

He didn't mention Liam—and neither did I. Wanted to see where he was going.

"Then you know all about the drownings, the clear sea. Empty ship floats ashore, sound as the day she was built, then burns for the sea to take."

"That's about right, yeah."

"Heard there was one fella who'd gotten onto the ship before she burned. Went mad from it, to hear the tale," Barley said.

"You talk to him?"

"Killed himself two nights before I got out there. Drunk himself silly on rum, muttering to all who'd listen that the Devil was going to sing him a lullaby. Then he stepped right off one of the piers in the harbor just before midnight. They pulled his body up the next morn—it'd floated up against a cod boat."

The rain eased up as the thunder moved east of the valley.

"Whole town's been locked up tight since," he went on. "The nights are still and the streets are empty. Strange fish been coming up in the nets. Water birds crying out at night, shrieking and restless. A darkness sits on the harbor."

"You've a way with words, to be sure—but that's Gloucester."

"Not just. It spread inland. Hunted down more tales. A pale

figure creeping around houses at night, on the roads. Couple of houses in Topsfield found empty, the families that live there gone, up and fled for no reason. An old woman claims she saw a shadow near twelve feet tall moving down a moonlit road, accompanied by a pale man."

"You put that in your paper?"

"Every word verified."

"Stories like that sell newspapers, too, I'm guessing."

"You think it's bunk?" he said.

"My heart melts for a good bogey story as much as the next Irishman's."

"Not what I asked."

"Notice you're not in Topsfield or Gloucester," I said.

"The trouble's come to Lawrence."

"And the trouble is what?"

He tapped the pencil against the note-booklet.

"There's our question," he said. His eyes were clever, All right —he looked at me like he might have been seeing Sister Ieva and me picking our way through the most downtrodden and abandoned spots in the city until the dawn broke. "Couple of murders —nothing new, especially among the Irish. Bit noteworthy in method."

"Fitzgerald."

"Fitzgeralds—three of them. Now, we've got some missing lasses. Prostitute. Mill girl from a Peabody family. Spinster near St. Mary's. People are jumpy."

"Noticed," I said.

"Tales going around. A pale man by the canals, singing at night. Shades haunting the cemetery on Gale's Hill. Variations on that."

"But here you are, talking with me, Mr. Barley."

A smile from him. "You happen to be a unique piece of the puzzle, worth talking to."

"Unique."

"Far as I can tell, you're the only person in the city who has ties to the *Jack Ketch*, Gloucester, and the Fitzgeralds—all at once."

"Maybe I'm missing what the Fitzgeralds have to do with that ship or Gloucester."

"Ah," he said, tapping the note-booklet like it had all the answers. "About that. Tavern out in Gloucester, place called the Shorebird. Burned to the ground week and a half ago. Fella came into it on a Thursday eve, pale fella. Unclean. Asking around for anyone who'd been on the *Jack Ketch*. More'n one person told me he was as pleasant as a corpse, shuffling through the crowd claiming something of his had been taken from the ship. Didn't go over too well with the fishermen, who thought to teach him some Gloucester manners. Time it was over, three of them had broken skulls and the place had flames that reached thirty feet into the harbor air."

I leaned back. All I could picture was Liam.

"And to all appearances," Barley continued, "the very same fella shows up at the Hemlock Street Tavern here in Lawrence not a week ago. Asking around for survivors from that ship, again. Night later, he's out in the shanties, searching for something."

"You think it was the same fella," I said.

"Had half a dozen people tell me so. They'd been at the Hemlock. Recognized the fella as he was prowling through the shanties."

"Still don't see how the Fitzgeralds are connected to any of it," I said.

He nodded and tapped his pencil to his notebook. "And therein lies one of the knots of this mystery."

One of my mechanics rapped his knuckles on the doorframe of my office.

"Sorry, Mr. Carey," he said. "Mr. Harriman sent me to fetch you. He's in the fourth storage bay, needs you."

"Be right there."

I stood up.

"If we're all done, Mr. Barley—I've a floor that doesn't stop. Wish I could help, but I may not be quite the puzzle piece you think."

He stood up, tucked the pencil behind his ear. Extended his soft hand once again. I shook it.

"If you think of anything else," he said, "you can find me at the paper, over on Essex."

"If I do."

I escorted him out of the office, to the stairs. His glance took a lot in. Waved him goodbye and headed off. Couldn't help but notice that for all his notes, he hadn't taken a one as we'd spoken.

SOUTH SIDE of the mill had a storage end to it, eight floors worth, next to the six floors of the main mill. Ceilings were low, still fresh with the smell of pitch pockets in the planed beams. Woolens and the like were stacked and binned, made easy to get in and out. Found Mac with the day watchman in a far bay. Small window let the gray afternoon light in.

"What do we got?" I said.

"Murphy here noticed this," Mac said. One stack of dyed wool sheeting was roughed over.

"Stack them bad?"

"Behind."

I braced a hand on the pile and leaned over, careful not to knock my head on the low ceiling. Streaks of blood smeared the flooring, a handprint clear in the mess of it, drag marks coming off the fingertips.

"Who left this?" I said.

"Looked around, top to bottom," the watchman said. "Can't find nothing."

"Anyone hurt themselves, wander off?" Mac said.

I shook my head. Seen it happen before. Woman on one of

the spinning mules once had her thumb torn right off. She picked it up in her other hand, excused herself before anyone else realized what'd happened. The floor boss found her a while later in the water closet, trying to stick it back on with a bit of plaster, white as the paint on the walls by then.

"No one on the fifth," I said. "Don't look too fresh."

The blood had gone to rust.

"Perfect," Mac said. He caught the bridge of his nose between his thumb and forefinger.

"I'll get a count on mine, have the others get a count on theirs. Put it up against anyone out today," I said.

"Make it fast. Mr. Winthrop is coming by tomorrow. He's not happy."

"You'll have it by evening, Mac."

Was on the stairs heading back to the fifth, thinking about who was missing. Started me thinking about what was missing.

Still don't see how the Fitzgeralds are connected to any of it.

Stopped in my tracks.

And therein lies one knot of this mystery.

Hit me clear, in a flash. I turned around, started down the stairs, taking them two, three at a time until I came out on the second. Saw Ben Hambry standing by one of the rag pickers. He came over when he saw me.

"What's this about a count?" he said.

"Where's Nell?"

"Over to first bay, where she should be."

"Need to talk to her. It's important."

"Course."

I cut through the fabric bins, moving in and around the lasses sorting and folding. Nell was by herself, a tall pile of worsted trousers next to her. She yawned.

"What was it?" I said.

She started at my voice, gave me a look. "What?"

"What'd you take?"

Saw something flash across her eyes before she hid it.

"Buttons. Like I said."

"Nell."

"Bag of them."

"You're not in trouble," I said. I knelt, took her by the shoulder to face me. "Just tell me one thing—was it from the ship?"

A guiltier look couldn't have passed her face.

"It was a key, wasn't it?"

"Found it. That's all."

She chewed on the inside of her cheek, then looked me in the eye. "Someone find it?"

"Jesus, Nell."

I sat back on my heels.

...He'd been going through the galleys and holds, asking around after the girls.

Came clear right then, like a kick right in the gut.

...shuffling through the crowd claiming something of his had been taken from the ship.

I stood up.

"Come on, we're leaving early. We're getting Maggie."

I dragged Nell by her collar, ignored the stares it got me.

15

A MASTER SO CRUEL

No one was happy as I drove them across the city, each of them with only an armful of their things, grabbed fast from the McAllisters. The sun dropped below the clouds and sent its late afternoon rays across the dripping streets and roofs, into the steam that rose where the summer heat burned off the rain. I pulled the carriage to a stop in front of the King Street Boarding Rooms.

"You're sure about this?" Maggie said. In the sunlight, the peeling paint and rotted window frames didn't quite make it to charming.

"I'd say the word 'sure' don't have quite the weight it used to," I said. "But for the time being, this'll do."

"We'll make the best of it, somehow." She kept her voice light, but I could tell that she had her doubts. She wasn't the only one.

"Kitty," Rose said. She pointed at a rat the size of a puppy that squeezed behind a wooden barrel against the front of the flophouse.

"Rat," Nell said. "The kind that bites your face off when you sleep."

"Nell," Maggie said.

"Not mine," Rose said.

I hitched the team and helped the girls from the carriage. Our shadows spun out along the muddy street. I gathered them at the door.

"Now you're not to mention to anyone we've moved."

"You said we wasn't moving for good. Not really moving, you said," Nell said.

I held my hands up. "Look. I don't want anyone—not from the mill, not around the city—to know where we are."

"He's right," Maggie said.

"How do you know?" Nell said.

"Feel it."

"Well I hate it," Nell said. "Smells like puke."

"I don't recall anyone asking for your thoughts," I said.

"They're my thoughts. I can have them."

"And you can keep them in that hard head of yours. Ain't making it any easier on your sister, talk like that."

I was harder on her than I might have been, but there we were, the lot of us unhappy as we marched into the flophouse.

Nell hadn't been wrong. The room smelled of cooked vegetables and piss and stale sweat. I put their things on one of the two musty mattresses, the pleasures of which, along with the nasty water closet down the hall, would cost me near as much as it cost to keep the horses in feed.

"Hope they have enough snakes to eat the spiders," Nell said.

"Snakes?" Rose said.

Maggie swatted Nell. "There's none. Your sister's being an arse."

"It'll be fine," I said. "We've all been through worse, and this's just for a spell."

"How long?" Maggie said.

"Until I clear up a few things around the city. That's all. Couple of days. Week, maybe."

Maggie turned to the girls. "You heard Finn. Get your things unpacked. Take whichever bed you like."

While the girls tussled over who got which bed, Maggie turned. "You're staying with us, right?"

"Have to watch the carriage house. Too much to do and worry about you at the same time."

"I can help," she said.

"Maggie."

"Got a sense about things, don't forget."

"Need you to take care of the girls."

"Want to take care of you, too," she said. She said no more, but there was a lot in her eyes. Was footsteps coming up the hallway that snapped my attention away. As I'd expected, it was Sister Ieva, heading back to her own room, just down the hall. She stopped when she passed the open doorway.

"You're early," she said. Her tone wasn't happy.

Maggie looked at her, then back at me.

"Change of plans, Sister," I said.

"Who's this?" Ieva said.

"Sister—this is Maggie Lane. She's helping me with the girls. Maggie—this is Sister Ieva. I'm helping her."

I turned to Ieva. "Got my two sisters here, too. Ain't safe back in the Plains."

Maggie looked at Ieva, her fingers twisting a fold of her skirt, this way and that. The two of them gave each other an eye. At the same moment, they both glanced at me.

"She's a nun, Maggie," I said. I turned to Ieva. "And she's fine. Trust her with my kin."

Ieva nodded, though I could tell she still wasn't happy. She looked thrilled compared to Maggie, however—you'd have thought I'd just handed her a return-trip passage claim for the *Jack Ketch*. Nell poked her head out the door.

"Rat turds under the bed," she said. She looked at Ieva.

"My sister Nell," I said.

"You cut your hair without a mirror?" Nell said, staring at Ieva. Ieva frowned. Introductions went well all around, I'd say.

Not long after, I drove the team fast through the streets. Maggie stayed behind with the girls.

"It's the key you mentioned," I said.

"How?" Ieva said. She had her bag with her and looked better rested than I was.

"The ship. Nell. She's a mind of her own, and—sad to say—she's a bit of a thief. Must've crept around in the holds, come across it somehow, snagged it."

Ieva shook her head. "He had a verg. He would watch over such things."

"Wasn't with him the whole time, is my guess. Maggie said he'd caused a ruckus with the other passengers. So Nell swipes it, he finds it missing during the storm, goes all over the ship, somehow works out it was Nell. But bad luck for him and for our friend the veln—he gets swept overboard."

"And the master would need a new verg," Ieva said.

I flipped the reins, speeding the team along. Nodded.

"He would," I said. "And who comes along, hot-tempered and out to protect his family, but my brother. This rotten, bloody devil took him. Makes him his newest slave. But in the chaos, Maggie and the girls jump ship. Nell's still got the key. Brings it with her back to Lawrence."

"And now he's drawn to it," Ieva said.

"Exactly. That's why he makes his way here, with Liam in tow. But by the time he gets here and closes in on it, Nell doesn't have the key anymore. The Fitzgeralds stole it, no idea what they were taking, they were just out to harass me." We crossed by the Common, riding to the hills west of the city where the sun was heading. "And they have the bad luck of having the key when our friend finally gets to it. He takes it back, slaughtering them."

"Vengeance," Ieva said.

"For what they stole. And what if he doesn't stop there?"

"He comes looking."

"Looking for Nell," I said.

She nodded. "So you hide them."

"That's a start."

"He doesn't forget."

"And neither do I, Sister."

I turned onto a road that wound up to Gale's Hill. Off to the south, a swampy bunch of acres stretched to the river, but along the hillside stood several large houses in the sunlight. Chestnut and willow trees stretched up bright against the sky.

"You know where to look," Ieva said.

"Newspaperman mentioned something to me. Talk been going around about shades haunting a cemetery up here. All I've got."

Winding lane ran farther than the houses, through patches of woods, and came out to a cemetery along the hillside. Shadows reached across the slanting ground. Along the far side stood a half-dozen crypts set into a terraced ledge of the hill. Family mausoleums, or storage for winter months when the ground was too frozen to bury the city's fresh dead. Pulled the team to a halt by the gates. Horses didn't want to stay still. I got down and patted their flanks. Ieva climbed down and I followed her through the stone gate in the wrought iron fence.

"Tombs look sealed from here," I said.

We cut our way between the headstones. Mosquitoes and floating weed pollen glowed in the rich light of sunset. I sniffed. Humid air carried up from the teeming city below mixed with the scent of the Merrimack, with the soil and dry grass around the stones. Nothing more—not the stench of rot and offal that had filled the hold of the *Jack Ketch*. Our shadows trailed us, reaching back to touch the wall fence. We stopped at the crypts. It was quiet, the hillside keeping the sounds of the city at bay. No signs that the overgrown grass had been disturbed. Ieva reached a hand and touched the stone door and the rusted iron hinges of the first crypt, cool in the humid air. Locked. I searched the ground, but nothing had passed the dark thresholds. Ieva turned.

"Not here," she said.

She swept her gaze across the headstones and fence, across the city falling into purple shadows of evening, running the back of a fingernail along her lower lip, squinting out past the fence and the headstones. In the gold from the western sky, I saw her face for a moment how Maggie must've—beautiful. Her dress was ridiculous as was her hair. She wasn't nothing but business in her behavior. In the time we'd spent scouring every deserted nook of the city, I'd never heard her make a joke nor a light comment. But looking at her in that moment, struck me again that she weren't any older than me. In her way, she was just as driven—more, even—than me, and her features showed it, but that didn't entirely hide the young woman she was.

"Nothing. Let's go."

She started back to the gate. I was about to follow when a noise behind me stopped me in my tracks. A dog ran along the outside of the cemetery, scrambling and frothing. Behind it, at the edge of the trees where the hillside slipped into twilight gloom, half a dozen deer bolted from the underbrush. A buck and some females, a fawn struggling to keep up. They zigzagged out of the darker woods. One by one, they leaped the low stone wall that bordered the cemetery, forcing Ieva to duck back out of their path. Once in the cemetery, they grew more panicked at the profusion of headstones and they spread apart, still racing. The fawn found the gate first and was followed by the others. The buck made the mistake of leaping in a panic over the wrought iron fence that fronted it. His back legs tangled on the ornamental spears that tipped the fence and his weight came down; he impaled himself with a bellow, the iron plunging deep into his underside. His legs kicked and scrambled, but he sank lower, screaming horribly.

By the time Ieva reached him, his struggling stopped. Blood ran down the white underside of his legs, slicked the iron of the fence and the wall beneath, ran in bright streams out of his nose and mouth. His eye was black and shiny, a white around it showing. Beyond, the rest of the herd raced down the hillside, disappearing into the evening.

"Aw, Christ," I said.

Ieva looked into the direction that the dog and the deer had come from. "They fled something," she said.

To the west, the horizon darkened against a fiery orange sky. The day was almost gone. We looked at the woods, and then at each other.

"It's why we're here," I said. She nodded.

We found a stream and followed it through the trees. A fingernail moon rose in the blue of the east, its image broken by branches as we went deeper into the woods. The stream became a braided twist winding between mossy rocks, smelling of minerals.

"How far do these go?" she said.

"Never been in them. Think they wrap the far hillside."

We pushed through prickers. The sun touched the ground through the trunks to the west—I figured it'd be down to a glowing smudge within a quarter hour.

"Wait," I whispered. I spotted a pair of low buildings, draped in the shadows of trees. Looked abandoned, judging by the empty windows and sagging roofs. As the wind stirred leaves and creaked branches above us, I realized that there was no other sound beyond that and the water. No frogs, no crickets, not even any mosquitoes. Nothing moved through the underbrush and pine-needled earth. "You feel it?"

"Yes," she whispered.

We followed the stream, stepping from stone to stone while

the water gurgled underfoot. A clearing fronted the buildings, overgrown with bramble and a carpet of dank leaves. The stench hit us from twenty paces. We didn't need to say a word, just exchanged a glance. Kept going, keeping silent, taking careful steps. The woods around the buildings dimmed blue with dusk. As we got closer, I noticed something hanging above the darkened entrance to the building. I reached and took Ieva's arm, stopping her. She looked where I pointed.

A body arched, impaled on an iron pole. A boy dressed in frayed pants and a dirty shirt. Fading daylight fell across his pale face and hands. The blood on his shirt had dried dark, as though he'd been there for at least a few days. Ieva leaned in close and spoke in a whisper. "This is it. The ground of a lair is always defiled with a killing."

Couldn't take my eyes off that dead lad. A child from the shanties. Or the streets. Maybe even one who'd stolen his way onto a ship bound for America, strong-headed and on his own. Took me right back. Scrounging. Hungry. Cold in the winter. Spending days collecting the ends of cigars thrown away by smokers, cutting off the burnt part to sell to a tobacconist for pipe use, or collecting cinders from coal ashes, or raking for rags and dish cloth in the gutters to sell to paper makers. Long, hard road, lots of forks in it—and I felt how slim was the difference between one route and another.

Ieva pulled me out of my thoughts by starting forward, pushing through witch grass. I took one more glance at the dead lad and followed. We reached the tumbled fall of beams and rotted boards below the body. I peered inside. Mud and leaves stretched into the dark interior. Stalls and splintered shelving lined the side while a pair of rusted circular saw blades leaned against the wall. I guessed that it'd once been a sawmill. The reek of rotting flesh hung in the air. We ducked under the canted beams. Half a dozen paces in, we stopped. On the splintering flooring, dead leaves, wet and rotted undersides showing. A trail was visible, dozens of drag marks through them. I tapped Ieva on the arm and whispered.

"Not much day left."

Ahead of us, chinks and spaces between the planks of the walls shone high with the last rays of sunset.

"We look, hurry. Ten minutes," she said.

The work areas were empty but for flotsam: a rusted lantern here, some dusty tin plates there, a stool with a broken leg and the seat missing. At the passageway's end stood a sagging doorway. The silence was heavy. Ieva stepped up to the doorway. My pulse trip-hammered in my ears. Felt a poison in the air, a dark hatred flowing out like a vapor from beyond that doorway. Ieva turned and looked at me. She raised one eyebrow. I nodded, then stepped through the doorway into a larger space of columns. The roof sagged at the far end. A broken workbench stood askew beside a pile of rusted machine parts, a group of rotted palates, clamps for the old planing station. Across the space, the daylight faded deep orange in the bays, hazy through the dusty windows.

Ieva stepped in behind me. I held up a hand and pointed to the corner, to a bay beneath the sagging ceiling.

Bodies. Limbs and hair and closed eyes, stacked into one corner in a tumbled heap, near a dozen of them. They all looked like lasses. Their skin shone pale, thatched with muddy streaks and cuts. Behind me, Ieva dropped her bag on the floor and popped the latches, rooted through it. I turned to her.

"What're you doing?" I whispered.

"Taking this opportunity."

"Thought you said we weren't going after him at night. He's strongest now."

"We hurry."

"Hurry it is, then. Where is he?"

"Underneath the bodies."

She pulled out a pair of metal spikes wrapped in cloth, handed them to me. Next, she handed me a mallet that I tucked into my belt. She took out a silver flask. I watched the sunlight fade from the holes in the wall.

"Sun's going down."

"Pull the bodies aside."

We both hurried across the space. An unclean, meaty tang filled the air.

"Don't listen to anything, sing to yourself, hum, talk. Don't look into the veln's eyes. Do exactly as I say," she said.

I reached the pile of bodies. Instead of finding them cool and stiff as I'd expected, they were warm. I moved in closer and laid a hand on the nearest back. The lass took in slow breaths.

"They're alive," I said.

"Their bodies. Their souls have been devoured. No more as they were."

I shook the one I touched, not able to believe what Ieva said. The lass didn't stir, didn't flicker an eyelid, didn't move. Nothing. Not a one of them moved so much as a pinky. I pulled my hand from her in revulsion.

"Move them. Now," Ieva said.

Slipped the spikes into my back pocket and pulled the bodies off. "Can we help them?"

"Just pull them aside, hurry."

I did it, didn't think about it—closed my mind down on it like I'd once closed my mind down on the fact I had nothing to do but carry sixty-pound crates of shoe leather up and down six flights of stairs at the Everett for the next twelve hours, for not even a penny. The lasses came off easily enough. I dragged them by their armpits off to the side. Didn't recognize any of them, but I knew their types from seven years in Lawrence: a prostitute, a mill girl with arms dyed blue from coloring cloth, a pinched-faced woman dressed for Mass, a stick-thin lass from a poor neighborhood, timeworn clothing.

"*Muusu teevs debesiis*," Ieva said.

Glanced over at her as I took the next body off the pile. She held her arm out, a medallion hanging from a steel chain. The long room sunk into shadow as the last of the sunlight disappeared. Sunset. Right away, the air changed, and a baleful hatred flooded from out of nowhere. I hurried, took off the last of the bodies, a narrow-shouldered girl who wore an apron.

The veln was behind her, wedged into a space behind an iron column.

A devil he was, ripped straight from all the nightmare tales. Skin scorched and cracked, showing wide splits of raw flesh, seeping liquid. Was hard to tell his height, but the arms, fingers, and legs were grotesquely long. The stench of putrid corpse hit me strong enough to force me back a step. His face turned to us, yellowed eyes snapping open. A mouth wide enough to stick my foot into opened into a terrible smile.

"*Lai naak tava valstiiba, tavs praats lai notiek,*" he said, the words crawling from that dreadful opening.

"*Sveetiits lai top tavs vaards,*" Ieva said. Her voice was commanding. The veln laughed and turned his cruel gaze to me.

"And you're her mongrel dog," he said, in lilting English that sounded like he'd grown up in Kildalkey. "Sniffing around at the heels of this ridiculous false priest. Have you an ounce of sense?"

"Where's my brother, you sonofabitch?"

"Don't listen, don't speak!" Ieva said. "Remember."

The veln laughed, moved. Ieva stepped forward and doused him with water from the silver flask while calling out: "*Mūsu tēvs, kas esi debesīs, svētīts lai top Tavs vārds.*"

The flesh scalded where the drops struck it, and the veln howled in pain. A chorus of female screams erupted, the lasses spread out around us yelling in one giant voice. A wave of foul air washed into the room, gagging-strong.

"*Izraidīt Jūsu pekles ļauno atpakaļ šahtā!*"

Ieva kept the medallion in front of her, kept shaking the flask and spraying the water as she shouted the words. The veln rose in the darkness, his eyes shining with a will-o'-the-wisp light. I put him at over ten feet tall, lean and angled and carrying a long head with eyes like a goat and curls of black horn twisting wild from the sides of its head. The face of a fiend. He pinned Ieva with his gaze, long fingers gripping the column. A tongue came out from the stretched mouth. Bits of red glow raced along the cracks in his skin, the last huffing flames tracing embers in a fire.

"Shall we play, children?" he croaked. The voice was mocking, cruel. He locked his gaze with Ieva, then smiled. The fiend raised his hand. The shackled bodies of the lasses jerked. Ieva stepped forward, holding the medallion up. I noticed that the devil's eyes kept landing on that worn piece of metal, and each time they did, the bits of faint flame along his body blazed, tracing the contours of his vile shape. He spun and slouched to the back corner of the long room. Ieva followed, taking measured paces.

"*Debesu gaismu ir zaudētas jums, veln.*"

Another scream burst from the veln, echoed by the women—their mouths bellowing in agony, even as their eyes remained closed, their faces expressionless. The veln scrambled up onto a heap of palates and turned to us.

"Your time is almost over, Little Bear," he said. His voice was strained and rough, his breath beyond foul, his words in flat English.

"Back to the Abyss with you, veln," Ieva said. She swung the flask and another spray of water landed across the fiend, smoking and raising up tongues of flame. He yowled, along with the women, loud enough to shake the floorboards. He leaned his head forward and snarled.

"Poor Little Bear, trailing death wherever you set your feet," he whispered, his voice grave-soil. "The soldiers came. They ate your village."

I edged around to the side, watching Ieva. She held her ground.

"How your mother screamed," the veln said. "How she threw herself before them to protect you. She screamed for you to run.

And you were such a fearful child. Frightened of the forest. Frightened of the storms. Frightened of the shadows and the scuffling outside the door. You heard a noise, didn't you? It terrified you, but they didn't believe you."

He leaned back.

"The soldiers so enjoyed your gibbering terror. You ran from one corner to the other, from one dead sister to another, to your dead father, your precious dead mother. You peed all across that shabby little house. So they spared you."

He stepped forward.

"And again, the kind sisters—all killed around you. No one is safe around you, are they, Little Bear? And how have you repaid all this unearned mercy? By murdering my poor siblings, prisoners already, hunted already, suffering already. Digging for them. Attacking them when they've starved for a thousand years. Serving a master you don't even understand, a master so cruel you'd run into my arms if you only knew, Little Bear."

The voice—terrible as it was—pulled me in. I wanted to keep listening, I wanted to slip into the rumble of it, wanted to hear what it had to say next.

Ieva straightened. "You turned your back on mercy long ago, veln," she said. She raised the medallion. A faint light ran over its worn surface, the first bit of dawn shining on white marble, a winter moon shining on a clear lake. The fiend arched his back, raised a long hand before his face. "*Ko, ņemot vērā Kungs, tavs sods ir mūžīgs, neatsaucamu, un tikai. Pazūdi uz elli!*"

Flames erupted on the skin of the fiend and he let loose a yell that carried again into the throats of the lasses. The veln staggered backward. I got my first glimpse of the grotesque wings that sprouted from its back, draping it. It lowered its head, swaying back and forth, its eyes trained on the light that fast grew blinding. A river of chill air flowed into the room and the skin up and down my spine rippled into gooseflesh. All around Ieva's medallion, light swirled, blue-white and glimmering, rising off her outstretched arm like sea-spray in a fierce wind. She looked straight at the fiend. He bowed his head.

"I don't forget," the fiend whispered. Before Ieva could get another word out, the veln whipped his arm, sending the bodies slamming into the back wall. When Ieva turned to look, he sprung forward. One, two, three strides and he was upon her. The veln stood over her, fire dancing across the surface of his arms, his face. He lifted his head back and opened his immense jaws. His forked tongue curved. The light from the medallion flared.

"*Ak, mama, kāpēc Dievs tik dusmīgs, dara to pārtraukt. Tas nekas, bet vētra, maz vienu. Jūs esat droši. Nāc, mama ir jums,*" the veln said, his tone affected to sound like a child.

I picked up the first thing I could find: a four-foot length of rock maple. Ieva tried to scurry back, but the fiend moved in on her, striking fast as a serpent. He didn't get to finish her off—not when I cracked his head sideways, driving it with as much Irish as I could get into my swing, connecting so hard that I thought for a second I'd also broken my own wrists. The fiend's head swung to the side, and he grunted. He turned on me. I swung the board right at his face again. This time, he darted out of the way. Rather than swing again, I shot the board forward, as though stabbing with a sword. Got him right between his ghastly eyes, and it snapped his neck back. Before I could ready yet another hit, the board tore from my hands, leaving me with a cruel patch of splinters in both palms.

"You prick," I said.

Ieva used the distraction to spring forward, reaching up and pressing the medallion into the charred flesh of his neck, shouting out something in Latvian. The flames leaped up, but even they weren't as bright as the lightning-bright glow of that medallion. Our shadows stretched crisp across the wreckage. Ieva lifted her other arm, palm raised. With that, the fiend slammed to the floor, pinned against the stones. Wails rose from the tumbled pile of bodies on the chains. She turned to me.

"Spike," she said.

The fiend thrashed, but couldn't move out from underneath the burning medallion. I flung open the cloth, pulled out one spike. Had weight to it—looked to be made of silver. I tossed it to her. She caught it smoothly and laid the tip on the side of the veln's head, next to the black horn. I stretched my arm to her, holding the mallet by the head of it. She grabbed the handle, and with one fluid movement brought it down onto the spike, bashing it with a strength I hadn't expected.

The veln erupted into flames. Skin blistered and cracked, the insides glowing bright red like the heart of a forge. Ieva leaped free of the flames. His limbs flailed, the lasses voices rose in a terrible shriek. Ieva walked backward, graceful around the junk on the floor. The flames rose to the ceiling.

"Step back," she said. I didn't need to hear it twice.

She pressed the medallion to her lips, and spoke: "*Var jums ir pienākums atpakaļ uz bezdibenis, ko aizzīmogojusi spēku Kunga un Debesu gaismu. Jums ir uzvarēts, veln.*"

The air changed, the way it will before a thunderstorm, and my ears popped. The veln stopped moving, the flames shrunk down to trace his entire, foul outline—and then he winked out of the spot he'd lain on, leaving nothing behind but a brimstone stench and the silver spike, glowing molten white and dull red.

Behind us, the lasses stopped their screams, their exhales dropping to sighs, the only sound that filled the darkness.

16

ONLY HEARTACHE WHERE THE VELNS TREAD

The darkness was broken with moonlight falling in through the collapsed part of the ceiling. As it cooled, the glow of the spike faded. Gusts of night air weren't strong enough to push out the terrible stench which lingered, acrid in my nose and on my tongue.

"We did it. Jesus, we did it," I said, finding my voice. "Think I told you—you have a Carey on your side, you get it done."

Ieva hung the medallion around her neck, tucked it underneath her collar. In the faint light, she looked weary.

"It wasn't him," she said. She knelt and wrapped up the spikes in their cloth, gathered up the mallet, looking back the way we'd come in for her bag.

"Come again?"

"That was a baby. Just released, and rather weak."

"That was a baby?"

"Bad word. What's the English—fresh? New? You understand."

"Not a bit."

She stood up, wiped her palms on the sides of her trousers. "You weren't listening, earlier. This is what he does, the veln I'm after. With the key—the one from the ship. *Signum Profundum.* Key to the Abyss. He stole it. Your sister's not the only thief in this story, you see."

She walked past me.

"The centuries are dim on the matter, but the story as I've come to believe is this: When the prince of the veln, the leader of the fallen, the Devil as you say, when he escaped and was hunted and killed, he had the key."

"How?"

"I don't know. Tricked an angel, perhaps. Stole it, most likely. That led to his destruction. A battle seen for miles, a storm, lightning like the world has never seen. Happenstance, that the abbey was not far off. Or maybe not so much happenstance. Who's to say?" She gathered the items from her bag. "And after, in the wreckage that cut a scar through the deep forests, the Sisters of my Order found remains. They also found the key, with no idea of what it was. So they took it all—a few strange bones, a skull with horns, and the key. All treated as relics. Stored away in the catacombs beneath the abbey. Over time, they lost their significance, save as part of a tradition. Each Sister had a watch in that chilly back hallway, under flickering lantern light. Tiresome. Rote."

She placed the items into the bag, pressing each to her lips as she did.

"Until this other veln found us. How he escaped, I do not understand. But he was drawn. We weren't prepared, we'd grown forgetful over the centuries, lost in our daily affairs. He stole the key. He killed the Sisters, save for me."

"You had that medallion."

"A medallion of the archangel Uriel. A relic different from the others. Made from molten metal from the site of the battle."

"Powerful thing."

"Just saved our lives." She latched her bag and stood.

"Then where is he, the one we're after, the one who took Liam?" I said.

"We're too late, he's gone. He's done his job and moved on. As before."

"Where to?"

She shook her head. "I must find out. It takes time."

The breeze moaned through the decrepit sawmill, stirring the air through the uneven and cracked beams and walls. Heard the sound of crickets from the woods outside.

"Sister Ieva—how'd this one know about you? Was all that lies?" I said.

She looked at me. "They weren't lies. My family was slaughtered when I was a child. The sisters at the abbey , also."

"But how'd he know?"

"They have channels into this world, I believe. They can feel and know things that are strong inside us. Their vision is far different from ours."

"But he said your time is almost over. Like he knew just who you are—what you're doing."

"The veln I hunt. He's aware. He passed that on to this one."

"You're not worried?"

"I'm always worried, Mr. Carey." She lifted the bag.

"What'd he say to you—when you fell?"

She took a deep breath, hesitated.

"You don't have to say," I said.

"No. They are cruel. I'll tell you. From my childhood, something I said, something my mother said."

"If it's private."

"He was correct—I was a very anxious child. Dogs. Darkness. Storms most of all. The one before the soldiers came, that was the one. 'Oh, Mama, why is God so angry, make it stop,' I said. And my mother, she said 'It's nothing but a storm, little one. You're safe. Come, Mama has you, tiny bear.'"

She cleared her throat.

"Well, you just did something that most of the hardest men I know would piss themselves over. Never seen nothing like it."

"Thank you, Mr. Carey. You're kind," she said. "I'm fine now, and I'll be better when the last of these veln are back in the pit."

She turned to go, heading for the sagging doorway we came through.

"What about the lasses?" I said.

"Leave them. There is nothing we can do. As I told you, their souls have been torn out."

I headed back over to the bodies of the girls. The one with the apron lay on her side. I knelt. Her skin was warm, her mouth open, her ribs rising and falling.

"Seems a hard thing to do, just leaving them like that."

"This isn't a lark," Ieva said.

"A doctor could look at them. The hospital here is three years old, they could do something."

"Mr. Carey."

"Finn."

"Fine. Finn. There's only heartache where the veln tread. This I know."

The moonlight brushed the still features of the lasses. Ieva shifted the bag in her hands, the spikes knocking together with a muffled click.

17

TAKE THE LORD FROM THE WORKPLACE

Dawn was hours off when I stood at the narrow back doorway of the Shay Hospital at the foot of Prospect Hill. Light shone out of the nearby windows. I took a minute to gather up strength before going back and getting the last of the lasses. Carried her in my arms over to the others, who I'd placed on the ground, one next to another. I couldn't leave them, even with Sister Ieva staring at me like I'd lost the last of my good sense. They deserved better than to wither away, starving, dying on the musty floor of that old sawmill. Missing and lost.

Five women. Their faces were blank, their eyes closed, their mouths open. Ieva said their souls were gone. Something was gone, no mistaking it. Whatever makes a living, breathing person more than fleshy bellows and gears and columns and a forge—that most important piece of life—they didn't have it.

Stepped around them and went to the door. I found the bell pull on the right side. Gave one look back at the lasses and gave the pull half a dozen good yanks. Heard the clang from somewhere inside. Rapped on the door with my fist, loud. I turned and ran over to the carriage, swinging up into the driver's seat and setting the horses off with a word and a flip of the reins.

"Thanks for not stopping me," I said.

Ieva shook her head. "You are determined to ram your head into a brick wall—who am I to stop you?"

"One of the many benefits of a thick Irish skull." We crossed over the river. Mist clung to the edges as the sky lightened. "Hard to think there's no hope for them."

She said nothing, even though the way she looked off into the coming dawn as much as said there wasn't. We had little else to say as I dropped her off at the boarding house. I headed back to the Plains. Looked after the team and fell into an exhausted sleep for the remaining sliver of the night.

WITH THE RAIN MOVED ON, the leaden heat of summer blanketed the city once again. Garbage in the alleys, bushels of horseshit in the hot dust, rotten sewage and night-soil—the streets grew cloying. Up in the Everett, thick sunlight deepened the color of the bricks and warmed the wooden floors as the temperature climbed. Noticed gouges and awls slipping in people's hands from the sweat. Was around three o'clock when Mac Harriman showed up on the fifth. He gave me a quick once-over.

"You look like hell," he said.

"Lovely choice of words, Mac. Thanks."

"Winthrop is on his way up here. Hearing the recommendations of the engineers and reviewing the figures for the last four months." Mac shook his head. "And he's fuming. Not happy hearing how much the improvements'll cost. Not happy about missing his targets. Yesterday his runners brought me seven notes, each note more pissed than the last."

"And now your head is his favorite bed-pan," I said.

"That's about the size of it."

"Well, maybe those engineers he's had about could rig you a shielding device of sorts."

"Be the most useful thing they've suggested. What I need is a cure for Winthrop," he said. He gave a twist of a smile and wiped the sweat from his brows with the back of his hand. "The other thing that's got him bothered is the religious stuff. He's seen it all over. Rubbing him the wrong way. Have your people take it down, get it out of sight—whatever it takes."

"Done," I said. "The Lord'll have to understand."

"Good, because Winthrop won't. He'll be up this way in half an hour. Hoping he sees your crew last, it'll put him in a better mood."

"Most Godless crew of Irishmen he'll ever see," I said. "It'll warm his heart."

I started with Theo and the upper-makers, two dozen of them in a U-shaped area. Got up on a low crate.

"Listen up," I said. "We need all this religious stuff out of sight, right now. And don't give me those looks—I'll go confess at St. Mary's on behalf of the mill, so your own souls are in the clear, boys."

They weren't happy about it, but pulled down a few medallions, tucking away pictures of saints and whatnot. Used to look at such things as nothing but cheap trinkets—not being a church-going man myself—but after what I'd seen the night before, I gave it another think, remembering how that medallion had shone, an ice-blue star.

I took Theo along with me to help get the word out. I went down one side of the floor, he went down the other. Got my side done. Reached the end and saw Theo standing and arguing with a fella by the name of Williams. Now, Williams had twelve brothers and sisters working at the Everett, always getting grief from me and the other floor bosses for praying too much at work—Polycarp prayers, Mary's Consent, Our Blessed Mother, meal prayers, various devotions and prayers to the Cross. All prayed in place of working, mind you. And of everyone on the floor—maybe in the mill itself—Williams' bench won the prize for most resembling the Holy Father's dressing table: bits of cloth, rosaries and medals, printed cards with saints on them. Wouldn't have been surprised to see a giant, homemade Papal Tiara stood up in the corner, in case he needed it to defend the faith more formally. More, he'd made it clear every day since he'd first started that it chafed him to rub elbows with those that'd be spending eternity roasting in the lake of fire—which, sadly, included myself and Theo and nine out of ten men up on the fifth. Williams shook his head.

"There's an unholy stain on this place," he said.

"Only unholy stain here is on the inseam of your trousers," Theo said. "Now get it down, will you."

"You skinny lapdog, you'll burn with the rest."

Theo's cheeks flared. He headed over to him.

"Feel like praying now, righteous prick?" Theo said. "You're going need to."

"Easy," I said. I reached out and grabbed Theo by the shoulder. "I believe Mr. Williams here understands that he's bound by the same rules as everyone else on the floor. Should he wish to retain his employment, that is."

Theo slipped out of my grip. "Here. I'll help," he said. He quick-stepped over to Williams' workbench and snatched medals. Before you could say Hail Mary, full of grace, the two of them were trading punches. One of Williams' brothers jumped on Theo's back. I waded in to break it up, yelling at them to knock it the hell off. Got the younger Williams off of Theo and tossed him to the ground. Snagged Theo by his collar and pulled him out of reach, long arms and all. He'd gotten one good hit right in on Williams, broke his nose from the blood streaming over his lips and chin.

"Prayers didn't do you much good, did they?" Theo said. His cheeks were alight with the bright red spots he got when he was angry. Two men held him back. A crowd gathered to watch as Theo and Williams egged each other on.

"Your doom is in the fires," Williams said. He spit a string of blood to the floor.

"Really," Theo said. "Because the Lord didn't say a word of that when I spoke with Him this morning—in fact, He said I was doing just fine on account of I'm not a self-sure sonofabitch who thinks he's got it all figured out."

Well, that set Williams off and he went in at Theo, fist swinging, crying out that he shouldn't use the Lord's name and some other helpful tips while he landed a pair of punches of Theo's jaw. Took five of us to pull them off of each other, and they were still yelling and spitting at each other when a voice erupted across the floor.

"What is this?"

Was Mr. Winthrop, standing at the top of the stairs, and none too pleased was he. With him were the engineers who'd come through the other day, looking around the floor as though they'd stumbled into a village in the heart of a dark jungle. Winthrop had his pudgy hands on his waist, sweat running alongside his sideburns.

"Mr. Carey!" he bellowed.

I shook myself loose from the end of the fight.

"Sorry, sir," he said. "Bit of a problem, they're all back at work now."

"You can't take the Lord from the workplace!"

Everyone turned. There stood Williams, holding a plaster crucifix with a chipped Jesus on it. His right eye had swelled up. "Any more than you can take Him from my heart."

"Is that so?" Winthrop said.

"You're a God-fearing Christian, aren't you, sir?"

"Amongst the most devout."

Williams smiled and his brother nodded his head. Winthrop

turned to me and pointed his finger at the group of men before us.

"Every one of these men not currently working at their bench is fired, Mr. Carey," Winthrop said, in a voice loud enough to reach the far corners of the department.

"Was a misunderstanding, sir," I said. "They'll all be back at their benches in half a minute."

"Am I being unclear, Mr. Carey?"

He looked at me calmly from beneath his white brows.

"No, sir. It's just that—"

"Are shoes getting made, Mr. Carey?"

Mac came up the stairs and hurried over to us. Winthrop didn't say another word, but didn't take his eyes from me. I turned to the men. The smarter ones had quick-stepped back to their stations, but a good dozen and a half of them were standing in a crowd around Theo and Williams. Floor was quiet. My gaze landed on Williams' crucifix. I looked up.

"That's it, boys—you're done," I said. "Pack it in. Right now."

Winthrop nodded next to me. I waved the rest of the fellas back to work, tucking my shirt back in, heading over to the ones I'd fired. Theo shook his head and fumed, opening and closing his good punching fist, having cracked it good on a few cheekbones.

"This is shit," he said.

"Tried to stop you."

Had more trouble with Williams. Couple of his other brothers had shown up from two floors down—someone must've hurried to tell them—and they was raising their voices, appalled at their brother's persecution. Williams shouted on about the entire mill being an affront to the Lord Himself.

"Get your things," I said. "You can preach all you want the second you're out of the mill."

"Don't you touch my holy items, you filthy sinner."

"Sod your junk, Williams," Theo said. He kicked over a stack of uppers, knocking over everything on Williams' bench. Perfect. That was all it took to get two dozen fired Irishmen to raise a holy riot. Tools flew, benches flipped, Mr. Winthrop and the scientists had to raise their arms to block the rain of shoes that pelted them. Two big jigs crashed to the floor. Someone hit me over the head. Men hurried over and soon there was a crowd bigger than before. Most were trying to suss out what was going on, and a few were just glad to have the chance to throw their fists around and settle some scores in the chaos, good Irishmen as they were.

As I tried to shut down the ruckus, an iron wrench sailed by my head, missing me by a whisker and clanging across the bench behind me. Another tool flew at me, this time catching my shoulder—it was the handle side of a chisel. We were in the part of the floor where we kept the lasts—them wooden foot-shaped blocks that repairs were done on—so I grabbed one of the thick bases and got up onto it as the yelling and crying reached a healthy roar.

"Hey! Knock it off!" I whistled loud as I could with my fingers. Pretty well caught everyone's attention. "That's enough! Leave your fighting for the saloons and get to your benches, or everyone else here is done, too."

"To hell with you, Carey," someone shouted.

I raised my hands. "I know you men. Know your families. Big city out there; there's work. Help you if I can—but you've got to stop this, right now."

Mac stood next to me, his shirttails pulled from his trousers, one of his suspenders come loose and his hair mussed in back. Took a few more minutes, but we broke the crowd apart. Theo shrugged off my attempt to calm him down. Williams and his brothers grumbled their way to the stairs, along with the other ones I'd fired. Damage wasn't terrible, save for the cracked jigs. Mr. Winthrop watched us from the doorway to my office. Mac and I headed over there once shoes were getting made again.

"It's all settled, Mr. Winthrop," Mac said.

"I'm surprised at the both of you," Winthrop said.

"It's my fault, Mr. Winthrop," I said. "I let the men forget what they're here for."

"I should say so, Carey. But you'll help them find other jobs in the city?"

"If I can, sir."

"Generous. While you're at it, find yourself one, too. You're fired."

"Sir, I—"

Winthrop turned to Mac. "I don't want any more Irish running anything in my mills, Mr. Harriman."

"Mr. Winthrop, I've put years in here—I love this place, I'll do anything for it. Please."

He stared at me, big nose lined with broken veins, hard eyes.

"Get out of my mill."

18

———

UNTIL THEY DIED

Ernst Glockner followed the doctor through the tuberculosis ward at Shay Hospital. He kept his mouth shut. The air was rotten with the breath of disease and unwashed patients. Sunset shone through the windows.

"They died," the doctor called over his shoulder.

"And there were four of them?"

"Five. Damnedest thing."

"You treated them," Glockner said.

"Such as I could."

"Anything work?"

"They died."

They passed out of the long room—twenty beds to a side, most full—and into a corridor where the floorboards creaked on thin nails and light fixtures hissed with gas flames. At the end of the corridor, a view that looked to Union Street, where the North Canal ran under bridges. Street lanterns and illuminated mill windows dotted the city as evening deepened.

"Tell me more about how they got here."

The doctor stopped. Glockner noticed stains of pus on his frock.

"Nothing more to say. Someone left them. That someone was gone by the time we found the women."

"Poison?"

"There was no distress. Breathing, pulse, temperature were fine. No vomit. No seizures. No tremors. Might have been asleep."

"Until they died."

"Until they died."

Glockner hooked his thumbs on his belt. "I don't like it."

"Nor do I, Officer Glockner. Yet there are living that I can attend to, so if you'll excuse me."

"Where are they?"

"The women?"

Glockner nodded.

"The morgue."

"No special precautions?"

"Against contagion, I presume you mean?"

"That's right."

"Yes—despite the outward absence of any symptomology. They are in a spare storage room. Normally only used for overflow."

"I need to see them."

The doctor gave him a curt nod. A black man with a ring of keys on his belt passed by.

"Charles, if you would," the doctor said. The man stopped. "Can you please escort Officer Glockner to the spare room of the morgue? I authorize it."

"Yes, sir."

The morgue was in the basement of the hospital, reached by a long corridor that ran past the building's coal furnaces, dormant now until the chills of late autumn would sweep in. The space was quiet save for the sound of occasional footsteps passing overhead. The man turned on a gas light fixture on the wall. A door to the left stood partially open.

"That it?" Glockner said.

"Main morgue, sir. Spare is at the end."

Glockner followed him. Despite the high humidity, the stones of the hospital's basement gave off a dank chill. They stopped in front of a low metal door. The man unhitched his key ring and sorted through the long keys.

"You see them?" Glockner asked.

"Seen a lot of dead folks."

"These."

"Believe I did, sir. Helped move them down here."

"You notice anything strange?"

"No stranger than them being dead. And that ain't all that strange, not around here."

He unlocked the door and pushed it open. He paused, turning on the gas lamp on the inside wall. When the glow widened, Glockner followed. The room inside was small, with unfinished stone walls, dark even with the hissing gas light. Wheeled metal gurneys lined up against one wall. The adjacent wall was for the bodies, four rows of four, each arched opening three feet by three feet. A scent of decay tainted the air, which was colder than the corridor. The man stopped, hooked his key chain back to his belt. Glockner went to the wall with the openings. Thick shadows from the faint lamplight stretched along the wall, into the darkened spaces.

"Which ones?"

"Bottom row, sir. And one above."

Glockner squatted, peered into the nearest opening on the bottom.

"It's empty," he said.

"No, sir. Put one of them in myself. Right there."

"Then am I missing something?"

The man came over.

"They was right—" He stopped. They both looked into the next space. Empty. No bodies, not a one. Glockner glanced at the man. "Doesn't make sense, sir. Put them here just after noon. Door's been locked since."

Glockner straightened up, looked around the rest of the room. One of the wheeled gurneys was askew. He went to the far side and felt a breeze of warmer street air. Up at the top of the wall, a narrow casement window stood open to the evening. The window itself hung open inside, on the hinges. The glass was intact.

"Why would someone steal bodies?" the man asked.

"This was open when you brought them in?"

"No, sir. Never seen that open."

Glockner looked at the window. Swung it back up into place. Tested the latch.

"Bring me over one of those tables," he said.

The orderly did, one of the wheels squeaking. Glockner pushed it beneath the window, then climbed up, coming level to the widow. Looking out, he put his hand through to the other side and felt around. A mesh wire screen had fallen to the ground. Glockner grabbed it. The center was pushed out. He examined it for a few moments, then closed the window, and latched it.

The window latched from the inside.

19

WINGS

"Couldn't have been more bored, darling. Altogether wretched waste of a perfectly fine evening."

"Sounds lovely to me. Beautiful."

Eve Winthrop dismissed her friend Prudence with a wave of her gloved hand. The coach hit a dip in the road and rocked on its springs. Prudence and Molly held on to the window frames; Eve let herself slide back against the front wall.

"Father wants me to be his little songbird," she said, careful not to let any brandy spill from the neck of the bottle she held. "And wanted my heart to soar at the spectacle of a fine night of opera. I'd have rather taken a quiet bath. Or chewed a linen napkin."

She took a drink from the bottle and passed it on to Molly.

"At least your father thinks you're fit for something other than keeping house," Prudence said.

"He's a businessman trying to make an investment that will bring a higher value to his interests."

Prudence laughed. "You're cruel."

"I'm honest. If he's to use my marriage as entry into the

Beacon Hill aristocracy, Pru, he needs me to be more than just a well-off Lawrence girl."

"You're more than well-off, love," Molly said. She passed the brandy on to Prudence.

"Perhaps. But never say I'm ungenerous." Eve turned and knocked on the ceiling of the coach. "Caution to the wind, sir! We're still quite shy of exciting."

Aye, Miss, came the muffled reply of the driver. The coach picked up speed. All three girls looked out the windows as the darkened countryside flew by. The moon paced them over the meadows, ducking in and out from behind the wooded hills, ghosting its image briefly on the surface of the Spicket River as the coach sped across a wooden bridge with a clamor of hoof and wheel on board.

"That's more like it," Eve said. She held her hand out for the bottle. Prudence handed it to her, slipping nearly off her bench to do so.

"You could have a darkly handsome instructor. Fall passionately in love as he sculpts your voice," Molly said.

"It wouldn't be a he, it would be a she—and she would have a mole the size of a mushroom, and cruel breath. Be assured, these things never work out as one would wish. That—" she paused, taking a sip of brandy, "is why I've learned to make my own excitement."

"Your father won't notice we have his coach?" Prudence asked.

"Father wouldn't notice if a crow landed on his wide head, these days," Eve said, then raised her voice. "And why are we slowing down again?"

She knocked on the ceiling again. The coach slowed, then bumped hard.

Prudence grabbed hold of the window frame. "We're going off the road."

"Driver!" Eve yelled.

The coach bucked and swayed, tossing Molly from her bench.

Eve cursed as the bottle slipped from her hands, spilling brandy across the floor.

"Driver!" she yelled again. "What are you doing?"

After a moment, the coach lurched to a stop, still rocking. The sweet bite of brandy filled the air.

"Maybe father has a point about being unable to find good help," Eve said, lifting her shoes from the sticky puddle that spread across the floor of the coach. She leaned out the window.

"Did we evade night-robbers?" she called out. "For any other excuse for this incompetence will fall short of the mark, Mr. Nash. Well?"

Wind rustled the trees next to the motionless coach.

"Perhaps he swooned," Prudence said.

"The only thing that would make Nash swoon would be more of those rat-catching dogs he's always breeding and going on about. Or a meal bigger than a morsel—he looks like he's made of broomsticks."

She leaned over and picked up the brandy bottle. Only a sip remained inside. She swigged it, then held the bottle by the neck and knocked it on the ceiling of the coach. No reply.

"Idiot," Eve said. She tossed the bottle out the window and threw open the coach door. "If I have to step out of this coach, Mr. Nash..."

She turned back to Prudence and Molly, made a face, then held the handle next to the door and slid down. Ignoring for the moment that she was more inebriated than she'd realized, she stepped around to the front of the coach, her hands on her hips, her skirts tossed by the breeze. The heights of Prospect Hill stood silhouetted against the moon, a mile off on the other side of empty fields, and stretches of woods that bordered the Spicket. Turning back to the matter at hand, she saw the two horses of the team off the road, standing in knee-high goldenrod. Stout birch trees lined the side of the road, just ahead.

"You couldn't see white trees, Mr. Nash?"

The driver held the reins. He moved to turn—and kept moving, falling shoulders-first from the driver's bench, tumbling nearly to Eve's feet. Blood—black in the moonlight—spilled from his neck, where his head had been. Eve opened her mouth, but no words came out.

"Don't tell me he's drunk too?" Prudence called from the coach.

Eve put a hand to her mouth. She turned and looked down the road in the direction they'd come from. Twenty yards back, indistinct in the darkness, but unmistakable in shape: Nash's head. A thud brought her gaze back to the coach. She thought Pru must have fainted—but both her friends leaned out the door. On the roof of the coach, a figure stooped. Still as a statue, it filled Eve with dread. She stepped back.

"Get out," she whispered.

"What about the driver?" Prudence said.

"If he's not up to it," Molly said, "I'll take a turn at it. Always wanted to drive one of these."

She smiled. The figure on the roof squatted and extended a slender arm. In an instant, it grabbed Molly by the hair and yanked her head up, smashing her into the frame of the coach's door. Prudence screamed. Molly groaned, and the figure let go of her, releasing her to fall from the coach and slump to the road.

"Run, Pru!" Eve screamed.

The figure swung itself into the coach, crashing into Prudence, who screamed in a tone of terror such as Eve had never heard. A wash of unreality took hold of Eve. The coach shuddered as Prudence's screams ended. A shoe kicked out of the door. At that, the shock that had held Eve frozen broke.

She turned and ran into the field, leaping over a low stone wall, tugging her skirts through grabby underbrush. She lost a shoe of her own, but kept running, her breath coming in heaves. Reaching a stretch of the field with rows of low vines of small pumpkins and squash, she looked over her shoulder. An inky shadow flew through the sky ten feet over her head. Eve stumbled in the softer dirt of the field, landing on her knees. The figure dropped in front of her and stood swaying back and forth. With the moon behind it, Eve couldn't make out any features beyond the thin arms and legs, unkempt hair that reached past narrow shoulders. Eve struggled to her feet. The smell of rotted garbage came off the figure in waves.

"My father has money," Eve said in a breathless whisper. She backed off. The figure came closer, slender, stretched, hunched.

"You have a new father now," the figure spoke in a gallows whisper. Something opened behind it, translucent skin caught by the moonlight, stretching past both shoulders.

Wings, was Eve's confused thought right before the figure fell upon her.

HOURS LATER, as dawn broke and the first touch of sunrise lit the brass weathervane that topped the Winthrop house, the handle to the front door jiggled. The maid—harried and cursing silently after the chaos of the night just ending—stopped on her way to the stairs, a tray of breakfast in her hands.

"What now?" she said, keeping her voice quiet.

The door opened. Eve Winthrop stood trembling, her clothes torn in spots, smudged with dirt in others, with what looked like dried vomit crusted to her chin and throat. Her skin was pale as cream. She took four staggering steps inside the entryway and collapsed. The maid dropped the tray in a clatter that cut through the quiet house.

20

THE DEAD MEAN NOTHING

Morning came, and I drove my wagon through the steam that rose from the warming brick and tamped streets crowded with people headed to the mills. First workday in over seven years I wouldn't be surrounded by weaving, warping, carding, beaming, fulling, and the rest of it. Thought—again, a hundred times again—of Winthrop looking at me like I was a piss-puddle in the dirt as he fired me. Seven years and not a man in that mill worked harder than me, and he'd probably forgotten me by the time he sat down to his supper.

Well, sod him.

And, of course, sod me, as I wasn't sure what in the hell I would do to keep the family fed and housed. I crossed the South Canal and the river, into part of the city that had street after street of tenements and three-story row houses, wooden and painted in mustard browns, barn reds, chalk whites, tavern yellows, cut through with streets of the city's other business: cabinet makers, soap makers, dealers in chaises and harness, stores to buy boots and shoes, trousers and hats, buildings set back that made bellows, guns, barrels, and bricks. Rode across train tracks and pulled the team to a stop alongside the train station. Yard out in back had dozens of cars lined on branches of steel rail hot enough by mid-day to fry bacon on.

Climbed down and knocked the dust off my trousers. Steam whistle blew on a huffing engine that pulled out, filling the blue above it with roiling black smoke. I hustled along the front and ducked in through the station's wide entrance. Rows of benches lined the inside; another door opened to the train platform. Two ticket counters and a newsstand stood on the other side. Looked around. Half a dozen folks bound for Boston fanned themselves in the heat—businessmen, looked like, and a woman with two smartly dressed children. I approached the fella at the newsstand.

"Anyone buy a ticket and a bunch of papers this morn, different ones? Short-haired lass dressed like a Father?"

"Was just here," he said.

"The train that left?"

"Not that one. The number forty-one, be here in a quarter of an hour."

I stepped out onto the platform. Long area was shaded, and beyond that were more benches. Out there, a group of men stood in line, gathered round a pair of Union officers at a little table, signing up for the Union Army. Headed over that direction. Around the corner, I saw Ieva, seated by herself on a bench that ran along the wall of the station. Her lone bag sat by her feet. The strong morning light had the whitewashed walls glowing. When my shadow dropped across the paper she read, she looked up at me.

"They're gone," I said.

Ieva shaded her eyes with her hand. "Who?"

"The girls. Asked around after them first thing over at Shay."

"I told you they wouldn't live long."

"Well they didn't. But now they're gone. Fella I know works

there, told me the police'd been there after all five of them disappeared, right out of the morgue. Gone."

Ieva squinted.

"I don't understand," she said.

"Nice to know it's not just me, for a change."

She thought for a moment, her gaze tracing the rooflines of
the buildings across the tracks, flitting across the men joining
the war.

"They're husks, after the veln is killed. No use. But dead—
nothing. The dead mean nothing to veln."

I nodded to the papers—they were from Boston, Portland, up
in New Hampshire.

"And you're sure he's gone?"

"He raises a new veln and flees, searching out the next. Across
Europe, into Africa, this is true."

"That's what the papers are for."

"Unexplained disappearances. A body found, the desecration
of a lair. Signs, yes."

"You find any yet?" I said.

"No."

"Then he might not have moved on."

She shook her head.

"The bodies tell us nothing," she said.

"Unless they're telling us something we don't understand yet."

"You're making my neck ache. Sit," Ieva said. She moved the
newspapers, and I sat next to her. I could still see the smoke from
the train that'd left.

"Let me ask you this, Sister. He knows you're hunting him. He
knows you've killed some of these raised veln. If it were me, I
might try to do something about you, if you know what I'm
getting at."

"I'm more cautious than he realizes."

I nodded my head—but also recalled how fast she'd reached
for the spikes even as the sun went down back in the sawmill.

"And more dangerous," she added.

"You think he's afraid of you?"

"He knows what I can do, and what I have. And I've learned to keep myself safe. He can't reach me at night. I stay nowhere I can't escape from in a minute. I have little, as you see. His verg have tried in the past year or two to find me, but they are rather easily dispatched. Soon, I will find him."

She leaned over and unlatched her bag, rooted around in it a moment, coming up with a fold of yellowed newspaper clippings.

"He's more and more drawn to the cities, where gathering souls for his released brethren is easy, quick. But he leaves a trail he doesn't even realize. I see it."

She handed me the clippings. They were in languages I couldn't make sense of.

"You read all these?" I said.

"Of course."

"How many languages you speak, Sister?"

"Six, plus Latin."

"Weren't for all this," I said, "you'd be like one of these modern women—writing novels, painting pictures, traveling the world."

"Or I'd be a nurse and tend to the suffering."

"Course. I meant it as a compliment."

"I know you did."

We shared a look, for a moment. Single-minded drives close off a lot of doors in life. I handed her back the clippings. She put them away and stood.

"Come, Mr. Carey. This ticket will wait. We'll look into these missing bodies. I think you have sharp instinct."

"Finn, remember."

"Yes. Finn. Ieva. You may call me Ieva."

"Carriage is out in front, Ieva."

She nodded. I got her bag for her.

"I can carry my bag," she said.

"Didn't say you couldn't," I said.

She let a hint of a smile touch her mouth.

"Fine," she said.

21

UNTIL YOU'RE AS COLD AS ME

The afternoon had gotten long by the time the mourners filed away from the graveside, off to the coaches and carriages that lined the road. Near as I could tell, the whole affair had not gone smooth. Crowd had filed into St. Mary's around two o'clock. Half an hour had gone by, men in dark suits coming to the door and peering out, stepping out into the street to glance toward Prospect Hill. Another hour passed like that, and the Winthrops' coach pulled up in front of the church. Mr. Winthrop climbed heavily out, while Mrs. Winthrop was escorted in by a man whom I guessed to be her physician; poor woman looked too weak to stand, and had the vacant look of laudanum about her puffed eyes.

Catholic funeral Mass started, and continued for well over an hour. Ieva and I sweated it out underneath a pair of wide chestnut trees in the lot of the funeral home across the street. At one point, she looked over at me.

"You lost your job."

"Prefer to think my job lost me."

"Unfair?"

"So unfair that unfair isn't even a good enough word for it."

She was quiet a minute.

"Sorry to hear," she said. "You're a good man."

I took a sip from the canteen of water I'd brought along. Offered it to her. She took it and drank.

"Yesterday it felt like I was a steaming train racing across a bridge, and then I suddenly ran out of bridge," I said.

"Maybe you already reached the other side. No more bridge needed."

I took the canteen back.

"Wouldn't it be lovely to think so," I said.

"Maybe is true."

"Maybe. I'm getting my livery business started. Fella from the mill—also without a job—will join me. We'll see what we can make of ourselves."

"I would not count against you," she said.

"I used to think the same thing."

"You have a good soul. Your heart and your words and your deeds work close, as one. Rare."

The bells rang, the Mass over. A quartet of men carried the coffin out into the sunshine. People gathered on the church steps, followed it down. Saw Mrs. Winthrop sink to the granite steps, crying out, lifted back to her feet by some of the men in the family. Pallbearers carried the coffin around the side of the church to the raw grave dug in the cemetery that ran alongside the church and rectory. It wasn't long.

"Children die," Ieva said.

"Sadly, they do."

"But this is different, this child?"

"Her friends disappear. She falls ill, no one knows with what. She dies. Young lasses, all of them."

"Just right for veln."

"That's what I'm thinking."

"But she's dead. Being buried."

"Call it a hunch," I said.

After the last of the mourners left, we watched as the gravediggers came out from where they'd waited out of sight. Wasn't long until they had the dirt filled back in and a couple of yards of grassy sod tamped down over the soil. Their shadows stretched across the grass. After a time, the cemetery was empty.

"We should be closer," I said.

"Where?"

"Over the other side of that stone wall," I said, pointing. We set off across the street. Late afternoon sunlight brightened the steeple atop St. Mary's sloped slate roof and the gray granite front beneath. As we passed by the steps and arched doorway, Ieva paused.

"Wait."

She looked up at the doorway, and started up the steps. I stood at the bottom.

"What happened to the church losing its way?" I said.

"It has. But there is something here." She put her hand on the door. "A longing, from time to time, takes me. To slip inside a church, to smell the dark wood, the incense. To kneel before the altar, to bow my head in prayer. Wrap myself in the embrace of communion with God."

She pulled the door open.

"But I never do. Tell myself I might as well wish to be a child again, held tight against the fury of a valley storm."

"So what are you doing?"

"I'm not sure."

She stepped inside. Now, I was no fan of churches, nor those who claimed they had private words with God Himself and could only point to the fancy tablecloths they were draped in as proof. No less ridiculous than any other Irish superstition, and the lot of it papering over the inevitability of death, was how I saw it. The inside of the church still held the dark aroma from the incense from the Mass. Above our heads, the light from the stained glass window fell across the rows of pews and the marble floor, the colors deepening with the late afternoon sun. Behind the altar, the figure of Christ on the Cross looked down at us from the stained glass mural.

He looked like he'd just been fired.

Our steps echoed. I looked over at Ieva. Her face had a soft look about it I'd never seen. While she didn't take in a deep breath and sigh it out, I could tell that she was soaking up the feeling.

"We need to pray?" I said.

"I'm always praying." She stepped forward, looking around. At an aisle, she turned. Held out a hand behind her. "Canteen."

I handed it to her. She twisted off the metal cap and poured the water out on the floor, shaking out the last drops. At the stoup on the wall next to the side door, she dipped the empty canteen into the water. The gurgle was loud. As an Irishman—even one who hadn't stepped very many feet into churches since last being dragged by my ma as a child—a jolt of primal fear coursed through me. Even if it weren't a sin, it would surely bring down the wrath of a priest—and while they might not have the Ear of the Lord as they claimed, most of them were ace with the switch and cutting with their tongue.

"Holy water," Ieva said.

"That's what you're after?"

"I think so, yes."

A door opened at the other end of the nave. Course I was right. Priest came out. Father Flaherty, seen him around the city, plenty of the folks who worked in the Everett attended St. Mary's, so I'd heard his name about. Wasn't a white-haired, red-faced hammer of the Lord yet, but he was well on his way.

"Can I help you?" he said, in a way that said *What're you doing?* Ieva topped off the canteen and put the cap back on, muttering what I figured was a prayer as she did. That's when the priest got a good look at her outfit.

"You can't do that," he said.

"That's not for you to say," Ieva said.

Father Flaherty pulled up. Didn't imagine he was used to being spoken to like that, least of all in his church.

"Excuse me?" he said.

"There is a battle being fought," Ieva said. "Here. Now."

He came walking down toward us. "I don't know who you think you are, but that is sanctified by the Church."

"A higher sanctification has happened, Father. Do you not feel it?"

"Put that back."

Ieva started toward the door, ignoring him. I followed her. She stopped at the doorway, turned back to the priest.

"You're not worried? You don't sense it?"

He stopped. He shook his head as if clearing out a daydream.

"I have no idea what you're referring to, Miss."

"*Fiant aures tuae intendentes*," Ieva said.

He said nothing. Ieva shook her head, then went back out the door. I turned to the priest.

"Sorry, Father."

Couldn't help myself. As I may have mentioned, the Irish ran strong in me.

When I caught up with Ieva, she was at the gate to the cemetery. Shadows drew nearly straight across the ground and it wouldn't be too long until the hills ended the daylight.

"What was all that?" I said.

"A lesson."

"For who?"

"All of us."

"What'd you say to him?" I said.

"Something he's familiar with."

"Which is?"

"Let thy ears be attentive."

"He's going to have someone fetch the police."

"He's terrified. He won't."

She sounded confident, but I wasn't sure. Kept glancing back at the church. The door was closed, and I didn't see anyone come hurrying out. We went through the graveyard. Noticed that several stones were missing, squaring holes in the ground left where they'd been, while others were in process of being repaired. We reached the fresh grave of Eve Winthrop. Wasn't a stone up yet. Sounds of the city were quiet right there and wasn't much beyond the wind sighing through the trees, some crows arguing with one another some ways off.

"Do you feel that?" I said.

"Yes."

Was as though the finger of a dead child brushed the back of my neck.

"Sawmill," was all I got out. Was all I needed to. Ieva nodded. She squatted, laid a hand on the fresh sod of the grave. She nodded her head.

"This is concerning," she said.

The sunlight slipped beyond the horizon, leaving the cemetery and church in evening shadow. Only the cross atop the steeple shone fierce with direct light.

"Doesn't feel like we're alone, does it?" I said.

"No. I fear we're not."

She stood up and eyed the rectory of St. Mary's. I followed her gaze. A figure stood at the window, then disappeared. Flaherty. Didn't see any lights coming on.

"You were right," Ieva said.

"Wish I wasn't."

A thud came from below the fresh earth. We both felt it through the bottoms of our shoes.

"Now I really wish I wasn't," I said.

Ieva muttered something in Latvian. Another thud. I thought back to the coffin on the *Jack Ketch*, with the scratches dug away from the inside of the lid.

"Is she one of the servants like Liam? A verg?"

"That's only for the living. This is different."

Another series of muffled thuds started. Worse, a voice joined in. No words, just guttural yells.

"This isn't good," I said.

"Nothing like this has happened," Ieva said. Her frown deepened.

"The ones that went missing, the bodies. Police think someone stole them."

Another burst of knocks from below the ground.

"Thinking that's not the case," I said.

Ieva looked around, scanning the edges of the cemetery. A pair of lamplighters started their rounds down the road, pushing the dusk back. A stray hound sniffed around alongside them.

"One way to find out for sure," I said. I jogged through the headstones, coming to a small shack near a standing crypt where the gravediggers had stored their tools. Door was locked, but a side window was left open, and I shouldered it up. Reached around inside and came up with a spade-headed shovel, took it out. Hurried back to the grave. Ieva stood silhouetted against the sky as it drained out. I sunk the shovel into the earth.

"Keep an eye out," I said. "Been a bad enough week already without getting arrested for grave-robbing."

The dirt was loose, and it didn't take me much time to make a dent in the grave, tossing the soil to the side opposite Ieva. We didn't talk, and the only sounds were the heavy slice of the shovel biting in, the whump of the dirt I threw, and the sounds from below, growing louder as I went deeper. After I got down another foot, the sound of scratching became clear. Thought came to me and I paused, heaving breaths and leaning on the shovel handle.

"What about your tools—the spikes? I think we'll need them."

Her features were lost in the dusk.

"Those are for veln. I have the medallion though. And the blessed water."

She pulled the worn medallion from beneath her collar.

"Better do the trick," I said. "Otherwise, this is a terrible idea."

I got back to shoveling. Didn't say so to Ieva, but I was getting unhinged listening to the screaming coming from below my feet, the knocking and the grunting coming up in rotten waves. The shovel crunched into an inch of dirt, then slammed to a stop against wood.

"There," I said.

Coffin was askew at the bottom of the grave, the head of it slanted up. Took more shovel work to clear away a span of wood. The sounds all stopped. In the sudden silence, a heavy, watchful feeling filled the grave.

"Sister," I called up. She crouched at the edge.

"Can you open it?"

"Should I open it?"

"Wait."

She held out the medallion, closed her eyes. Stars were coming out overhead in the rich blue.

"*Launo garu, Kungs atrodas šajā svētajā vietā. Zinu tavu vietu,*" she said.

I scraped the dirt from the top half of the coffin, pushing it away with the shovel, finally using my hands. I looked up at Ieva. She nodded. My fingers found the latch along the side. I slid back until my knees were off the top half, then I flipped the latch and got a bite of the front edge of the lid, pulled it up. Soon as I cracked it open, a rank stench billowed out, enough to gag me. I turned my face away, looking for fresh air. I got the lid open. Dirt fell down into the silk lining.

Young Eve Winthrop stared up at me.

"Hold me—I'm so cold," she said. Her voice grated like a rusty hinge and a fetid stink rose from her mouth. I scrambled back on the coffin, my shoes scuffing and sliding. She sat up.

"Stay with me. Stay with me all night, until you're cold as me."

Her pale features rose in the gloom, free of the coffin. Something terrible had happened to her, no longer the sweet young lady I'd seen at the Winthrops' lawn party. Her mouth stretched down, her jaw protruding in a narrow point, the skin taut, bloodied, while her brows turned up on the outside, and stuck out the width of a finger, leaving her eyes to glint from dark hollows. Wasn't just her face that'd gone strange, either. Her arms extended out past the cuffs of her funeral dress, the wrists long and bony, the fingers warped and near to six inches long apiece.

"Ieva!" I shouted up.

Eve Winthrop tilted her head and lunged, scrabbling out of the coffin and straight for me. I tried to hold her off with my feet, my shoulders pressing hard into the dirt walls of the grave. Above, Ieva spun off the cap to the canteen, then held it out over the grave.

"*Jauda Kunga liek tev! Atpakaļ savā caurumā, veln. Problēmas nav šajā pasaulē!*"

With that, she shook the canteen, flinging water in arcing showers down onto Eve Winthrop. As the water touched her bone-white flesh, she shrieked, thrashing around. Ieva shouted again and water hissed across the body of the young lady, sending her into such a spasm that it made me think of a rat dropped onto a hot stove. I shot up to my feet, grabbing at the side of the grave, kicking my feet into the dirt to get purchase to climb out. As I lifted myself up, a long hand grabbed my ankle in a crushing grip. I kicked but couldn't free it. Got pulled back into the grave. I let go with my right hand, let it fall to the handle of the shovel which was upright in the corner of the grave. I grabbed it and swung it, hitting Eve in the face. Another spray of holy water and she let me go. I clanged the spade of the shovel hard against her head and the howl she sent up was probably heard across the city. Dropped the shovel.

Ieva took my forearm and wrenched me up. Between the two of us, I was out of the grave in one breath. She stumbled and my

face mashed against her chest. I rolled off, and we both hurried to
our feet. She put out an arm, kept me behind it.

"Take this."

She handed me the canteen. She took the medallion off from
around her neck. It shone with the same faerie light as when
we'd killed the young veln. From inside the grave, the sound of
shoes on dirt-strewn wood. Eve's screams stopped.

"My father is coming."

The words were cold bone. I looked around the cemetery.
One edge of it bordered a strip of grassy common. Stars were out.
Looking back over my shoulder, I saw that the sunset had gone
down to a line of ember that traced the far hills, dimming even as
I watched.

"Who are you?" Ieva said.

Girlish laughter broke from the grave. White fingers crept
over the edge, pushing into the piled earth. A movement from the
edge of the cemetery caught my eye. A shadow stood by the far
length of wrought-iron fence. Another moved along the corner.
The hillside beyond had yet a third shadow sliding between trees.

"Ieva," I said.

She looked up. As she did, Eve Winthrop lifted herself from
the shadows that had taken watch in the grave, a horrid smile
turning her face into something out of a nightmare. I heaved the
last of the holy water at her. It splashed her in the face, sizzling,
turning her smile into a grimace of agony. Her mouth opened
wide enough that I could have put both fists into it and her eyes
rolled back in her head.

"We have to run," Ieva said.

"We'll get more water—we'll fight them."

"No. We're in mortal danger." She grabbed my sleeve and
pulled me back. The figures closed in on the gate. One climbed
the curved spikes. In the dim light, I caught glimpses of them—
and it didn't take long for me to spot that at least some of them
were the lasses I'd brought to the Shay.

"Now," she said.

We both turned and ran. I glanced over my shoulder. Shapes hurried into the cemetery and voices called out. We sprinted, heading for a lane. When we hit it, I stopped, looked back. In the graveyard, the pale form of Eve Winthrop climbed from the grave and turned her ghostly face toward us.

We fled.

22

TOUCH OF THE GRAVE

Maggie peered around the tattered blanket she hung in the window of the flophouse room, watching Nell and Rose heading off down the street, holding hands, on their way to the market a few streets over to buy apples. Once she was sure they wouldn't return for having forgotten something she let the blanket drop and turned back inside. She had twenty minutes, maybe less. The window still let in a muted daylight. Still too bright. She searched through her bag and came up with a shift to hang alongside the blanket, to further darken the room. She cleared a spot on the splintered boards in the middle of the room.

Better.

She opened the small box she had and pulled out a candle, a scrap of paper and pencil, and a few trinkets. A string necklace went over her head; she pushed her hair aside so it rested on her skin. She put a river stone on the paper and a rusted nail from a good-luck horseshoe next to the candle, then lit the candle and got herself settled.

The trick was to keep her mind shut tight once the séance began. A stray thought, an odd memory, an urge—those were the spirits looking for a way into the world, knocking at the door, trying the knob. *When there's spirits about, don't wander*, her mother had taught her. She rocked, straightening out the hem of her dress, taking a deep breath. Cupping her hands, she gathered the heat from the flame and pressed it over her eyes.

"Spirits, I call on thee," she whispered.

Outside, beyond the walls, a dog barked. She settled her shoulders.

"I seek your insight, humbly, with love, with gratitude. May I receive it as the soil does the rain, as the flowers do the sun."

For a time, there wasn't anything more than the huffing of the flame. A calm descended on her, a relaxing of her neck, her shoulders—as if a warm shawl draped across her. The channel was open to the other side.

Don't ask for Liam. Not again.

She tried to keep even that thought well hidden. The last time she'd sat with the spirits, she'd asked after Arthur; a song had come to her lips, a childish rhyme they'd sung as little ones back in Kildalkey, and the scent of pumpkins had filled her nose. It was him—and she'd known then he'd passed on, beyond the burdens of the world. Her tears had been heartfelt, but the touch of his spirit had comforted her. Then, she'd asked after Liam Carey.

She wouldn't make that mistake again.

"What is Finn Carey searching for?" The candle fluttered, nearly going out. Maggie opened her eyes and glanced at it. "I ask for a sign, so I might help him."

She kept herself from fidgeting. The sign could be anything: a word coming out unexpectedly, her hand wanting to scrawl something on the paper, objects moving. Minutes passed. Muffled sounds from outside the room—wheezing laughter, a slamming of a door, footsteps heading to the water closet— fought with her concentration.

"Is it in the city?" she said.

A knock on the floor. Maggie breathed deep, kept her hands

folded. In a spasm, her stomach tightened, her throat tightened, her lips closed shut—and words came out, in her voice, but not hers.

"Miss Winthrop?"

Maggie kept her eyes closed. Winthrop? Another wave of clenching muscles rose from her belly. The words burst out.

"Got fresh sheets, Miss."

A series of images dropped into her mind's eye, shifting like the blue heart of the candle flame: the city spread out in a tumble that followed the sinuous curve of the Merrimack, seen from on high; smoke from a dozen hundred-foot-tall smokestacks filling the air with black and gray smoke; a nightgown cradled in arms, folded and clean; a door.

The stink of urine filled Maggie's nose. She felt more words well up to her mouth.

"Poor child, we'll get you cleaned up."

Urine and unwashed skin, so strong that Maggie gagged.

"Where are you, child?" she said, her voice lowering to a soft call. More images flashed: sunlight slanting across a wall; a bed; a closet door. Fear stabbed at Maggie's heart. She shook her head, but the spirits weren't done yet.

"Miss Winthrop?" she said in a whisper.

Maggie stiffened. She saw a body sitting up against the wall inside a closet, draped with fine dresses, hands in fists, knees pulled in front. Still as a stone.

"Oh, child," Maggie cried out. The shock brought a tingle to the skin on her arms, her forehead, her neck. A spasm twisted through her body. She shifted—the spirit had left her, leaving her with the half-dream sensation she felt after every channeling. With a glance at the light coming in around the edges of the blanket in front of the window, she focused her mind once more.

"Why is Finn Carey with Sister Ieva?" she asked. A twinge of guilt passed through her mind. At first, there was nothing. She wondered if the spirits knew she was asking for her own selfish reasons and were ignoring her. As she was about to say never mind, a snapping noise grew. She opened her eyes. The flame of the candle had stretched to four inches, the end of it tearing and popping in the air, sending little bits of light up above it.

"Will she help him, or not?" she said.

A blackness touched her, starting in the middle of her forehead and pouring over her face, her throat, her heart, sending a coldness into her limbs: the touch of the grave. For a few terrible moments, Maggie couldn't move, couldn't take in a breath, couldn't seem to get her heart to beat another beat. The cold end enveloped her—until she leaned forward and blew out the candle.

"Jesus," she said. She scrambled to her feet, panting, shaking her head. Trembling, she hurried over to the window and ripped down the shift and the blanket. Her gaze landed on the steeple of one of the city's churches. Behind it, black smoke belched from the chimneys of the great Everett mill. For a moment, it appeared as if the spire itself was burning, wreathed in smoke. Behind her, the door to the room opened, startling her. Maggie spun around. Rose stood in the doorway, a half-eaten apple in her small hand.

"I told her it's a no-no," Rose said.

"What's a no-no? Where's Nell?"

"Where the stealers are."

Maggie shook off the last of the séance.

"What stealers? You mean thieves? I'll have her head if she let you walk back here by yourself," she said. She crossed to the door and knelt in front of Rose.

"Where, Rose—where'd Nell go?"

"She heard the apple man talk about the houses at the river. Where the stealers are."

Maggie looked at the girl, then at the empty hallway behind her.

23

THE NIGHT SANG WITH BELLS

She stuck close to the flickering street lamps and made her way up to the great stone dam. As Maggie got closer to the shanties, a barricade of rough-hewn rails blocked the road. A quartet of police stood nearby. Beyond, more clusters of police gathered—on foot, on their black horses. She stepped to the barricade.

"You seen a young lass go by here? Ten, thereabouts?" she said.

"You can't be out," one policeman said. "Curfew. Move off."

"She snuck out—I have to find her."

"No one goes in or out down here."

"So you didn't see her?" Maggie said.

"Curfew, I said."

"Please. You can't let me through?" Maggie said.

"You don't want to be in here tonight, trust me. Mayor's night-stick festival. He's about had enough of this lot."

Maggie turned and headed back the way she'd come. When she reached the corner, she turned—and then hurried into an alleyway that led back and past the barricade. At the end, she turned down a wider stretch of alley that extended behind a line of businesses and dwellings, spills of light falling from back doors or windows. She darted out and slipped close to the banks of the river itself, to the darkness and squelching mud. The shouts and raised voices from the police sweep echoed out across the water.

"Of all the nights to go out doing who knows what," Maggie whispered.

The dirt lanes were empty save for police shouting back and forth—no folks spilling from the shanties, gathering around fires, talking, playing tunes on an old fiddle. Shadows passed across curtains drawn in the windows and doorways of the shanties. Maggie stuck to the water's edge until she reached a point where she could cut between the flimsy shacks and huts. The smell of cooking onions and lard smoked up the humid air. A few people marked her with suspicious eyes as they milled about outside their homes, huddled in their doorways and on the edges of lanes. Maggie caught fragments of their talk. The barking of dogs and clang of pots carried in the still air. A group of women stood by the doorway to a tin-roofed shack, hair tucked under kerchiefs, plain faces and threadbare dresses.

"You seen a young lass around here, maybe looking for the Fitzgeralds?" Maggie said.

"Fitzgeralds have gone."

"And good riddance," another of the women said. "Take their curse with them, is fine with me."

"But you ain't seen a lass, on her own?"

"Seen a few too many strange faces through here this eve."

"Well then where'd they live? The Fitzgeralds. Before they left?" Maggie said.

"Down that way," one of them said. "The more garbage and dog shit you smell, the closer you're getting."

Maggie pushed her way farther in the darkness. No fires nor lanterns burned. She passed black doorways and windows, and wondered how many Fitzgeralds had left, because the whole place appeared to be empty. She peeked into a few hovels and was just about ready to give up when she spotted someone slide out from a doorway up ahead, pausing before crossing over to the next doorway.

"Nell," Maggie said.

The girl stopped.

"I bloody see you," Maggie said. "Right there."

"Maggie?"

"What if I'd been the police, or worse? Get your skinny arse over here."

Nell paused, then slow-walked to her. As soon as she was in range, Maggie grabbed her by the arm.

"Do you know what could've happened to you?" she said.

"No one asked you to come after me."

"No—but I asked you to watch over your sister. I asked you to hurry back to the room. Christ, Nell. Why are you even down here?"

"No reason."

"No reason?"

"No. No reason," Nell said.

"You're just wandering around the most dangerous neighborhood in the city on your own. For no reason."

"Wanted to."

"Well, Finn'll hear about it, and he won't be any happier than I am." Maggie started back the way she'd come, marching Nell alongside her. "This is about them Fitzgeralds, isn't it? Well, they're gone."

"Where'd they go?" Nell said.

"What's it to you?"

"Thieves."

"Don't see how it matters."

A pair of young men came running, nearly plowing into them.

"Coppers," one of them called. Maggie paused for a second, then ducked behind an empty shack, yanking Nell with her. A moment later, a tall policeman sauntered by, using his nightstick to smack the sides of the huts he passed, breaking glass where there was some, just knocking out oiled paper where there wasn't. Shouting from up ahead grew louder. Maggie wound through the buildings, heading toward the river again. Just as the black strip of water came into sight, Nell stopped, dragging her heels. To their left, an orange glow built, embers lifting into the night. The breeze was heavy with smoke.

"Come on, it's just a fire," Maggie said. Nell still didn't move. Maggie turned. The girl wasn't even looking toward the fire—she stared back at the way they'd come.

"Liam," she said.

"What?"

Nell just pointed. Maggie looked. By the edge of a hut, a thin figure, skin like moonlit paper, dark hollows for eyes, matted sideburns.

"It's not him," Maggie said.

"It is. My brother."

Maggie stared hard at the man.

Don't even think about him.

She pulled at Nell, turning away from the man.

"Come on, we're hurrying."

"But—"

"Forget it. Run. Now!"

She broke into a run, pulling Nell with her. They stumbled along the muddy banks of the Merrimack. Maggie glanced back and saw the figure slip after them. The bridge and main road shone in lantern light one hundred and fifty yards up—but the riverbanks were lightless and black. After a quick debate, she changed direction, cutting left, into the heart of the shanties where the shouting and flames rose.

They stepped out into a fight.

Police formed a line a score across, nightsticks and pistols out, some of them with torches. Three shanties burned, bright flames reaching up, plumes of reddened smoke drifting off over the dark river. A group of Irish men, a few of them with kerchiefs tied across the bottom halves of their faces, faced off on the other side, hurling rocks and bottles, a few of them with axes and knives. Beyond them, a crowd of women and children hollered. Maggie watched as a policeman got hit in the face with a stone, his nose snapping in a burst of blood. The police surged forward. Maggie ducked and dragged Nell behind them, shouldering past more police. She took a swat from a nightstick on her shoulder-blade and had to let go of Nell.

"Hurry," she called back to her. Nell darted by a policeman. They cut behind the line, Maggie making sure she kept the fight between them and Liam. A wagon on its side blocked their way, so they skirted the edges of the lane.

"Wait," she said. Holding Nell's arm tight in her hand, she looked back and saw Liam come out next to one of the burning hovels, beneath the flames that rolled out from underneath the top of the doorway. His tattered clothing was afire, the legs and collar hung with bright blossoms of it. He stared right at her, walking through the fight, ignoring the Irish, ignoring the police —even as one brained him good with a nightstick, Liam only shrugged and kept walking.

"Fast as you can now," Maggie said to Nell. They broke into a sprint, hurrying up the rise until they reached the retaining wall of the North Canal and then racing alongside a pair of sheds used for controlling the locks. They veered off alongside a set of rails, following it to where it crossed Broadway. The street surged with a growing mob. Shouts carried up and down the street. In the commotion, Nell trailed Maggie, staying close.

A knot of men clamored and bunched up around a coach, rocking it. The two-horse team tried to rear up. A red-faced policeman climbed up next to the driver, shouting and pointing his arms. A lantern came out of the crowd and smashed against the coach, spilling flaming oil down the side of it, causing a little opening in the mob that was pushing it. Two gunshots barked and a furious roar swept the crowd. The policeman fired his pistol up into the air again.

"Next man who lays a hand on this coach is getting shot! Now clear the way, let them through. No more warnings."

Nell tried to rush forward, but Maggie grabbed her. Nell tried to yank herself free, but Maggie held on tight and pulled her back. Another group of policemen cut through the crowd, swinging their nightsticks like they were clearing their way through underbrush. Men staggered, hands to their bleeding heads, cradling broken fingers. Maggie dragged Nell forward, moving faster by edging around the thinner parts of the crowd.

She looked back and glimpsed Liam, coming up along the rails. Another couple of gunshots sounded—and the policeman on the coach fell over, shot dead through the heart by someone from in the crowd. A roar rippled through the mob. The horses were full panicked by then and the coach lurched forward, still flaming on the back. There was more yelling and the police tried to form a line, their guns raised. The coach's back left wheel snapped under the weight of the crowd and it reeled to the side. One of the horses screamed, twisted by the hitches and toppling, kicking a man in the head. The coach flipped onto its side, the crowd pushing back, and wails of agony coming from those caught underneath. Gunshots erupted from the line of police. Folks took cover behind the fallen coach, scattering onto the dark streets and bridge.

Smoke from the guns rolled over the mob. The toughest—or drunkest—of the mob wrenched open the door on the top side of the coach. Police fought to reload, and the few policemen who reached the coach were yanked down by shouting men. An angry cheer went up from the mob as they dragged a figure from the back of the coach. Nell strained to see, but Maggie clamped her hand around her wrist and stood up, bringing her along, winding through the crowd diagonal to the current.

"It's the mill owner!" Nell said.

Maggie looked. Nell was right—Mr. Abbot Winthrop tried to stagger to his feet, shoved to and fro, trying to duck under a flurry of blows from fists and at least one cane. Behind him, his wife climbed out of the door, her hair undone, a bloody cut under her eye.

Winthrop got himself up onto the side of his tipped coach, putting himself between the mob and his wife. A hand from the crowd grabbed his ankle and pulled, sending him sprawling. The mob surged. Though Winthrop tried to right himself and fight them off, there were dozens of hands on him, pulling him by the legs off of the coach, fire now bright orange along the back of it. His chubby fingers grabbed at the latches and bars on the side of the coach, but it wasn't enough. He disappeared into the crowd. A tremendous roar rose.

"He's coming," Nell said. She pointed into the street. Liam came at them, slicing his way through the crowd. People got clear out of his way while others turned on him. Those that tried to stop him—rioter, police, or bystander—were shoved aside.

"This way," Maggie said, pulling Nell away from the street.

Back by Liam, a man spun up into the air, screaming before he slammed to the cobbles of the street. A momentary hush came over the mob. Another man flew into the air, breaking his neck against a lantern post. A gasp came up from the mob and they moved back. Liam stood in the light from the lanterns and yelled in a voice that shook the chests and quailed the hearts of all who heard it.

"Move!"

Coming down the street, a wave of police on horseback waded straight into the crowd, trampling anyone not quick enough to get out of the way. Shouting, screaming, bullets singing and ricocheting off the cobbles. Around Liam, the mob attacked, and he was swept under a wave of arms and fists. At one point,

Maggie saw an axe rising and falling in cruel arcs. Gunshots popped.

"No!" Nell yelled.

"Don't look," Maggie said. "This way, fast as you can."

She pulled Nell around the corner, to a wide alleyway. They ran. Soon, the clamor of the riot grew distant behind them, even as bells rang across the city.

24

ONE HELL OF A HEADLINE

A warm wind stirred up the soot that hung over the city even as evening came on. I had the team and wagon hitched behind the feed store, and I walked up Common Street and then cut over to Essex. The Everett rose like a cliff at the end of the street. I used to love the look of that building, that place where I made myself into something more than a penniless Irishman. Had to turn my eyes from it. There were plenty of folks out, draymen unloading their wagons at stores, shopkeeps talking in bursts in doorways. This stretch of the city had bankers and solicitors, barbers and tailors, but the place I was looking for had fancy lettering on the frosted window of the door that read *The Lawrence Tribune*. Walked inside. There were a few brass plaques hung, printed notices, and lanterns on the wall that weren't lit. From the other side of the building, upstairs, came the sound of the turning of a press. A heavy smell I took to be printers' ink hung in the air. A man sat on a stool beside a counter.

"Tom Barley here?"

"And you are?"

"Looking to talk with him. Name's Carey."

He looked at me, then nodded. "Wait here."

He got up and went off around the corner. Came back in a minute and waved for me to follow him. Led me up a flight of stairs and into a large room that extended the entire width of the second story, filled with enormous printing presses. Half a dozen men in black-stained work clothes leaned over various stations of the presses, readying them for the next morning's edition. Mechanic tools lined one wall, alongside a stack of round tubs, giant rolls of paper, and shelves of bottled and canned greases, oils, and inks. We skirted the edges, passing workbenches with cubbies full of stained, burnished letters, dozens and dozens of them, and came to an office. Barley stood in front of a long table with bits of printing paper and notes laid out across it.

Saw that wide, bald-headed cop from the Everett with him. Paused in my tracks, about to turn and head for the door—but the cop looked up and caught my eye, so I went on in after the doorman.

"Carey," Barley said.

I nodded hello. The cop straightened up and crossed his arms in front of his thick chest.

"I can come back if you're busy," I said.

"What would we be busy with?" the cop said.

"Run out of Irish heads to crack this morning, officer?"

He nodded to Barley. "So he's got a mouth now. Sad that he doesn't have a job to go with it."

"Maybe I'll join the police," I said. "They'll obviously take anyone."

He stepped closer, hoping I'd step back. I held my ground.

"I see you two know each other," Barley said. He sat by a roll-top desk covered with notes. The cop and I practically touched noses. Barley turned.

"You start that riot?" he said.

"Tried to stop it, as a matter of fact."

"Bet you did," he said. "Winthrop's got a trigger finger for firing."

"Barley here tells me you worked for Winthrop a long time," the cop said.

"I did."

"So you've no love for him after being fired."

"Not giving him another thought. More to the city than the mills."

"For some."

Barley watched me.

"Something happen?" I said.

"One of his daughters was found dead this morn," Barley said.

"Winthrop?"

"That's right."

"Dead of what?"

"Don't think they know yet. Couple of her girlfriends disappeared a night back, coach they were out riding in was found abandoned down by the Spicket. Maid said that, since, she'd been screaming, crying out, laughing, staring out the window at the sun. Then, she drops dead."

"Winthrop may be a sonofabitch," I said, "but I'd never wish ill against him or his children. In case that's what you're dancing around."

"You wished ill against the Fitzgeralds," the cop said.

"Keeping them away from my family, is all. Nothing else."

"And now their whole clan's cleared out from the shanties. No one knows where they went."

"Then the shanties are a better place for it," I said.

"You seen them?"

"No, and I ain't crying over it."

"Officer Glockner here thinks this is all part of a feud," Barley said.

And this one—this deadly, wily, thieving darkness—is on the verge of what he thinks is his time of renown, when he can finally stab at the eye of God.

"May be," I said. "But if it is, it's no feud that involves me."

"Just everyone who's crossed you," Glockner said.

"I notice you ain't slapping irons on my wrists."

He eyed me.

"Can if you want me to," he said. "And we can keep talking with you behind bars. We can talk all night if you want."

"Sounds enchanting, except you know I haven't done a thing."

Barley leaned forward, his fingertips bracing him on the edge of the long table covered in papers and notes. Leafing through them, he found and pulled out a large map of Lawrence. Ink marks covered it, notes on the edges. He spread it out on the table.

"Gals gone missing," he said, tapping several spots. "Bodies found. And most of them don't involve our friend Mr. Carey. People are talking, staying off the streets. Talked to the city's pastors this morn—attendance has doubled, half of them scared silly."

There were two areas he'd circled. I recognized the river and the canals and tried to make sense of the layout of the city. Glockner put his finger on a spot on the map and gave me a glance.

"What's that?" I said.

"The Shay."

I frowned and shook my head.

"Bunch of gals, near-dead, dropped off by an Irishman with a wagon," he said.

"Imagine that," I said. "A wagon driven by an Irishman in Lawrence."

"The hospital staff didn't say it was an Irishman," Barley said.

"Course it would've had to be, wouldn't it?" I said. "Never a crime did happen in this fine city until us Irish set foot here."

"Irish words are like Irish babes—always more of them," Glockner said.

Barley traced a circle around the spot where Glockner pointed.

"And then the bodies disappeared," he said.

"Disappeared?" I said.

"A disturbing turn of events discovered by Officer Glockner here."

From the big room outside the door, another door squealed and footsteps ran to Barley's office. A young man poked his head in, resting a hand on the doorway.

"Riot breaking out, down in the shanties," he said around heaving breaths.

"Who?" Barley said.

"Don't know. Police are swarming in."

Glockner grabbed his tall hat and dropped one of his meaty hands to his nightstick.

"Don't think I'm through with you," he said to me as he hurried out. Barley grabbed his vest off of a coat rack, put his cap on his head. I looked around and saw ashtrays full of stubs and burnt matches. Ceramic cups lined one of the desks, half-filled with old coffee.

"This is your big story, ain't it?" I said.

"Could be."

"They know what you're chasing?"

"Told the paper's owner I'd give him the biggest story of the century or he could fire me."

"Surprised he didn't toss you right then."

"Probably would have, save for his wife. Near as I can tell, she only leaves the church to take her meals these days. Thinks it's all a part of the End of Times. The dead are rising. As predicted in the Holy Bible."

"Didn't take you for the Bible type, no offense."

"I'm not. Sources aren't reliable enough for me."

I followed him out the door and through the printing room. We went down the stairs as Barley put his vest on, making sure he had his note-booklet and pencils.

"What do you think's really going on, Barley?"

"More than you're telling me."

"Sorry?"

We hit the bottom of the stairs and hurried through the Tribune's entryway. Stepping outside, we both squinted in the hazy sunshine. Saw a police wagon speed by, heading up Essex, the driver putting the crop to the horses, raising a cloud of dust. We both turned our gazes to the southwest where the river was hidden from our view. Smoke rose into the blue. We started up the street.

"Saw it plain when I talked to you at your job. You didn't blink at a thing I said. None of it surprised you," he said.

"I didn't see you put your pencil to your paper. Wasn't the only one surprised, apparently."

"Well then, Mr. Carey—it would seem that we're both holding our cards close to our chests. I wonder if they're the same cards?"

You'd have one hell of a headline, if they were, I thought.

"What about my friend in uniform?" I said. "He holding them, too?"

"Ernst has an instinct that's sharper and four steps ahead of his ability to put it all together. He's like a terrier, though—once he bites on, he won't let go easy."

"He doesn't think it was me."

"You'd be locked up if he did. But he knows you're in deeper than you're playing at."

"Not playing, Barley."

We cut through a group of businessmen coming out of a pub. Sweat ran in streams under my collar.

"And I'm guessing you didn't just wander into my office by accident," Barley said.

"Looking for people going missing," I said. "Or bodies being found. Around here, maybe as far down as Boston. If there's any kind of pattern."

"Because?" he said.

We reached Broadway, the widest street in the city. Theaters and saloons and bakeries lined the trampled sidewalks.

"Because this is something that needs to be stopped. Here," I said.

"And you're not spilling what you know because you're afraid it'll come back on you."

"Your instincts aren't so bad."

A water wagon on a four-horse team pounded up the street in front of us. Barley looked toward the smoke, then back to me.

"This part of it?" he said, nodding toward the shanties.

"Don't know. But I'm not getting anywhere near it. Way my luck's been heading, I'd end up getting blamed for the whole thing and more."

"We'll talk again, you and me," he said.

"That mean I can trust you?"

"Means I'm starting to trust you."

I nodded. He turned and hurried off to where a black stain of smoke dirtied the air.

25

FOR AN IRISHMAN TO LOSE IT ALL

When all of it was over, we would be better off, I vowed.

And we were getting out of Lawrence, where being Irish was enough to erase any hard work or loyalty a man could muster. That's why I was far out in the valley, in a town of thick woods and meadows crisscrossed with low fieldstone walls, waiting for Theo at the stables of a horse breeder named Rosenberg. Lot of the blue bloods wouldn't deal with me, but Rosenberg was a Jew, and didn't take issue with me being Irish. I leaned on the fence rail and watched a red-tailed hawk circling the fields. The air out there smelled of leaves and pine, warm grass and earth, wood smoke—no soot, no bite of industry—and the sounds were the wind and the clang of hammer on iron coming from a nearby smithy. Rosenberg came out of the stable run with a gray stallion of sixteen hands. Walked him over.

"He's no draft horse," I said. I reached out and ran my hand along the horse's nose.

"He's not," Rosenberg said. "Hot-blooded as they come."

"How much?"

"Seventy-five."

"Now you're killing me."

I lifted the horse's lip and looked at his teeth. He yanked his head back and stomped. Rosenberg patted him on his flank.

"Could sire a line of fine horses," he said.

"Lot of money."

"Lot of horse."

I nodded. Lifted my cap, ran a hand through the sweat clinging to my brow.

"Couple of weeks to think about it?" I said.

"He's not going anywhere."

"Appreciate it."

Behind, a wagon came up the lane, raising summer dust behind it. I waved when I saw it was Theo. He'd set the wagon for one horse—I'd ridden the other out. He pulled up next to the fence.

"That him?" he said. "Look at him. How much?"

"More than it cost to bring my family over," I said. "You get my friend where she needed to go?"

I'd had Theo bring Ieva to the train station over in Lowell, where there'd be daily papers from Boston and Portland. Lawrence station was under guard on account of the riots.

"She let me do all the talking," Theo said.

"I'm stunned. And the girls?"

"Got them to work," he said. "You'll be as glad as me to hear fat Winthrop ain't having an easy time of it, neither. Just barely escaped with his ugly wife from the riot, then the lads from the dye rooms walked out first thing. Found a bunch of dead cats floating in the vat. One fella said they also found a hand, but who's to say—them boys are all addled to start with, breathing fumes twelve hours a day. Wouldn't even set a foot back in, Mac running around, pulling his hair out."

"The lot'll be fired before the day's out."

"Well, Winthrop hasn't fired 'em yet. Hasn't shown his boozy face in the yard. Not in days. Holed up in his huge house, shaking and peering out the windows, waiting for the mayor to have the streets cleaned up of every last Irishman before he'll dare to, is what I'm guessing."

"Heard his daughter died," Rosenberg said. "His stableman told me."

Not quite, I thought, working hard to make sure that my face didn't betray the dirt I'd dug from her grave, nor the coffin I'd cracked open.

RODE back with Theo beside meadows thick with goldenrod, passing through the shade of elm and chestnut.

"Seventy-five dollars?" he said. "How we going to come up with that kind of money?"

"We could put your mouth to work powering one of the mills."

"Nice, and thank you kindly."

"But barring that, I'm afraid we'll have to work for it, hard as we can. Deliveries, fares, hauling anything we can get paid for."

"We could always join the army."

"I'm not in as much hurry to get shot at as you."

"Glory, actually. Hoover signed up, so did them Parker boys. I'm a better shot than any of them."

"Won't do you much good when you're looking down the maw of Reb cannon, loaded with grape."

"That's where bravery comes in," he said.

"That's where amputation comes in."

"Come on. You don't think about it?"

"Just another way for an Irishman to lose it all."

"Don't know who's worse," Theo said after a spell. "Old Jeff Davis or fat Winthrop. Both of them hiding, I suppose."

We crossed over a bridge that spanned the narrow Shawsheen River. The water moved brown and lazy, flecked with bits of mineral below the surface. Not too far up was the crossroad that'd take Theo back to Lowell to pick up Ieva. I pulled up on the reins to my horse.

"Wait," I said.

"What?"

"Give me the wagon, Theo. You take this one."

I climbed from the horse and hurried over to the wagon. We traded.

"Just make sure the girls get to the flophouse safe," I said. "Tell them I might be late."

"Where you going?"

"Can you do it?"

"Course. But why?"

I snapped the reins and didn't answer him, headed off west to Lowell.

26

PUT THAT IN YOUR PAPER

The mayor was ready to have Tom Barley tossed out. Underneath a wild hedge of black hair and sideburns that reached his chin line, the flush of Honorable Hiram F. Oliver's skin deepened—but Barley knew he wouldn't dare now, not in front of the other newsmen from as far off as Worcester and Boston huddled in the antechamber of the three-story brick City Hall.

"So you disagree with Reverend Prescott," Barley pressed.

"The good reverend's opinions are his own."

Barley flipped through his notes. "The exact quotation was, 'Our greatest sin was in allowing our fair city to become a beacon to wave after wave of unwashed Irish, with their allegiance to Rome's Papacy.'"

"The reverend doesn't speak for the city."

"Yet the city's police have been ripping down prints of saints and holy medallions and other Catholic charms, as we'd fairly describe them, all throughout the city."

"We're trying to quell a riot, sir."

"With actions exclusively aimed at the Irish," Barley said.

"We didn't choose the neighborhoods that'd riot."

"How many of the rioters jailed weren't Irish?"

That got the police chief to stop glowering at him and step forward.

"We jailed as many as it took to bring calm to the streets, and didn't concern ourselves with heritage or nationality," he said.

"The streets are calm, then?"

"They will be."

"Is there a connection between the crackdown in the riverside neighborhoods and the death of Mr. Abbot Winthrop's daughter Eve?" Barley said.

"Tragedy unrelated to last night's events."

"But many of the rioters were dismissed from the mills owned by Mr. Winthrop, were they not?"

"No one forced them to stoop to violence."

Barley nodded and flipped to yet another page in his note-booklet. "There's talk that a train-load of Union troops is on its way up from Boston. Is that true, and how many would that be?"

The police chief looked to the mayor and then stepped back, letting the mayor answer.

"Governor Andrew and I share the same determination to bring order back to Lawrence."

"And how many troops will that require?" Barley said.

"One hundred men from the Fifth Massachusetts Infantry Company will arrive this morning."

"Fifth Infantry."

"Correct."

"They're shipping out to Virginia next week."

"You'd have to ask the governor that."

The other newsmen scratched that into their own notes. *From the strife-torn city to the hellish battlefield—which will be a truer test of the noble Union soldier's mettle?* Barley could see them each forming their own version of that sentiment.

"Was it your request, or the governor's insistence?" Barley

said. "And at what point did you realize that the police force would not be enough?"

"Did you lose faith in your police?" another reporter asked.

Mayor Oliver clamped down on his cigar as he stoked it to life again in the flare of a match.

"We have a police force that's the equal of any modern city's," he said in a whorl of blue smoke, "yet the situation has grown to merit an augmentation of law enforcement."

"Will the soldiers have authority to shoot citizens, Irish or otherwise?"

"They're not coming to shoot the Irish," the mayor said.

"But they'll be armed?"

"Curfew goes into effect two hours before sundown. Rioters will be given a clear warning."

"So you expect more rioting?"

"We don't," the mayor said. "For the very reason we just elucidated."

They took a handful more questions from the other newsmen, most of them following up on what Barley'd begun. Barley looked out the lead paned windows. A pall of smoke still hung over the city, drifting out over the river. *As the ashes and scorched ruins of the once teeming shanty neighborhood smolders in a perfect vision of the sulfurous depths of Hell itself, the city girds for more unrest,* he scratched into his notes, already crafting his next dispatch.

"I'll take one more question," the mayor said.

Barley lifted his pencil and pointed. "Mayor Oliver, when you communicated with the governor and requested troops bound for the battlefields of Virginia, which of the following was at the forefront of your decision: the murders, the mutilations, the kidnappings, the arson, the riots, the unexplained deaths of seemingly healthy young ladies, the grave robberies, the claims that one of the rioters was seen to hurl men to their deaths and then took a blow to the head from an axe and continued on his way—or was it the talk that a curse has brought an unnamed evil to the streets of Lawrence?"

Mayor Oliver spun on his heels and made for the door, trailing smoke. "Hope you didn't expect a serious answer for such a ludicrous question, Mr. Barley."

"The talk is all over the city."

The mayor stopped. "Curses, evil," he said. "We've more important matters at hand, and you're asking about something Mrs. Oliver might grow hysterical over when she gets the vapors."

"How does Mrs. Oliver feel about nine missing prostitutes, three missing schoolgirls, eight missing mill girls? Or the voices some attest to hearing from outside their windows at night?"

The mayor waved the question off, his face grown deep red. He hurried under the transom, leaving twists of smoke to drift after him. The police chief pointed a meaty finger at Barley.

"We will catch the ones responsible, and their ruthlessness and butchery will be answered. Block by block, we're scouring the city—and we'll rest only when they decorate the gallows. Put that in your paper."

But do you even know what you're after? Barley thought. A few streets over, the clock tower rang ten. Barley closed his note-booklet and hurried out into the morning.

27

OURS FOR THE TAKING

I eva and I stood before the Winthrop house as the sky to the west faded to a sullen dusk, streaked with smoke. Dark windows stared back at us.

"This is possible," Ieva said.

"And only one way to find out," I said. I looked up and down the street. Wasn't nobody out strolling, so I led the wagon right up the drive and got the horse to a stop behind the carriage house. Bats darted around in the sky as it faded to a twilight blue. Below us to the south, Lawrence glittered with street lanterns and candlelight from the tenements and factories.

"Around back," I said.

We followed a brick path. The gardens and lawn stretched off to the back of the property, where we found the servants' entrance. The door stood open. Leaning in, I saw nothing move, no sign of supper cooking, didn't hear any knocking of steps or scrubbing of pans. The door led into a pantry stacked with tins, sealed jars of preserves, sacks of flour, and more. Ieva came in behind me. I saw she'd slipped the medallion out from beneath her collar. The stillness pressed on us.

"That graveyard was noisier than this," I whispered.

Beyond the pantry, a tiled hallway opened into a kitchen. I stopped at the corner. Shards of a shattered porcelain bowl littered the floor. I stopped and pointed. Where the kitchen opened up, a woman in the dress of a servant lay face-up on the floor—her fingers hooked into claws, her lips pulled back from dry teeth, and her eyes still open. I knelt and laid the back of my fingers against her cheek. No warmth.

"You were right," Ieva said.

We cut through the kitchen and up the stairs into the first floor. Furnishings were fine: long couches of carved mahogany legs and bases, cushions covered over in velvet; crystal vases on polished shelves; tables and corner cabinets with fine inlay work; paintings on the silk-papered walls. A month earlier, such lavish things would have whet my appetite to work even harder—but seeing them like that only made the lot of it look hollow, knowing only too well that Winthrop got most of it by being a bastard, and if any of it made him happy, no one would know it from the misery he spread around without a second thought.

Found no one on the first floor. I was about to head up the stairs when Ieva paused. She fingered the medallion with her eyes closed.

"You feel it?" she whispered.

"Not sure."

"We're not alone."

When she said it, I knew she was right. The feeling had grown, stealing in like shadows in the gloaming. I put my hand on the banister.

"Wait," Ieva said.

She knelt and opened her bag. Pulled out the wraps that held the spikes, pulled out the mallet, lifted a silver flask of holy water. Pressed each item to her lips and forehead as she did. She left the bag and handed me the mallet. I nodded, and we started up the stairs, going slow as to not creak the runners. At the top, a long hallway. The setting sun drew dull squares on the walls from the high-up windows of the second floor. To the left, the doors were closed. To the right, the door at the end was open a hand's-width, shadow beyond. I pointed and Ieva nodded. We walked quietly as we passed in and out of the sunlight. I glanced out the last window. Was the last spot in Lawrence to see the sun, Winthrop's house—and the molten plug of it slid below the horizon in a wink. Paused at the door, listening. Might as well have been listening to a tomb.

I pushed the door open. The hinges swung smooth. Giant four-poster bed took up most of the far half of the room, the sheets hanging off the side. A lantern lay shattered on the floor next to a nightstand and the heavy smell of whale oil filled the air. I stepped inside, also catching a whiff of old cigars and hair tonic. Underneath it, something stank, sharp and tangy.

"They fled?" Ieva said.

"Might've."

I headed for the closet—and then stopped. Mr. Abbot Winthrop sprawled across the floor on the far side of the bed, barefooted and wearing a long nightshirt. Though he was on his stomach, his wide face stared empty at the ceiling, eyes bulging.

"Jesus."

Went closer. In death, he'd soiled himself. A handful of sheet was still clenched in his stiff fingers.

"She came for him," I said. Knelt next to Winthrop. The skin of his neck was bruised purple and black, horrible-looking twists of skin from having been snapped all the way around. Whatever I thought about the man, he hadn't deserved this—killed by the horror that was once his own precious daughter. Behind me, Ieva searched the room.

"Look," she said. I followed her gaze and saw a strip of cloth caught in the double door to a closet. I got up and opened it. Dresses and skirts sat in a heap, wooden hangers and a rack of shoes kicked over—and Mrs. Winthrop sat at the heart of it, her fingers still gripping a flower-print dress. Her face was clawed up, her neck bruised from strangling.

"The wife?" Ieva said.

"Yes."

I left the door open and turned to her.

"But she didn't take them," I said. "What's that about?"

She shook her head.

"This I don't understand," she said.

"Vengeance—like with the Fitzgeralds?"

"Perhaps."

"But they didn't have nothing to do with the key the veln went after. With anything, near as I can figure."

Ieva stood over Winthrop. She leaned over.

"He has something in his mouth," she said. She reached and pulled on something. A silver chain spooled out from his still mouth, and then something came free and Ieva stood.

"A locket," she said.

"Bloody evil, that's what it is."

"Yes. I've not seen this."

"So what's different here?"

She placed the locket on the edge of the bed and grew quiet. I looked around the rest of the room, but found no other signs of struggle. I peered out into the hallway. The darkness pooled in the stairwell.

"It's not—how was it you said it—to mark a spot?" I said. "To raise a new devil?"

"Not like this. That's for ceremony, a desecration."

"Then she was a verg."

"I still don't think so. A verg is from a living victim. As we saw, this one was dead."

From overhead, a noise—the creak of a door. I pointed. Ieva nodded; she'd heard it. Neither one of us moved. A sly footstep started a board groaning, then went silent. Ieva came to the door.

"Where?" she whispered.

"That narrow door at the end," I said, pointing. She nodded. Looked like a way up into the attic. She motioned us both back and unwrapped the spikes, letting the cloth fall to the floor. She handed me one and then slipped back, out of sight from the hallway. I swung the door mostly closed. With a step, I got myself to the hinged side, where I could get one eye to the crack between the door and the jam, giving me a view of the hallway.

We waited. Minute passed with both of us no louder than the dead folks behind us. Then, at the far end of the hall, I watched as the door handle slowly turned. Heard the click of the latch and then saw the door push open. It swung out into the hallway. Though the sun had set, the western sky held the fiery sunset, and the four windows along the hallway let in the soft orange. The passage up into the attic was black, a smudge of pale coming into view.

Eve Winthrop stepped into the hall.

Her burial dress was torn and dirtied, a strip of the hem hanging off, a shoulder undone. She walked to the room where we were, moving with an uneven stride, passing in and out of the somber wash of fading sunset. Her face was a grim mask—elongated jaw, proud brows that left her eyes dark wells of ink, stretched mouth that gaped. My heartbeat galloped in my ears, for as she walked up the hall, I swore that she stared right at me the whole way, as if she could see me peeking out from the edge of the door.

She came closer, bringing the unclean air of death with her. She stopped. Her dark eyes fixed on mine. I didn't even breathe. A hideous smile cracked her face even more. I backed away from the door, raising the spike up.

"I see you, child."

Her voice was grinding pieces of shale. Out of the corner of my eye, I spotted Ieva moving near the door.

"I'll play with your ropes," the voice intoned. A horrid laugh followed. Before I could take another step, the door slammed into me, catching me so hard in the chest as to knock the wind from me and send me crumbling to the rug. She was on me, then—coming around the door like some oversized spider, arms and legs churning. Her flesh pressed on my own, hot and feverish. My head knocked on the floor under the weight of her—and I still couldn't get a breath in. Her mouth touched my ear, and I recoiled.

"So smooth," she said, her lips brushing my face. Her breath was rank, gagging-strong.

And she screamed and rolled off me. Ieva drove her backwards, pressing the medallion against her elongated face. The smell of burning flesh filled the room. As much as she scrambled back, Ieva stayed right with her until she had her pinned in the corner next to the door.

"*Sveetiits lai top tavs vaards,*" Ieva said. With her free hand, she splashed holy water on the girl. An animal howl broke from Eve Winthrop's lips. When the screaming ended, they stared at each other. I got up to my feet and grabbed the mallet and spike I'd dropped. Ieva held up the hand that gripped the flask.

"What do you want here?" Ieva said to the writhing girl.

"I want my mummy."

"Who are you?"

"Just a tired old wretch."

"Your name?"

"We know yours."

She leaned to the side, peering around Ieva's shoulder to meet my eyes.

"And yours, too," she said, that grin twisting her features again.

Ieva slammed the medallion to the fiend's forehead again, bringing forth another scream. The light from the medallion held her—it—back.

"Were you in the ruins outside Benoud?" Ieva said.

This just brought out a gravelly chuckle. Her stretched lips could no longer cover her stained teeth and split in several spots. Worse were her eyes—sooty where the white would have been, and her pupils shone as golden slices. Along the side of her head, a twist of black horn burst from the skin, crusted with dried blood. Ieva asked her a question in a tongue I didn't know, and the girl answered back in the same tongue. Ieva switched languages, and the girl followed her lead—I counted six languages, one of them I recognized as Latin, another sounding like German. Finally, the girl sat up, leering in the glow of the medallion.

"Such a tiring game," she croaked. "*Spel*, *gibier*, wild, *gioco*, *lek*…"

Each time she said the word, she switched languages, passing through and leaving behind all I—and Ieva, from what I could tell—had any knowledge of.

"Then answer me," Ieva said.

The girl pressed her face forward, a cunning look taking hold of her. "You command me?"

"I command you," Ieva said.

The girl smiled. Light—the glow of an ember—moved across her collarbone.

"You have no say," she said. "I'm the destroyer, and I appoint death to whoever I choose. Your time is soon. Your purity fails. Your efforts have failed. You've lost, false priest."

"Hardly," Ieva said. She flicked her hand and tossed holy water into the girl's eyes. Smoke rose, and the girl rolled her head back in agony. Ieva pressed the medallion into the flesh of her throat, where it sizzled. Ieva turned and motioned. I knelt and pressed the silver spike's point against the girl's temple. She thrashed. I struggled to keep it steady.

"Chest," Ieva said.

I did it in one swift movement, dropping the point of the spike onto the soft spot where the throat met the indent of the collarbones, slamming the mallet hard onto it. I kept the spike at an angle, driving it hard into the girl's chest. Thick, dark blood splattered out, and she wriggled, crying out, her face a rolling wave of agony. She crab-scurried out of our grip, along the wall below the window. Her limbs hammered the floor, jerking like a body being hung on a gallows. A croaking gurgle came from her mouth, which flapped and roiled.

She stilled.

Ieva and I both stared at her. She didn't move.

"Where's the flames?" I said, remembering the sawmill.

"Don't know."

Her voice wavered, and it gave me a start to realize how frightened Ieva was.

"None of this makes any sense," she continued.

"She wasn't a—" I started. A rustling sound behind us stopped me. We both turned. Mr. Abbot Winthrop stood up behind the bed, his chest facing us, his head facing the wall behind. With the sound of huge cracking knuckles, he turned his head around, coming to face us, a gloating smile breaking across his mouth.

"Such lovely forms I can have," he said. His voice box must've been broken, as it came out in a dry rasp. "And there are always more."

Without a pause, his body keeled over heavily onto the bed. A shifting and banging came from the wardrobe closet, and Mrs. Winthrop staggered upright, looking at us with the same ghastly grimace, her dry eyeballs spinning until they found us. She smiled, looking like she'd just swallowed poison.

"Ours for the taking," she said, "and so much fun."

She turned and grabbed the bedpost with both hands and slammed her forehead right into it—so hard that it shattered the wood. She looked back at us as though she'd done nothing more ordinary than sneeze. A sliver the size of a pencil jutted out of the space between her eyebrows.

"What is your heavenly name?" Ieva said, getting to her feet.

Red flared along Mrs. Winthrop's jawline, the heart of a coal beneath the skin. She walked around the bed, her eyes watching us.

"The sound of it would shatter your skulls."

"You can't say it, can you?" Ieva said.

"My name is freedom. My name is liberty. My name is legion."

"You're forbidden. Banished. It won't even form on your tongue, you've been so utterly stripped. Damned."

Mrs. Winthrop barked a harsh laugh. "Banished? Imprisoned? Damned? No longer. We're free, and this is just the start."

"Lies," Ieva said. "Your time is over, veln."

"It's just beginning, false priest."

Ieva advanced on her, the medallion extended. Mrs. Winthrop snarled. I searched the floor for the other silver spike, struggling to find it in the twilight that plunged the room into shades of charcoal and pewter.

"*Atpakaļ uz bezdibenis, veln. Tā Kunga spēks pārspēj savu tumsu,*" Ieva said.

Mrs. Winthrop groaned. Bits of her skin smoldered, hints of flame dancing across her thick neck, her cheek. She leaped, landing with enough weight to rattle the windows on the other side of the room. Her stench was foul beyond words.

"No more," she said.

I looked around and grabbed a porcelain water carafe, swinging it up and into the side of her head, hard as I could. It cracked her good, shattering. The water sizzled, steaming. She didn't even seem to notice, but spun and grabbed me. The next thing I knew, I was up in the air. She had me by my collar and the top of my trousers. I had just a split second to admire the fine furnishings from that perspective before I was hurled to the floor on my back, hitting it so hard that I couldn't even think. Next I knew, Mrs. Winthrop was astraddle me. She leaned into my face.

"We'll have so much fun—" was all she got out.

Ieva drove a spike through the top of her head. Mrs. Winthrop exhaled a blast of flame and her eyes shone with a strange glow as though the inside of her skull burned like a forge. She slid forward, slumping onto me. I wriggled out from beneath the dead weight. Ieva gave me a hand to my feet, and we both turned to the body of Mr. Winthrop, still sprawled facedown on the bed.

"We're going to need more spikes," I said.

Ieva approached his body. The medallion continued to glimmer. All three bodies were still.

"Where did he go?" Ieva said.

We turned and looked at the bodies. None of them even twitched. Full dark had taken the house.

"He's still here," she said.

"The same one—the one we're after?"

"No. Different."

"But he's not—it's not like the other," I said.

"This is bad," Ieva said. She looked back and forth from one body to the other, holding up the glowing medallion.

"He ain't hopping from one corpse to another, is he?" I said.

"We'd best hope not."

"Is that even possible?"

"I'm not sure. I've never seen it, never read of it. But if it is…"

"If it is," I said, "then stopping them just got a whole lot more difficult."

Ieva knelt by the body of Eve. She looked at the changes to the girl's head, her face.

"They don't just possess the body," she said. "The body itself changes. Grows diabolical."

"And if any dead body can become a new devil, this quickly, leaping from one to another," I said, "You know what that means."

"It's worse than that, I fear," she said. "It means they've grown more powerful. And it means that the gates to the Abyss might come down, releasing the remaining veln."

The room stank of burning. She put a knuckle to her lower

lip. A knock came from downstairs that practically had us jumping into each other's arms. More knocks, pounding on the front door. I left the bedroom and looked down from the windows of the front of the hallway. Saw a policeman on a horse by the gate out by the street. Another horse was empty.

"Time to go," I said.

"We're not finished—I feel it," Ieva said.

"If we get caught in here, we're finished. Nothing we can do if we're locked up. Come on."

I grabbed her sleeve and dragged her from the room. A panicked minute later, we tore out of the servant's entrance we'd come in through. Moonlight marbled the grass and the brick paths. The humid night air put a cowl around the moon. As we cut into the hedges, I heard, from behind us, the gate bang against the side of the lovely home of the Winthrops.

"Hey!" a voice shouted. "Right there—stop!"

We ran.

28

BEYOND THE CURTAIN OF DAYS

The third floor of the schoolhouse shone with lantern light.

"Why here?" Tom Barley said.

Ernst Glockner stood next to him, his uniform buttoned tight in spite of the heat, a toothpick wagging in the corner of his mouth. Evening settled on the city. They were south of the river in the residential neighborhood. A few stray hounds picked through a mound of garbage and the sound of a wailing babe drifted into the humid air.

"Mayor doesn't want word of this getting out."

As they watched, an iceman came out the front door, his tongs slung over the sackcloth on his shoulder. He chatted up the policeman who opened the door for him, then got onto his ice wagon and headed to the main thoroughfare. A figure stood silhouetted for a moment in one of the third-story windows, then disappeared out of sight.

"Haven't forgotten that I'm a newsman, have you?" Barley said.

"Matter of fact, I haven't."

"I'll print what I see."

"Wouldn't expect anything less," Glockner said. He crossed his arms across his chest, looked up at the lighted window. "Best police work this city's seen. Why sweep it under the rug?"

"Mayor won't be happy," Barley said.

"Might not."

They cut across the packed dirt yard behind the school, up granite steps to the back door. It was unlocked, the sunset behind them reflected on the panes of glass. Inside, a staircase rose to their right. Heading up from the second floor, lantern light crossed the railing. Voices reached them. At the next floor, Glockner led Barley across the hallway to a door that opened into a small observation room that looked out on a lecture hall. Half a dozen writing desks lined the side wall, along with a pair of portable blackboards, the green slate smudged with ghost lessons. Glockner stood back from the big window that opened on the hall, keeping to the shadows.

"There it is," he said.

Barley stepped to the window that looked out onto the lecture hall. "And you're sure it's her?" he said.

"Grave is dug up and empty," Glockner said. "Checked that myself. And she was at the house, along with both Mr. Winthrop and his wife."

"Both dead?"

"As doornails. Murdered. Cruelly."

Barley glanced at Glockner, who smiled as though he was discussing a favorite nephew. Barley thought—and not for the first time—that Glockner was about as well suited to policing as an arsonist would be to being Fire Chief. He jotted notes, his fingers zipping along even as his eyes swung back and forth, taking in the scene. The lecture room was now a morgue. The chairs and desks had been moved off of the risers and where the lectern would normally be, and blocks of ice in copper tubs kept the body cold. Lanterns burned on the table that held the metal autopsy instruments. Three men stood over the body.

"Who are they?" Barley whispered.

Glockner pointed as he answered. "Those two came up this morning from Boston, one of the colleges. That one yelling down there came in this afternoon from Newburyport. On the board of the Shay."

In front of the table, one man shook his head, reaching for his jacket.

"Preposterous, transparent buffoonery," he said, his voice raised. "You've wasted half a day of my time, gentlemen—for a cheap stunt not even worthy of a carnival. I will expect a full compensation for my time and travels."

"You've got it wrong, Doctor," one of the others said.

The man jerked on his coat and stabbed his finger at the body arranged on the ice. "That is a corpse—dead for a week. The other nonsense is repugnant. Insulting."

"You see it with your own eyes, sir."

The man stepped up to the body. "This? This is manipulation of a corpse. It sickens me—and it sickens me likewise that any of you have been coerced or bought into this charade. Remarkable that either of you can stand here with straight faces." He turned and stormed out of the lecture hall with a dismissive wave of his arm and a slam of the door.

"Doctor Bartholemew?" the other doctor said.

The taller man with a high collar and unkempt beard shook his head.

"If he wants to put his tenure before his science, then he has no right to the name of scientist," he said. He leaned over the body, lowering the magnifying piece clipped to the arm of his spectacles.

"You've never cared for the academy, Cyrus."

"Nor do I now." He picked up a brass pointer and indicated a spot on the girl's head, behind the temple. "Manipulation? Observe. Horn-like material, sprouting through the skin."

"Remarkable," said another scientist. "Resembles the buds of horn of a ram."

"Precisely."

Footsteps came down the hallway and the door to the lecture hall pushed open. A pair of policemen entered, accompanied by the mayor. Glockner slid back farther into the shadows of the observation room.

"Professor Emerson just gave me an earful on his way out," the mayor said. "Is he right?"

Dr. Bartholemew straightened.

"He couldn't be more wrong," he said.

"Good," the mayor said. He twisted his face up at the fecal-meaty stench of decomposition. "So are we ready to toss this mess into the river yet?"

"Not quite as simple as that," Dr. Bartholemew said.

"How's that not simple?"

"This is spectacular."

"Spectacular?" the mayor said. "I want everyone to listen to me. Half the city isn't showing up to work, the looms are standing idle, workers are fleeing the company housing. This is getting resolved, and the word better be that it was just something gruesome. Nothing else. This hysteria ends."

The tall scientist shook his head.

"This is something more than gruesome—though you're right that hysteria is an inappropriate response. Not surprising, given the uneducated nature of most of your citizens. However, Mayor Oliver, we're looking at something that can only be explained with science."

"Dr. Bartholemew, my uneducated citizens need not understand anything beyond how to make boots, belts, uniforms, and woolen garments—but they do need to hear something more comforting to them than all this talk of devilry."

Bartholemew grabbed his jacket from the back of a stool and

headed for the door. "Then you may tell them anything you wish, sir."

The mayor shook his head but swallowed his dyspepsia. "Dr. Bartholemew. Sir, I don't mean to discount your opinions. Your fee alone should speak to that."

Bartholemew stopped. "I don't deal in opinions," he said. "I deal in facts."

"Then pray tell me—what are the facts?"

Bartholemew headed back to the table and replaced his jacket onto the stool.

"Our esteemed colleague from Newburyport was correct about two things before he scurried off: this body shows every sign of having been dead for a week, and of having also entered an unheard-of state of transmutational post-mortem growth."

"Post-mortem?"

Bartholemew picked up the pointer again. "That means after death, Mr. Mayor."

"I know what the hell it means, Doctor. Go on."

"Now what could be the cause of such an implausibility?"

"Was she dead, or wasn't she?"

"Neither, is the unlikely answer. And, here—I'll spare you the struggle with that paradox by pointing out a few notable anomalies."

They got in closer to the body.

"Let's start with the skull."

Bartholemew pulled on a pair of thick leather gloves and hefted the head. The skin was bruised, yet the features were clear, even as they were unnerving in their distortion. A portion of the back of the skull had been sawed through.

"Notice right here," Bartholemew said. "The bone itself is thicker at the crown, and yet the density of the bone is lighter, which would indicate that this is new growth—not something this girl was born with. I'd put the radius of her head now several inches wider than anything that would be proportional to her overall size."

He turned the head so they might get a better view. Barley craned his neck, flipping the page of notes.

"More unexpected, you can observe that the brain itself is penetrated by dozens of spines of bone that appear to have sprouted from the inside of the skull cavity itself, winding ever deeper into the soft tissue."

"Good Lord," one police officer said. The mayor shut him up with a look. Bartholemew picked up a surgical apparatus and wedged it into the opening, breaking off a piece. The snap of it carried up to Glockner and Barley. Bartholemew pulled it out and held it up for inspection. It appeared as long as a sewing needle.

"Must have been agony," the mayor said.

"Catastrophic, no doubt. Perhaps not as painful as you'd think. Stranger still, observe."

Bartholemew lowered the head. He waved the pointer over the rest of the naked body, walking along the ice tubs.

"Singular deformities abound," he said, pointing or lifting the pieces in question. "The lower jaw is elongated, again with new accretion of bone material. Wrists and fingers show a stretching and new growth. In fact, nary a bone in the body is in a state I could describe as normal."

He put down the pointer and waved over his colleague.

"And along the back," he said, taking the body by the arm and lifting. "Let's flip her, Horace."

They lifted the body and rolled her first onto her side, and then her stomach, giving Barley a brief view of surgical incisions around the wounds between the young girl's breasts, the dark hair between her legs. Bartholemew leaned over the girl's upper back, lowered his magnifying lens. He pressed at two raised spots, pushing them this way and that with gloved fingertips.

"Doesn't feel like bone."

"What are they?" the mayor said.

"Let's see directly." He looked over at the table and pulled out a large scalpel. The men leaned in closer. Barley and Glockner strained to get a glimpse.

"That's revolting," the mayor said. The other policeman went pale. After just a moment, he bolted out the door and treated them to the sounds of retching.

"Impossible," the mayor said.

"Yet you see it for yourself."

"It's a damned wing."

Bartholemew leaned over the torso and, with a pair of tongs, stretched out what looked like a flap of dark skin.

"Mammalian in nature," he said. "A barb, right here."

He opened and folded it, noting the joints. With his other hand, he tapped a point at the bend. The other scientist leaned in and looked at the opening they'd made.

"The stretching of the skin—like a boil or a welt, the tissue bruised and pulled. This wasn't a slow growth."

"Would they have come out?" the mayor said.

"Almost certainly. And grown remarkably fast."

"But no one noticed it when she was buried?"

"One would suppose such conditions would have been well-noted," Bartholemew said.

"This is insane."

"We will document every last detail, and drag it into sanity," Bartholemew said. He let go of the proto-wing and wiped some of the blackened fluid off his gloves onto the canvas on the edge of the tub.

"Could it be a disease?" the mayor said. He stood with his hands on his hips. "Something she picked up somewhere."

"Not an illogical postulate, Mayor Oliver—though my rather extensive studies of contagion include no such symptomology."

He straightened out his apron and looked at the others.

"My thoughts take a rather different turn," he said. "Someone please run and fetch a blacksmith. Have him bring a cold chisel and small anvil."

Spread throughout the musculature beneath the girl's skin was a tough, black, thread-like substance that veined its way in and out. Flexible as stitching, yet strong enough that it took the summoned blacksmith two broken chisels and a dozen hard hits with a third to break it. As he picked up the piece, nothing but the hiss of the lanterns filled the room.

"You figure out how forge dis, we h'all be wealthy men," he said in a thick Quebecois accent.

The mayor sent him off with a handful of dollars and a promise to shut his business down if he so much as honked a word about it to his own wife and eleven children.

Up in the observation room, Barley whispered to Glockner. "Mayor looks like he's ten minutes from a heart attack."

"Two more lasses disappeared last night," Glockner said. "His Honor's political future ends if he doesn't stop this."

"And yours?"

"Just remember who got you into this private show," Glockner said.

The mayor returned to the others in the makeshift morgue.

"So it isn't a pox or distemper," he said. "I'm still waiting to hear what the hell it is."

Bartholemew had several lengths of the black substance before him. He held one closely and examined it with his magnifying lens.

"It appears alien to the host, which could indicate—"

He jerked his hand back, dropping the tread. It landed on the table—and even back where Barley and Glockner watched from, they could hear the scratching sound.

"My God."

Bartholemew reached for a pair of extraction clamps and with deft movements snagged the thread. It twisted and arched like a thorny worm. A clacking sound began, along with a bellows-like huffing.

"Dr. Bartholemew," the mayor said, loudly.

"Remarkable," Bartholemew said. The body before them shuddered, limbs bouncing on the ice. Eve Winthrop's head cranked sideways, and her jaws opened and closed, teeth clacking, dry lips and tongue making flapping sounds. The other scientist brought a lantern to where her back heaved—the strange wings on her back stirred, flapping with enough strength to tear at the flame, almost extinguishing it. The policemen pulled out their nightsticks.

"Everyone back," Bartholemew said. The end of the black filament he held whipped up at his face. The mayor didn't need to see much more than that. He hurried to the door and shouted for help. A few moments later, two more policemen rushed in.

"That's it, I want this thing burned!" the mayor shouted. "You men tie it up with as much rope as you need, someone find Claude Chesterton—it's going into the furnace at the Pentucket within the hour. Whatever it takes."

"Absolutely not," Bartholemew said. "Do you even realize what you're looking at?"

The mayor ignored him. "Grab it. Now."

Just as Bartholemew attempted to interpose himself between the police and the body, the heaving bellows sound turned to thick gurgles. The eyes of Eve Winthrop opened wide, staring at the window where Barley and Glockner stood, and the gurgles turned to screams of agony. Her back arched, and she pushed herself upright, sliding on the ice, the blood-freezing yells filling the lecture hall.

"Rope!" someone shouted.

Bartholemew leaped up, spread his arms wide, trying to keep the police away. "No! Lock the doors; let this process continue."

The nearest policeman tried to get past him.

"Get him out of the goddamned way!" the mayor yelled.

Bartholemew was no small man, a full two heads taller than the policeman. When he didn't move, the policeman lowered his shoulder and rammed him with it. In a moment, the two of them erupted into fisticuffs, and a moment after that the policeman upended the scientist and pinned him to the floor, kneeling on his back and wrenching the man's wrist hard enough to drag a scream from him.

"I'm giving the orders here, Dr. Bartholemew," the mayor said. The remaining scientist ran for the door. No one stopped him. The mayor pointed the other policemen toward where the body thrashed off the ice and onto the floor.

"By God, look at that," Barley said.

With stiff, jerky movements, the corpse of Eve Winthrop craned her neck around and dragged herself to her feet. One policeman approached, holding his nightstick in front. She stilled, her eyes fixing on him. The policeman's nightstick clattered to the floor. His hands shot to his face. A pair of points on his cheek below his left eye pulled out into little fins—two black cords stuck from them, dragging him forward to where the cords snaked from the wound in the girl's chest. His yell filled the room even as he tried to rip them free, but his face whipped back and forth and he fell forward. Before anyone could think to do anything, he slid forward into the waiting arms of the corpse— who grabbed him by the face just before tearing into his throat with her mouth. A moment of scrambling and an agonized scream were cut off as a fan of dark red blood shot across the floor, splattering the glass of the nearest lantern with a hiss. The policeman fell still, and the figure dumped him to the floor where he finished bleeding out.

"Don't just stand there!" the mayor yelled.

Eve Winthrop lurched upright in a marionette jerk. In the blooded lantern light, her flesh roiled as if infested with maggots. The policeman's blood dripped from her discolored chin and chest. At the sight of her, other policeman backed off of the scientist, who struggled to his feet. All eyes were on the corpse. The mayor was halfway out the door. Bartholemew raised his hands to the corpse.

"What do you feel?" he said.

Her head swung in his direction.

"Do you understand me?"

A guttural sound came from her mouth.

"Can you speak?"

"Doctor—back off!" the mayor yelled. "Everyone out, we're locking this thing in."

The corpse took an unsteady step. Her mouth worked. The voice that crept from those bloated lips was one that no one in that room would ever rid themselves of.

"I am death. I will pluck the life and this valley will stare upward, an empty socket in a forgotten skull. Each one of you is marked."

A curled finger raised, and the corpse looked at them each in turn. She even turned to the dark window that Barley and Glockner watched from. Barley wrote her words into his notes, not taking his gaze from the figure below.

"Out," the mayor said. The remaining police needed no other prompting.

"This's our cue, too," Glockner said. He and Barley backed away from the window.

"Bartholemew!"

The scientist looked back and forth from the mayor in the doorway to the corpse that had just minutes earlier been a collection of scientific anomalies.

"Who are you?" he said to the corpse.

"The one who's going to learn you some common sense, you soft little whelp."

Eve Winthrop's voice had changed, taking on a clipped northern Maine lilt. Bartholemew looked like he took a blow to the stomach at that. He backed to the door, knocking into the table, spilling his instruments in a crash. The corpse staggered after him. Bartholemew fumbled with one of the black leather bags on the table and came up with a brown jar of liquid. He unclasped the lid and tossed the liquid. It landed on the corpse and hissed, throwing off a white steam. Eve Winthrop shook her head and grunted. Bartholemew bolted to the door where the mayor himself pulled him through and then slammed the door shut.

Barley and Glockner rushed back along the dark room and into the hallway. The window next to the stairwell showed the western skyline of the city cut out against a line of deep sunset. They ran down the hallway just as a horrendous banging came from the room they'd just exited—the booms of heavy black-boards smashing to the floor, of desks being clawed past. They burst out of the shadows into the half of the hallway lit by lanterns.

"The hell is he doing here?" the mayor yelled, seeing Barley.

The policemen pushed two large oak desks in front of the lecture room doors. One had a pistol.

"She's coming out that way, Your Honor," Barley said, cocking his thumb over his shoulder.

Glockner, red in the face, helped slam the last desk in place.

"For the love of Christ," the mayor said.

Eve Winthrop stepped out of the smaller room at the end of the corridor, moving herky-jerky, framed before the fading light of the window. Barley pushed past the others, stopping a dozen feet from the corpse.

"Do you know your name?" he said.

The figure cocked her grotesque head.

"A lonely child from beyond the curtain of days," the figure said through shattered vocal cords.

"And what do you want?"

She raised a broken hand and pointed at them. "The grave is yours to taste, children. All of you." With that, she vaulted over the railing to the stairwell and landed in a tumble in the darkness below. Footsteps thudded, then the sound of the back door slamming open filled the empty schoolhouse. Barley was the first to move, running to the window, looking into the yard behind the schoolhouse. Glockner and the others raced after him. They glimpsed a shadow slipping into the blackness outside the street lamps. They all pressed in for a look. The stench of putrefying flesh was cloying, filling the air. Barley turned to the mayor.

"Care to comment, Your Honor?"

"You print a word of any of this and you won't find a job delivering a damned newspaper anywhere in the state, Mr. Barley."

"City has the right to know."

"My city has the right to be protected. They get wind of any of this, the city shuts down. Riots sprout up bigger than anything we've seen. Don't you be the spark that touches that off."

He was quicker than Barley—he snatched Barley's notebooklet right out of his hand. When Barley reached for it back, another policeman blocked him.

"You sonofabitch. You can't take that," Barley said.

"Take what?" The mayor looked hard at Barley. Daylight had faded to nothing but a purple edge on the horizon; stars shone clear above as they came out.

"Impossible," Bartholemew said, quiet and seemingly to himself.

Barley turned to the window. He didn't care about the notebooklet—this was the biggest story of his life, and everything he needed was right where he needed it: in his head. The mayor could grandstand all he liked. Barley looked out into the darkened city below and wondered how many other there were.

29
―――――

BAG OF BUTTONS

Curfew wasn't making things any easier, and as I raced through the streets trying to get everything done, I kept one eye on the lowering sun, and the other out for any signs of the veln. Another full day of searching had turned up nothing. Ieva told me she needed an hour for prayer, so I took advantage of the time as best I could, and headed over to home to gather up tack and other gear. The Plains were quiet, folk settling in for the evening. Pairs of soldiers set up watches on the bigger street corners, dressed in new-issue blues likely made right there in Lawrence. They didn't stop me as I had another half an hour until curfew began. Pulled the wagon up next to the carriage house and climbed down, knocked the dust off my trousers and cap. Went around to the big doors, getting ready to shove them open, and I paused.

Looked over at the house. The back door stood open, showing a rectangle of twilight beyond. I pushed the door open and stepped into the kitchen. Stopped in my tracks.

On the kitchen table, right in the center of it, sat a small cloth bag, tied shut. I picked it up. Something inside shifted. I undid the string and opened it. Inside, buttons, a few dozen of them. I dumped it out, watching as the buttons landed on the table, a few of them rolling to the edge.

A bag of buttons.

In a bolt, Nell's words came back to me.

DROVE THE TEAM HARD. Curfew came on and the soldiers and police waved me along, exasperated and irritable.

Down the street from the flophouse, a pair of them stood miserable in the sudden downpour that opened from the low sky. At the corner of the road they ordered me to stop.

"Right there, fellas," I said, pointing to the flophouse.

"Get the hell off the street," one of them said.

"You understand what nightfall means, don't you?" the other asked, helpfully.

I snapped the reins and pulled the wagon to a stop in front of the stable behind the flophouse. Everything grew indistinct in the heavy rain, lantern lights glimmering. Flashes of lightning threw the street into relief and I tried to tamp down my panic.

Not a candle nor lantern glowed. The entry stood dark and quiet. The watchman who gathered up the money each day between drinks and cigars that reeked like horse crap wasn't at his desk. I looked over the top—knowing before I saw it what I'd find: him, sprawled on the floor, hands up in the air in front of him, stiff, his eyes open in the sort of shock that told me he'd met someone who didn't care too much for his authority. With a sick feeling in my gut, I ran up the stairs. In the hallway, in the open spaces just inside the door, in and around the many cots within, folks were dead, locked in various poses of fear. I ran around the bodies to the room the girls had, fearing I'd find them dead. The door leaned open. I glanced down the hallway, to the door to Ieva's room. It stood open, too.

"Ieva?" I said.

My voice fell flat in that dead hallway. I ran to the girls' doorway, put my hand on the jamb. Rain spattered against the windowsill and onto the floor—the window yawned wide and the tattered curtain flapped on the wind. Gone, all of them.

"Christ," I said.

The two beds sat askew. Looked closer and saw that the sheets and mattresses were torn as though someone had ripped into them with knives. I ran to the window and leaned out, squinting into the blowing rain. Two stories down to the side alley, as much a mess as any other in the city. I looked around, but found nothing beyond the signs of struggle. In a panic, I darted back out into the hallway, to Ieva's small room. A window opened out onto an iron fire escape. Cot lined one wall, a scratched-up chest with drawers stood in the corner. Couple of rosaries draped it. At the foot of the cot sat a traveling bag.

The realization hit me in a thunderclap: The veln was two steps ahead of us.

Oh, we might have gotten a few hits in—before he'd known. Knew right then how foolish we'd been. He wasn't even striking out. He was toying with me. I was the prey. He had the teeth and the speed and the wit. He had me scurrying back and forth, just then gleaning how trapped I was, looking for a way out.

And I didn't see one.

"Sod, sod, sod," I said. I punched the plaster wall, hard as I could, knocking in a hole and nearly breaking my fingers. Ran back into the girls' room. My breath slipped away from me right then. Images hit me with the force of one of Conlin Nagle's hammers: Rose, Nell, Maggie, trussed up with cruel chains, struggling in some dark place while the veln got ready to feed their souls to a newly released fiend. Or maybe worse. I thought of young Eve Winthrop and the cruel fate she'd met. Shook my head hard, as though I could keep the images out of young Nell turning into a horrid fiend, her clever eyes and sharp mouth making the leap from delightful to nightmarish.

I'd have done anything right then to trade places with them, spare them the horror. I sank to my knees in the midst of that tossed-up room.

"Fuck me," I moaned. "You sonofabitch."

But he already had, the veln. I was a fighting Carey, and could take anything he threw at me. So he took everything from me. The rain drummed against the sill and floor as the warm air brought in the stink of the city. I got to my feet, went to the window. Maybe he—or one of his servants—was watching right then. I was about to give him a piece of my mind, curses and promises of revenge, shouting it out to the night. But I heard an argument. Raised voices, a pistol shot, the high-pitched voice of a lass hurling insults to make a soldier blush, all of it bouncing off the brick walls of the alley beyond the window. I turned and ran from the room, hurried down the stairs, not sparing a glance at the dead. Flew out the flophouse and into the rain.

"Maggie!" I yelled.

She had herself up in the face of one soldier who'd stood curfew guard, shouting at him. In his grip, he held onto Nell's collar. She kicked at his legs and spat at him, mixing in a string of curses as she did. Wasn't just them, neither. Theo got himself in front of the other soldier, waving his hands and loosing a river of words, raising his voice and jabbing his finger. It'd been that soldier who'd fired the shot I'd heard, his pistol still held up into the rain. Beyond them, Rose bawled.

I ran over, as much relief as I'd ever felt coursing through me.

"All right, All right, All right," I said, getting my voice up over everyone else's, no mean trick. "Let 'em go. They're fine. We're getting inside."

"Throw the lot of you into the city's jail," the soldier with Nell said. She wriggled free, but not before kicking a decent helping of mud at him.

"No," I said, grabbing her away. She fought like a rabid tomcat. "For Christ's sake, Nell. Enough."

The soldier got to his feet, slathered in thick mud. I pushed the family back, Theo helping me.

"We're done here, we're going inside. Misunderstanding," I said.

"Get off this street, right now!" the soldier said.

We herded up the gals and jogged through the rain to the stable next to the flophouse. The soldiers stomped after us, slowing as we got off the street. I hefted the girls up onto the wagon.

"But the streets are all guarded," Maggie said. Her hair was plastered against her face.

"Can't stay here," I said. I turned and lifted Rose.

"My fault, I brought them out," Maggie said, looking miserable for it. "Had a feeling. Bad feeling."

I took her by the shoulders.

"You saved 'em," I said. "Don't know how you knew, but you saved them."

Her gaze swung to the window of the flophouse. The dark square leered down at us.

"A vision did it, Finn," she said. "Terrible vision. Couldn't get it out of my heart."

"You've no idea how close it was."

I helped her up. Theo came up beside me, looking over his shoulder at the soldiers. They hadn't noticed us yet.

"How we gonna do this?" he said.

"Fast as we can, as many back lanes as we know."

"Where?"

"Shanties."

"For real?"

"Aye. For real."

We both climbed up and I took the reins, snapped them. The wagon lurched forward, the wheels not going easily out of the mud. I took up the crop and gave the team some inspiration. A moment later, we set off through the back lane, bumping out onto the cobbled road, thunder tearing the sky apart over our heads. The slate roofs and smokestacks of the city shone in the lightning.

"You seen Ieva?" I shouted, looking over my shoulder at Maggie. She held Rose, while Nell leaned into the wind and rain.

"Why you always so obsessed with her?" Maggie yelled back.

"Just have you seen her?"

"No. Not all afternoon."

Rain sluiced off every roofline and gutter as we raced through the least travelled roads of Lawrence.

30

GHOST VISIONS

Shanties were under special lockdown, what looked like half the city's police ringing the edges. Far as we could see, though, the police weren't stepping foot inside. Mayor must've realized that keeping a powder keg from going off meant keeping the flames away. Theo knew a path that twisted through briars and witch hazel, down past a stony pasture and into the riverbank neighborhood. He said he'd take care of the wagon, meet us back at first light. I watched as he and the team disappeared into the midnight rain. Maggie held Rose in one arm; I took Nell's hand.

"Well, I promised you all the good life, and I meant it," I said. "So keep that in mind—because we're taking a little detour first."

As Theo'd said, we came out near the far end of the shanties. The houses weren't houses as much as crude huts put together of river mud and sod and sticks. That hardest neighborhood of all stood silent and haunted, smudged with mud, like the whole of it sprang to life from the river itself. A few gaunt people watched us pass, their eyes hard. Used to think what separated my path from theirs was hard work and nothing more. Fool I was. Now I'd had bad luck following me with the single-mindedness of a starving wolf, snapping and tearing at everything I'd worked for, I knew different.

Chatter came from some of the huts lining the path, smudged firelight inside, people passing by windows, the smell of cooking roots here, the smell of weak fish soup there. Down near the water, where I remembered them from the night I'd gone looking for the Fitzgeralds, I found the empty hovels pressed up against the rocks. Told the girls to wait a minute while I took a closer look. Entrance to the nearest one was practically a hole, scraps of slat wall patched up with river clay, muddy bits of old rope, and rags. Had a musty stink. Cleared away the cobwebs and stepped inside, keeping my head down to avoid scraping the low roof of old boards. Couple of rodents scratched by me and darted off into the darker corners. I chased them out, stamping my feet. A low doorway with a moldy sheet separated the inside of the place into two rooms. Back room of the place was dry enough, lined with old leaves and a pair of filthy blankets. It would do until morning. I went back outside.

"Right," I said. "Here we are."

None of them said anything. Looked at me miserable and wet.

"Pile of mud," Nell said.

"So you'd care to continue standing outside, getting soaked?"

The rain sang on the water and the sound of the nearby falls mixed with the thunder as it rode off west of the hills.

"Everyone in," I said. "And I don't want any fussing. This is only for tonight."

"Well what are we gonna do?" Nell said.

"You're gonna sleep. We're all gonna sleep. Now go."

Nell stomped right in, commenting on the stink of mouse crap. Maggie ducked inside with Rose asleep on her shoulder. I looked around for a minute and turned back to the hovel. Never once in seven years did I imagine I'd end up in a shanty—and I was banking on the hope that, for a night at least, neither would the veln.

Maggie and I got the girls settled in the back room as best we could, fashioning a bed of sorts out of the blankets, and ducked through that low doorway again to hunker down in the front room.

"Like the Winthrops'," I said in a whisper. "All it needs is a touch more silk wallpaper."

"How much trouble are we in?" Maggie whispered back.

"If you don't count our lives or our souls, not much. We'll need a sight more luck than we've had so far."

"Because of her?"

"Who—Ieva?"

"Thought so."

"She's the one that will save us."

"Finn."

I turned to her, making out her face in the darkness.

"Listen. Maggie—she ain't no one you need to worry about."

"I'm not."

"She's not."

"Fine."

She shifted. Water dripped in the corners.

"You should sleep," I said.

"So should you."

"I'm gonna keep an eye out."

"For what?"

"Don't worry about it. We'll be fine."

"That's not an answer."

"Sounded like one to me," I said.

"Fine. And then what?"

"And then we leave. Tomorrow."

"We leave?"

"That's right," I said. "Fella I know over near Ballard Vale is going in with Theo and me on the second wagon. We've been talking. He's thinking about growing his stables. Full livery. Needs help—man has nothing but a house of daughters."

"Must be terrible."

"Spirit nearly broken."

She swatted at me, but let me continue.

"We can earn our keep," I said. "Small wool mill on the little river they've got out there. Pretty soon, we'll be doing better than we did here."

"How'd you manage all that?"

"I just did."

"And then what?"

"We scrape together some land—a meadow, a field. Breed horses. I've an eye for them, always did."

"You never stop, do you?"

"I'll give it a thought once we're living the fine life."

"We?"

"Maggie. You think I'm going to leave you to fend for yourself? Got news for you: you're part of this family now." I glanced at the doorway. "Whether you like it or not."

Lines of rainwater fell across the doorway to the hovel. Lane beyond was still. Listened for the sound of thunder, but all I heard was Nell snoring behind the curtain. I couldn't keep my eyes from the dark shapes of the nearby shanties and beyond. Was too easy for me to imagine dark figures moving out there, see them coming up looking for us.

"You can't stay up the whole night," Maggie said.

"Who could sleep with a breathtaking view like this?"

She came over and sat down next to me, her arm pressing against mine. The curtain behind us fluttered on the damp breeze.

"You think he'll find us here?" she said.

"Who?"

"Liam."

A wind picked up in the night outside, sending thin clouds scudding fast in front of the moon.

"I'm not stupid, Finn," she said.

"Was he what you saw in your peepstones?"

"He's been in my thoughts. Feelings. I've been having ghost visions—something that's never happened. It's why I took the girls from the room. Never felt the *sien begeondan* so strongly."

"Second sight."

"More than that. I tried to reach him. I shouldn't have," she said. "Didn't even want to tell you."

She shifted against me.

"I did a séance," she said. "When we first got here. And it didn't go well. In fact, it went horrible. Kept seeing terrible things. Kept feeling as if my heart was about to stop. Came back, lying on the floor. Bloodied my lip. My head full of death."

"Death?"

"You don't see things like that in a séance. Been terrified ever since. I touched it, Finn. Death, the grave." She grabbed my hand. "All I've been doing is worrying about you. And with you traipsing around with that nun, all I could think is that I'm seeing —well, your death."

I reached an arm around her shoulders, pulled her closer.

"I'll be fine," I said.

"But what I saw."

"They always come true, these visions?"

"Not always."

"Then there you go."

"But there's always truth to them—even if I don't understand."

"Well, there's plenty of the grave about," I said. "More than I'd care to let you know of. But listen—I'm quick, I'm watching out for all of us, and I'm going to take care of this. That's a promise."

She turned her face to mine and kissed me. Everything else disappeared—as though we weren't sitting in a stinking hovel, as though we weren't running from a nightmare. After a time, she swung her leg, straddled me, twined her fingers with mine and sat looking at me. Behind her, the moon began its long dive to the far-off dawn. She leaned down and kissed me again. Her hair fell over my face. Her kisses were cool dew on morning leaves, her skin was like home. Soon, our kisses grew harder, and she fumbled around with the front of her dress. She pressed into me, and I pressed back, both of us trying to push ourselves together into one person. Her breathing grew heavy.

"Every night," she said, "all I think about is falling asleep in your arms."

She pressed forward and moved her dress until it fell down around her hips. Her dark hair fell in a lovely tumble over the tops of her breasts, pale in the faint light, her nipples dark. We kissed again. Not the hungry kisses we'd just done, but something more tentative, more searching.

"Don't say you don't feel it, too," she said between kisses, her voice barely audible.

Something came loose in my heart right then. Our kisses took us somewhere, there in the light of the moon that hung above the silvered city, in the shadows of that hovel. Didn't fight it. My heart slipped free of my will, it did, and that changed everything.

31

DON'T NEVER FORGET

I wrenched from sleep with a start, cursing myself for having drifted to sleep. I lifted my head. Maggie and I lay half in our clothes, half sprawled on the dirt floor. She was warm against me, and we were both sweaty, our skin cooling in the night air. Everything else had washed off me for a time—but it came crashing back in the time it took for me to come awake. Swung my gaze over to the hovel's doorway. Rain stopped, replaced with quiet dripping. The sound that'd woken me wasn't there now.

I sat up on one elbow. Maggie's skin looked ghostly in the shadows, eyes dark, her soft lips inches from my arm, the curve of her pale hip, the slope of her belly pressed against my side. Turned to the curtain and still heard Nell's snores. Slid myself out from beneath Maggie's arm without waking her. Quiet as I could, I pulled on my trousers. A knot formed in my lower belly, realizing how foolish I'd been, how much more danger I'd put Maggie in. He was after everything, the veln—and the closer someone was to me, the more he'd try to hurt them. And there Maggie was: lovely, incredible.

I'd just handed him another terrible weapon.

That's when I heard two steps from outside, mud squashing beneath shoes. I froze. Listened. I went to the doorway. Saw the mud and huts nearby, black shapes beneath the stars. Farther off, a few low fires had burned down, and everything was silent, making the flowing of the river loud. Didn't see no one.

Moving slow, I leaned out the doorway, looking to both sides. Nothing but dirt and the faded bits of old lumber, gray and sodden in the starlight. Thought back hard on whether there was any other way into the hovel. Closed my eyes and remembered an opening in the wall, some excuse for a window, blocked over by rotted boards. I crossed in front of the doorway, going across the mud to where I could see along the side of the hut. Brambles and a broken wagon wheel lined the slanted mud wall. I stepped quietly. Was but a pace from the back corner when a figure stepped out in front of me, fists up.

Tried to see who—what—it was, and that pause on my part was a mistake, and one hell of one at that. My pa'd been right about just a few things, the main one being that the world was a hard place and a fella'd better count on toughening up his fists and being ready to use them before he ought to put much faith in trying to use the mind to solve problems.

Before I could even register a thought, the figure smacked me so hard right in my face that I believe I saw the backsides of my eyeballs. I staggered back. He rushed me, getting in a solid hit to my ribs, and another to the side of my head. Tried to get my legs under me to hold him off, but he barreled into me. Like getting caught beneath a falling chestnut tree. I twisted, but he sent me slamming face-first into the mud, and straddled me. Had to have outweighed me by a good hundred pounds. I couldn't wriggle out, only twisting far enough to get my face mostly in the mud. His knee crushed the small of my back. I groaned.

"Like it, do ya?" he said.

I tried to buck my back, but he pressed down harder on me until I was sure that my spine would snap. He grabbed a handful of my hair and yanked my head back, then mashed my face hard into the mud. Once he'd done this a few times, he smacked the back of my head again. Nearly blacked out on that one—hanging on to wakefulness through a tunnel that'd be tight for an ant. In a moment, the weight was off me, which gave me a second of relief before a boot slammed hard into my side, cracking a rib and driving the wind out of me. I couldn't do much more than croak out a thin gasp.

"Fitzgeralds don't never forget, now do we," he said.

As his boot worked me over, I heard the muffled thuds of it echoing off the lightless shanties, all around.

32

TOUCHED BY THE DEVIL

Father Ralph's stomach woke him up, sour. The rich beef stew and glasses of wine the O'Briens had made him for dinner had turned into burning bile in his stomach. After a time, he sat up, swung his feet to the worn floor. Being upright forced the dyspepsia back, which was something.

He squinted at the mantel clock on his bureau. Quarter past three. The wind outside knocked a loose gutter against the outside of the rectory, tap tap tap. He stood up. He had a packet of bicarbonate powders in the water closet, and would wash it down with a glass of warm milk and cream downstairs. The humid night air stifled the sounds of his slippers on the floors. The only light was from the front end of the building, where a small window at the end of the hallway caught the glare of the street lantern out front. He passed the hall window that looked out over the graveyard and kept his eyes straight ahead.

Because they're restless under the earth, in the black of their rotting coffins. Go out and listen. Put your head on the ground. You'll hear them.

Father Ralph stopped before the water closet. His heart rate jumped and the burning flared in his throat.

"Stop it, stop it, stop it," he said. He took a deep breath and went through the door. He found the packet of bicarbonates and turned back to the door, recoiling at the prospect of the chalky powder mixing with the milk and cream into a runny paste.

A sound from the hallway stopped him.

He froze with his hand on the edge of the water basin. Something clacked on the stairs, coming up, quiet steps. He turned his head to the door. It wasn't the pipes, wasn't a loose gutter outside. Father Ralph closed the door to the washroom and swiped the latch closed. The steps—*hooves, you coward, hooves*—reached the top of the stairs and stopped. Father Ralph stepped back, bumping against the toilet. Step by step closer, pausing on the other side of the door. From under the door, that dark half inch, sniffing—quick inhalations, a dozen of them, followed by a louder exhale. Then the door moved, nudged from the other side. It didn't give, just creaked.

Father Ralph dropped the packet and sat, shaking, on the toilet—and double-checked that he wasn't dreaming, feeling the porcelain, rubbing his fingers along his knee. A low groaning sounded from the other side. The water closet had no window. He grabbed a wooden-handled plunger next to the toilet. Outside the door, the groaning grew louder. Something raked across the door and then rattled the handle.

A fetid stench hit him, seeping in under the door—decay, of desiccated flesh gone bad in the sun. His heartbeat thudded in his ears. Father Ralph stepped to the door and smacked it hard with the plunger, hard enough to rattle the door.

"Get out of here!" he yelled.

Clattering steps moved away from the door and the groaning turned to whispers. Father Ralph hit the door again. This time the steps didn't move off. The whispers grew louder. The sound of them sent a wave of dread over Father Ralph.

"You did this to me, Father."

He flinched so hard that a few drops of urine dampened the front of his undershorts.

"And all I wanted was to serve you. Every way, serve you. I still can, Father. Would you like that? You and I, finally embracing, tasting one another."

"Be gone," Father Ralph said.

Miss Constance? *Impossible*, he thought.

His heart jumped like one of those horrible crows, trapped in the cage of his ribs. The door shuddered and claws raked the other side.

"We'll watch your graveyard grow."

The stench grew overwhelming, rank skin and foul breath. Father Ralph stood and hit the door with the plunger, yelling as he did. It didn't seem to do anything more than amuse the owner of the voice. He looked around, desperate. There was a ceramic cup on the corner of the wash basin. He grabbed the cup, turned on the water tap. Off in the distance, the plumbing knocked.

"Come on," he said. A thin spill of water gurgled out of the iron faucet. He held the cup beneath it. As the water filled the cup, he whispered.

"*In nomine Patris, et Filii, et Spiritus Sancti.* Amen," he said. He made the sign of the cross above the cup. The door behind him boomed, startling him enough to spill half the water. He refilled, and then struggled to recall the prayer, the Latin jumbling over itself in his mind.

"Oh God, grant this water may be endowed with Divine grace…to drive away devils and cast out illnesses, that whatever in the houses or possessions of the faithful may be sprinkled by this water will be freed…from everything unclean. Banished by this sprinkling water by calling upon Thy Holy Name," he whispered.

Outside the door, the voice screamed.

"Father Ralph, Father Ralph, Father Ralph!"

He finished blessing the water and turned to the door. The shaking stopped. The voice outside the door went silent, but Father Ralph sensed it—he could feel the rage, feel the threat. He leaned over and swung his arm forward with the cup, shooting the water generally under the door. Laughter tore through the silence. Father Ralph shouted another prayer.

"*Adjuro ergo te, omnis immundíssime spíritus, omne phantásma, omnis incúrsio sátanæ, in nómini Jesu Christ,*" he said.

He listened, but heard nothing. He reached over and turned off the running water. The pipe knocked hard in the walls and then everything was silent.

Nothing.

He listened for a full minute. The only sound was the faint tap tap tap of the loose gutter. The stench had faded, the rectory gone quiet. Father Ralph watched the door and listened. Minutes passed this way before he did anything. He stood by the door, saying a quick prayer to St. Michael the Archangel, then bent his head to it. Still nothing. He grabbed the knob, turned it so it wouldn't make a sound. A quarter of the way into the turn, the lock snapped free. He grimaced and swung the door inward. His hand shook.

The hallway was empty.

Outside the door, a puddle spread across the floor. Father Ralph leaned out and looked both directions. Towards the front of the building, before the light spilling from the window, nothing. In the other direction, shadows. No wet footprints. He took a step out. The smell of putrescence, so strong just minutes before, had faded to a musky hint. He looked at the cup still clenched tight in his hand.

A quiet knocking came from downstairs. The door.

Father Ralph looked around one more time, then hurried to his room, put on his pants and a black shirt. He stepped around the puddle on his way back down the hall. In the entryway below, he saw someone outside, their figure blurred by the glass panes on the slim window beside the door. He opened the door. Before him stood a young man, his clothes filthy, his face pale and unwashed.

"May I come in, Father?" he said. Irish.

"It's the middle of the night."

"Realize that, Father. It's just that I fear I'm ruined. Stained. Been trying to go see you at Mass, but I can't pass beneath the lintel. Hand is keeping me out."

"It's still the middle of the night, son."

"Think I been touched by the Devil, Father."

He bawled like a child, snot running down his unshaven face, eyes lost in dark circles. Father Ralph looked at him, then glanced back over his shoulder at the dark second floor to the rectory. He turned back to the young man, put out a hand and motioned for him to come inside. The young man stopped crying, nodded. Gave him a smile as he passed into the rectory. When the door shut, Father Ralph turned on the gas lantern on the wall; it came on with a hiss. When he turned around, the young man was standing right next to him. His eyes glimmered.

"Let me give you something for your trouble, Father."

He reached up and wiped something across Father Ralph's lips, his cheek. Father Ralph recoiled. He saw that the young man's hand was dripping with a dark fluid.

"What did you just do?"

"Little something my Father needs, Father."

Father Ralph stepped back. A smile broke across the young man's face, a dark crack. From the stairs behind, clacking steps descended.

AGNES MURPHY WENT INTO ST. Mary's ahead of Deacon Samuel, passing him as he struggled to get the key from the lock. She knew it irritated him when she did so—he believed his status granted him the right to be the first in; he believed being a deacon entitled him to too much, in her opinion. She clutched the organ music for the Mass and crossed herself while he propped open the doors behind them. A sigh of wind carried from the front of the church, breaking the quiet.

"Father Ralph?" Agnes called out.

Her voice carried across the wide space. Across the rows of pews and beyond the altar itself, a ten-foot-high triptych of stained glass windows filled the wall, stretching up to the arc where the angles of the ceiling met. The images were from the Gospels, the center one of Christ up on the cross.

"Oh dear," she said. Deacon Samuel passed by her.

"What now?" he said.

"Look."

Agnes pointed to the stained glass. Deacon Samuel hurried to the altar, kneeling and crossing himself before stepping onto it. He leaned over and came up with a piece of colored glass the size of a playing card. There was more on the floor. Agnes looked back up. The crucifix and other images shone with the fire of morning sunlight—except where blue sky shone through. Christ's face was gone, and so were his hands. The crown of thorns was still there, the arms, the cross. A crow flapped by the space where the Lord's face had been, leaving a patch of empty sky.

"Fetch Father Ralph," Deacon Samuel said. "I think the police will want to know about this."

"Wait," she said. She turned and stared now at the organ loft above the entrance.

"This is no time to—" he began.

"Samuel," she said, cutting him off. She looked up, and he followed her glance. Above her. She craned her neck.

Father Ralph hung across the tall arch of organ pipes, his

arms splayed and his back horribly broken. Eyes open, mouth slack, throat slit open from one side to the other. Blood crusted in his hair and darkened the keys of the organ. Flies had already found him, whirring about in the surrounding heat.

Agnes couldn't get a breath in. The sheets of music she held spilled to the floor in a soft flutter.

33

HOURS AND HOURS OF DAYLIGHT LEFT

Came to, wracked with pain. Couldn't see out of my right eye, couldn't get in a good breath, couldn't get my split lips to close properly—and then there was the real pain. Deep in my back, my kidneys.

"I see the inside of your lip."

I cracked my good eye and looked. Nell leaned into my face, giving me a look like I was some new bug she'd found. Strong sunlight told me it was late morning. I leaned up against the side of the hovel.

"Give him some room, Nell."

Maggie came over, pushing Nell aside. She knelt and dabbed at my bloodied face with a rag damp with river water.

"Now that hurts," I croaked. My mouth didn't want to get the sounds out right.

"Who did this?"

"Who do you think."

"Police can all rot in hell," she said.

I went to shake my head. Felt like my skull was a collection of cracked bricks and nearly passed out again.

"Fitzgerald. One of 'em," I said. If my stomach hadn't been

empty, I'm sure I'd have heaved up my last meal. Nell looked down at me over Maggie's shoulder.

"Give me some matches," she said. "I'll burn their hut down."

"Leave it be, you," I said.

Maggie touched the edge of her sleeve to her tongue, wiped more blood from my cheek.

"You looked done for," she said. "We dragged you over here after we found you. All you've done is groan."

I put a hand to my face. My right eye was swollen like the worst bee-sting I'd ever heard of and the rest of my face had a whole new set of contours to it. With my left eye, I looked over the shanties, out past the river, to the roofline of the Everett. There I was, sitting in the mud, bloodied, nothing left to my name but a grubby handful of hope that I treated like the Queen's own jewels. Look what hope'd gotten me so far. And there the Everett was, quarter mile of brick, six floors of grinding work, year round. Hadn't been but a couple of weeks since I'd walked those floors, thinking I had it all under control, that I could grab hold of hope itself and use that giant mill to lift me where I wanted to go.

How ignorant I was. Ignorant.

As Maggie got up and wrung out the bloody rag, I marveled at how fast it'd all fallen to shit—and that brought my mind back to Tommy Fitzgerald and his gruesome end.

The animals.

The disappearances.

The accidents.

Hit me right then. I sat up, the deep pain in my lower back telling me I had a date with the mud if I kept up with moving so. Pushed myself farther, grunting.

"Nell," I said. I held my arm out. She got under it and helped me. Was getting to my feet when Maggie saw, on her way back from rinsing the rag.

"Oh no you don't. Back down," she called out.

The world swam on me as if the shanties were wreckage riding the surface of a stormy sea. Held on tight to Nell, who complained that I was breaking her shoulders. Feeling cleared up after a moment.

"What do you think you're doing?" Maggie said.

"Come on. Gather up the girls."

"You're talking nonsense."

"We're leaving."

"Ridiculous. We're getting you to a doctor," she said.

"Got to get Theo. Can you do that?"

"Finn."

She got herself right in front of me. Looked me right in my good eye. Reached out and ran the backside of her fingers along my cheek.

"You're not going anywhere like this. It can all wait," she said.

"Can't wait. Only have today," I said.

"Don't forget what I said last night."

"I didn't forget. Not a word, Mag. It's why I've got to get you and the girls out of here—and why I've got to take care of the rest of it. Today."

Theo was a gem, no doubting it. He came racing back with Maggie before the clocks of Lawrence struck noon. Horses groomed, wagon cleaned, and he did everything I wasn't able to. Chattered away the whole time, he and Nell arguing about something I didn't catch.

"How many was it? Jesus," he said, inspecting my face.

"Just one, but that was one too many."

"Those lousy pieces of garbage. Don't let nothing go 'cause there's always more of them. Fertile as they are stupid, them goddamned Fitzgeralds."

"We got everything?" I called over my shoulder to Maggie.

"Don't have nothing."

"Then we got all we need."

"Hard to believe you're leaving Lawrence," Theo said.

"Not through with it just yet. Got one more thing to do. Owe it at least that much."

"What are you talking about?" Maggie said.

"Now don't stop for a single thing. I'll be there when I'm done. May take a day, two at tops. Theo will get you there, got everything set." I turned to Theo. "Rosenberg's expecting them. Once you get there, wait with them. Offer him a hand with whatever he needs. Sunset comes, keep everyone inside. Don't forget about that."

He nodded.

"You're in no shape to do anything," Maggie said. "You can barely hold yourself upright."

"I'll be fine."

"You think I'm going to let you do this on your own, you forgot how stubborn I am," she said.

"Trust me—I ain't forgetting a thing. But this is how it's got to be."

Glanced back at her—every muscle in my back complaining —and she shook her head. Not happy. Rose sat trying to look at the back of her elbow, and Nell had her hand in her pocket, staring off over the river, talking to herself as she often did. I turned to Theo.

"Don't stop for anything. I'll catch up soon as I can."

He clicked his tongue, and the team started forward. I watched them go, keeping a smile on my face until they were out of sight. Then I groaned, the pain too much. Around me, the shanties dried out in the summer heat, the warmth stirring up the smell of rotting food and piss. Was a Sunday, so no one was at work, and I was marked leaving by folk standing in dark doorways, out cooking over pits. Soon enough, I reached the empty shops and saloons that ran that stretch of Broadway before the bridge by the dam. Streets were full of workers and tradesmen off for the day, police and soldiers making themselves known at the corners of the shanty neighborhoods. Each step sent a stabbing pain into my kidneys.

Gave an eye to the sun. Hours and hours of daylight left.

I needed them.

34

BACK TO HELL

Only one place Ieva would think to meet up with me, so I made my way to the train station.

"Christ," I muttered more than once, struggling not to double over in pain. When I walked inside the station, I didn't bother checking the benches nor the ticket counter, cut straight through and turned left along the platform. Around the corner and I stopped. Ieva looked up at me. Her eyes widened.

"Don't worry," I said. "Just a regular fight."

"What happened?"

"Someone got the jump on me, nothing to it. Been through worse. Did us a favor, truth be told." I stepped over and lowered myself down to the bench next to her. "Because I got to thinking about how much fun I've had with a lovely family by the name of Fitzgerald, and then it hit me."

"Something hit you."

"Well look who's found a sense of humor," I said. "Listen. I know where he is. And he's been watching us. Toying with us."

"Where?"

"A lair is always being prepared with a killing. You said it. We saw it."

"Defiled," she said.

"Defiled. Well, it was right in front of my eyes, I didn't even think about it. Not once. Not even when I should have, when more started."

"I don't understand," she said.

I raised my better arm and pointed.

"Those two smokestacks. The Everett Mills, where I worked. Started going bad right after we found a body hung at the door. Got worse from there."

The river gleamed, and the sky was free of smoke. There—across the brick, the water, the iron—was where the veln had hidden since he arrived in Lawrence, hunting after what Nell had stolen on the *Jack Ketch*. Ieva nodded.

"This is all much worse than before," Ieva said. "So much I've missed. My mind was stuck in what had been. Before."

"The bodies," I said. "That's different."

"Very different. Very concerning. I thought hard, back through Rabat. Through Europe. There were hints—but nothing like here."

"What's changed?" I said.

"I walked the city last night. In the rain. There's a feeling, a tug on my heart, a shadow touching my soul. It's him." She turned. "And that tells me he's grown more powerful than ever. He has more strength—and he's using it to release other veln differently than before. They're no longer bound to their infernal form. Their essence can leap—from one body, to another, to another."

"Like Eve Winthrop," I said. "And her parents."

"Exactly."

"The gals I dropped at the hospital."

"Those, too. Not souls to feed a new veln."

"Moved from feeding to housing them, haven't they?" I said.

"And all that means. You understand?"

I nudged my fat lip with my tongue and nodded.

"What was hard just became tenfold harder," I said. "They can spread farther, faster. Harder to catch. Harder to kill."

"And more to protect him, the one I've chased. To do his work."

"He doesn't need any more verg, like Liam."

"Or he could have a hundred verg, controlled by the ones he releases, the ones who can move effortlessly from corpse to corpse. A thousand. All doing his bidding. Striking out at anyone who tries to stop him."

"Like us."

"Indeed. Like us. I thought he took you and your family last night," she said.

"Nearly did. Bit of intuition saved us. And luck."

She reached over and put a hand on my knee. Found I was holding my breath against the pain. I let it out, slow. I put my hand on hers. We sat that way for a minute, not saying anything. I bit down on a groan as I got to my feet.

"But he didn't count on a heap of Irish and Latvian grit, now did he?" I extended a hand to Ieva, and she stood. "And I'm betting he's resting smug somewhere down in the basements right now, thinking he's nearly got us. So let's pay him a surprise visit—and send him back to Hell."

35

———

NOTHING IF NOT A FIGHTER

The Everett was still in the Sunday afternoon light, quiet. We watched it from the towpath that ran alongside the canal. Couple of seagulls rode the warm air above us, their calls echoing off of the bricks. I watched the guard shack, the stable and hayloft next to it. Didn't see anyone. I pointed to the spot where the body of Tommy Fitzgerald had hung.

"Was right there," I said.

Ieva nodded.

"It's closed?" she said.

"Sunday, yeah. Unless you know someone. Come on."

We crossed into the yard between the Everett and the Stone Mill that connected to it, a couple of Sunday strollers—never mind she dressed like a priest and I looked like I'd been trampled by a herd of cattle. Soon as we slipped into the shade of the mill, I hurried to a side entrance, down half a dozen steps. Big door painted barn red was locked. Fished around along the top of the granite lintel over the door until my fingers hit one of the spare keys some of the floor bosses used.

"They shouldn't forget about these things when they're firing floor bosses," I said. I slid it into the lock and turned. Door opened. As Ieva stepped past me, I remembered how much trust I'd had to earn to learn about that key—and how fast it'd all disappeared. I shook my head and tossed it out onto the granite steps. Shut the door behind us. That part of the Everett's basements had narrow windows every twenty yards or so, at ground level.

"This is where you worked?" Ieva said.

"Seven years. Come on."

I led the way. We followed the short corridor that extended out by the storage end of the mill and past a couple of the offices that the fellas who worked maintenance used. The sunlight coming in was dulled by the dust on the windows.

"Problems, the past month," I said. "Injuries. Death. People starting tales about a curse. Didn't pay enough attention to it."

"Would have seemed unlikely."

"Unlikely don't hold quite the meaning it used to, Ieva."

We reached one of the main corridors. It ran the length of the center of the building. Even in the middle of a sunny afternoon, it was dark. Took down a lantern from a hook and lit it, handed it to Ieva. Lit another for me. The darkness extended back further. At intersections with side corridors ahead of us, filmy sunlight shone in the gloom.

"These'll help."

As we walked, I told her about the bag of buttons I'd found. She didn't take much convincing. Above our heads, I caught the sounds of the Everett settling, of wind chuffing around the upper floors. There was a weight to the empty bays, stairs, and floors above us, all of it warm and stifling in the humid July afternoon. Mill'd never made me feel that way before—as though I was walking along in the belly of a beast. Didn't notice my bruises anymore, nor the pain in my back. My attention focused on the growing dread that came in like a tide.

"You feel that?" I said.

"He's here."

We passed into the coal cellars that fed the massive boilers during the cold months, walls, floors, and ceilings dusted in black. One of my first jobs at the mill was shoveling hunks of coal from the chutes into the wheeled bins, twelve hours at a shot. For a year, I found coal dust on me in places I won't mention. Boilers hulked across the middle of the room, piping coming off of them like a forest of iron. Went out a side door, into a narrower corridor. I paused.

"Down this way is the sub-basement. Got a door that extends out to the end of the building, all the way to the canal. That's where I'm guessing he is."

We both looked over to the nearby window as if to reassure ourselves that it was still broad daylight. The lanterns we held whispered with their flames. We hurried along the hall, passing by the spot where Ruby McKenna fell to her death, a sprinkle of old sawdust still marking the spot. On the inside edge, a doorway opened to a set of stone stairs. A pair of crates blocked the door. I put my lantern down and put my back into them, gritting my teeth against the pain of my bruised ribs. I opened the door, needing a bit of shoulder to get the rusted hinges to give, sending a squeal off into the stairwell. A stench filled the air, coming up from the darkness.

"You're sure about the daylight keeping him still—it's awful dark down there," I said.

"I'm sure."

"I might point out that 'sure' is another word that hasn't held up so well lately."

I held the lantern in front of me and started down. The walls were damp and moldy. Beyond the stench, I caught the stink of the canal and mud. I reached the bottom first. Low brick arches lined one side of the brick tunnel. A skinny passage ending in a rotted wood door that marked where the mill above ended and the passageway stretched out beyond. The light from our lanterns found stores of stone and brick stacked up, cobwebbed in the corners. A chill came off the stones of the walls and low ceiling. I stepped forward, shining my lantern. Dirt floor had tracks in it, but how old they were wasn't clear.

"Wait," Ieva said.

She put down the lantern and her bag, and pulled out the spikes, pulled out the mallet, pulled out a worn Bible, pulled out spare clothes. Her movements grew frantic. She looked at me.

"What?" I said.

"It's gone."

"What's gone?"

"The medallion. Of Uriel."

Remembered the bag of buttons at the McAllisters—left out for me to see, left out to tell me that the veln knew exactly what we were doing, while we were blind to his every whim.

"He took it," I said.

"He can't."

"Then his servant did. Liam."

She knelt, shaking her head. "Not possible."

"There's been a lot that's not possible, you said so yourself. Question is—can we do this without it?"

Ieva closed her eyes.

"Because this might be the only shot we're going to get at him where we can surprise him," I said. "Sundown is hours off, but I don't think either of us wants to risk running around, wasting any more daylight. Another night with him and his brood taking the streets, spreading this. We don't even know how many others there are. Could be dozens. More."

She looked more unsure than I'd seen before.

"We've got power, right now. We can get the jump on him," I said.

"No, you're right," she said. "And if it's gone, it's gone."

She picked up the wrap of spikes, the mallet. We went forward. Passageway wasn't much wider than our shoulders, ceiling just above our heads. Bits of lichen hung in spots and little curls of wayward roots pried their way between the stones here and there. Twenty paces on, the stench was so bad I gagged.

"Wait," I said.

Ieva stopped. Our shadows loomed up on the curved walls. Another set of storage arches opened along the left side. I saw something. Picked it up. It was a shoe, not a big one. I knelt and peered into the arch.

"Bodies."

My voice fluttered off down the passageway. Ieva knelt beside me, peered in. A bigger space opened after a yard, and the lantern light caught a hand, several pairs of feet, bits of neck and cheek. Wave of gooseflesh ran along my spine, and a voice deep in my gut told me to run, to get away from there. Ieva ran her hand across the front of her collar again and on the back of her neck.

"I'm not sure," she whispered.

"Plenty of daylight left. Hours and hours."

She kissed her knuckle and pressed it to her forehead. Her eyes looked past the brick and the bodies. Realized she'd been chasing after the veln as long and as hard as I'd chased after the dream of bettering my life, and my family's. We weren't as different as we looked—which was why we understood each other so well.

"We can do this," I whispered. She nodded. She started forward on her hands and knees. I took the lantern and her bag, and followed her. She crawled into the far space.

"There are more," she whispered.

"You need the light?"

"Pass it to me."

I slid it forward to her. She dragged it past the far side of the archway and lifted her head.

"The bodies," she said. "They're—"

The ceiling came down.

Stones, brick, long scraps of rusted steel and iron. Ieva cried out for a moment before her voice vanished beneath the rumble of all that weight. Dust billowed out, heavy with mold, choking me, blinding me. The sound of it went on and on, shaking my guts, filling my ears with hissing. When it subsided, blackness.

"Ieva!" I screamed. I scrambled forward, but met a heap of brick and board. Pulled and grabbed away at anything I could, wracked with coughs, the inside of my mouth coated with brick dust. As the dust spread out in the corridor behind me, the faint light of the other lantern showed me a horrifying collapse of stone and iron. Wriggled forward, bloodying my fingers and hands as I tore at the pile. I found Ieva's leg.

She was buried. I kept calling her name, trying to pull her loose. She didn't move. My hand grew sticky with warm blood. Ieva's blood.

"No!" I yelled.

Tried to calm myself, tried to think of a way to turn this around. I stopped moving for a moment, frozen. Felt along her ankle for a pulse. Didn't find one. I pounded my fist on the dirt and stone. Then, I heard a crackling. Looked up. Through the small gaps in the broken wood and brick, I saw fire. The lantern had shattered. Smoke reached me.

"No, no," I said.

Shoved my way forward, pushing aside wreckage. Moved a stone and came face to face with a corpse, dusted with fallen brick. The lips were shriveled and pulled back, the eyes sunken, the flesh rotted. Wasn't one of the changed corpses, like Eve Winthrop. Wasn't one of those soulless bodies, like with the new veln we'd killed. This was just a dead body.

A lure.

A trap.

"You sonofabitch!" I cried out. The fire found something it liked because the heat bloomed out at me and the smoke grew so thick I couldn't breathe. Pictured where I was in relation to the mill—and realized that we were below the wool and yarn stores, where the fear of fire had haunted Winthrop and the rest of us every single day, the one bit of the mill that had twice the number of galvanized iron fire buckets as the rest.

It's so near. Death, the grave. Maggie's vision came back to me.

I fought to move an armful of bricks, but the smoke choked me, had me gasping. I couldn't get Ieva from beneath that heap. She hadn't even had a chance to put up a fight—and she was nothing if not a fighter. Maybe that was the cruelest part of all.

I crawled backwards into the air of the corridor. By then, the roar of the fire had taken on an evil of its own—and I feared that the gas from the city gas works lines had caught. I stood up, not able to get a good breath of air, not able to slow the frantic pounding of my heart, not able to wind back the hands of time a paltry two minutes to where I could've—should've—been able to keep this from happening.

I could only run.

Smoke filled the corridor. I grabbed Ieva's bag and staggered back, blinded by the choking smoke, my eyes teared up. Held my shirtsleeve to my nose and mouth. Pushed through the wooden door and ran. Reached a second wooden door that opened out at the canal, kicked it open and stumbled into fresh air. Leaned over, hands on my knees, as I hacked and spat, wiping the snot and tears and sweat off my face. I turned. A towering pillar of black smoke roiled up into the blue sky from the Everett.

The sun was halfway to the horizon, and the veln had won.

Somewhere nearby, a fire bell clanged.

36

HERE, HERE, HERE I AM

Theo and the others reached the far side of the river, heading south. The wagon rocked as the wheels passed through gullies left by the rain, now hardened in the sun. Rose stood behind the bench, saying *bye-bye smokestacks* every time they slipped further from view. Nell squinted in the sunlight.

"I'm thirsty," she said.

"You'll have to wait," Maggie said. She sat next to Theo on the bench up front.

"Just saw a pump."

"We get where we're going, you can drink all you like. Not now."

Nell turned away, shaking her head. The road went up a low rise. Near the top, a church rose, gray granite and slate roof reaching up to the sky. Nell heard growling. In front of the church steps, two mangy dogs fought, their hackles up, their ears down—rising on their back legs as their jaws snapped at the other's throat. Nell turned around in the wagon for a better view. The growling was flat in the thick air. Her gaze scanned the church.

There weren't any pigeons lining the edges of the roof. On the steps outside the high front door, a dozen little candles burned, weak. Flowers had been arranged.

A feeling came over her—practically making her palms itch.

She patted her pockets. All her things were there—secrets, every one of them. An awl from the mill. Pocket watch chain. A pipe. Twist of silk ribbons. Necklace. Brass cufflink. A few more tucked into her spare clothes. They were charms to Nell. Caught her eye, caught her imagination, caught whatever that dark part of her couldn't resist. Having them made her feel better. Hiding them was a guilty, sneaky thing, yes—she could live with that, to keep her charms safe. But there was one charm she'd lost. Stolen. And since, it'd become the one charm she couldn't shake from her thoughts. The one charm that still gave her that tight sensation in her stomach.

The one charm that called out to her—she was sure of it. Sure as if she'd looked up and seen her own mother waving her over.

"Wait," she said. "I have to pee."

"You can't wait?"

"Can't wait."

Theo pulled the team to a halt and Nell climbed off the back before the wagon even stopped. She jogged toward the church, past the fighting dogs.

"Jesus, not up there," Maggie called after her.

"Hold on," Nell called over her shoulder. She ran up the steps.

"Nell!"

She ignored her call and yanked at the doors. They were locked. She bit her lip and ran off to the side, going around the corner. A pathway extended to a smaller building attached to the back of the church. To the right, a graveyard, shadows of the stones stretching to the east. She felt it again—the pull, the sound that no one but her ever seemed to hear. Nell slowed, looking at the church wall. Windows. Some tilted open.

She gave a quick glance back at the street, then reached up and got her hands on the nearest sill of an open window. She lifted herself up. The dark inside practically sang *Here, here, here I am*. Nell got her leg up and wriggled over the sill, into the cool hush of the church.

37

TO THE BLACK

Theo fanned his face with his hat, swiping off the sweat from his brow.

"Got six sisters," he said, "and ain't a one of them takes this long to make water. You sure that's what she's doing?"

Maggie watched the corner of the church. She didn't like it.

"Who ever knows what that one is doing," she said.

"Well, if she's doing more than making water, doing it on a church just doesn't seem right. My ma wouldn't even let me sneeze if I was in church without getting a smack to the side of my head, let alone if I'd pulled down my breeches and dropped a turd."

"Theo, please."

"Oh. Right. Sorry there, Rosie."

"Where's Nell?" the little girl said. Her cheeks were flushed from the heat. Maggie shaded her eyes and looked at the church, craning her neck to look all the way to the top of the steeple. Her breath caught.

...the steeple of one of the city's churches...as if the spire itself was burning, wreathed in smoke.

She realized that it was the very steeple she'd seen from the flophouse window, after the séance.

The touch of the grave.

"That's it," Maggie said. "I'm getting her."

She jumped from the wagon. Looked at the church, then up the street.

"Bring the wagon up there," she said to Theo, pointing to a turnoff farther up the street, in the shade of a block of shops. "Get Rose out of the sun. I'll be up in a minute."

"Finn said to hurry."

"Well Finn ain't here, is he? Just go, I'll be right there."

Theo didn't need to hear more than that, just smiled tight and snapped the reins. The wagon started off again, Rose watching Maggie from the back. Maggie climbed the steps of the church and found the doors locked. The flowers on the steps had wilted in the heat. Her pulse raced—all the feelings from the séance flooding in.

"Nell," she called out. Nothing. She hurried to the corner of the big church and scanned the walkway. No sign of the girl. Maggie walked that way, cursing and trying to stay calm. She spotted the graveyard and gave it a good look, sensing that Nell might find that place interesting—or an appropriate spot to make her business. Nothing moved. A noise floated out from inside the church, a shoe scuffing against marble.

"Damn you, Nell," Maggie said. She stepped over to the church and squinted in the open window she found. The outside was so bright that her eyes only let her see shadows. An ill feeling rubbed her sides, a touch of the blackness that embraced her, squeezed her breath.

"Nell?"

Her voice jumped around in the big space. No answer.

"If you're in there, you're in so much trouble. You ain't going to be able to sit for a week."

The sound of something crashing over inside the church clattered out the windows.

"That's it. Right now," she said. Still no answer. She took a slow breath, working to keep her panic down, fighting the unease that played at her limbs, her throat as she put her hands to the sill. A lift and a wriggle got her inside, dropping in a heap, hearing her dress tear as a corner of it caught on something.

"We have to get out of here, Nell. Now."

Her voice surprised her, the way it bounced off the high walls and ceiling, the marble floors and windows. The inside of the church was shaded, the colors of the stained glass above the altar dark plum, dusk blue, pale gray. The smell of old incense hung in the air. She took a step in and cut between the pews, looking around. Up above the altar, panes were missing in the stained glass.

"Nell."

Even with the windows open along both sides of the church, the air was breathless. The fear that came over her was pungent, the concentrated version of what she'd felt when she'd taken the girls from the flophouse. She started down the center aisle to the entryway and spotted muddy tracks on the otherwise spotless floor.

"Welcome."

The voice carried all around the church. Maggie looked up. Liam stood before the altar, gaunt and filthy, his eyes lost to dark circles. He had Nell in his grip, lifting her up, one unwashed hand clamped over her mouth. She kicked and struggled, but he held her as easily as if she were a doll.

"Liam," Maggie said.

Nell yelled, but Liam's hand muffled her cry.

"Let her go," Maggie said.

"Snap her neck?"

Liam's voice was broken, pushed sharp out of his mouth. Nell tried to slither out of his grip, but he used his other hand to press into the skin at the side of her throat. Her muffled cries were of agony, and she went limp.

"What happened to you?" Maggie said. "We'll get you help."

A ghastly smile wound Liam's mouth into a curve. He dragged Nell up onto the altar.

"Come," he croaked. When Maggie didn't move, he put his other arm around Nell's head, grabbing the back of her head with his hand, getting ready to break the girl's neck. Maggie raised her hands.

"No, don't!"

"Come."

The air where he'd stood smelled of milk gone bad in the heat. As she stepped onto the altar, she took a split-second glance around, registering a heavy brass candlestick at the edge of the altar itself.

"She didn't do anything," she said. Her voice shook. "Just put her down. Liam. Do it."

Nell looked at her with terrified eyes. She kicked at Liam, but the blows didn't even get a grunt out of him. Maggie snatched up the candlestick. Liam moved in closer, his gaze never leaving her own.

"Oh, but she did," Liam whispered. "And the master will teach her what happens to thieves."

He hurled Nell right at Maggie. Nell's head caught her right on the side of her face and the force of it sent them both tumbling. Maggie lost her grip on the candlestick and it skidded off the altar onto the floor below. Liam rushed forward. He grabbed Nell by the back of her dress and threw her into the wall, where she yelped and then fell still.

Then he was on Maggie. She tried to keep him off with fist and feet, but he pushed through her efforts and straddled her. Maggie yelled. He leaned forward and grabbed a thick handful of her hair and pulled her head up.

"A gift," he said into her face. His breath stunk of a bog.

He slammed her head onto the marble floor. She held on for a moment after the first crack, but the second time he hammered her head onto the floor sent her to the black.

38

IRISH KILLER

The sky over the city darkened as the smoke from the burning mill smudged out the sunlight. Flames shot high into the air, traced the length of the Everett. Even as dozens of fire bells spread their call from neighborhood to neighborhood, there wasn't anyone who thought there was much of a chance of putting it out until the flames had their greedy fill. Folks had come out and filled the streets. As I wandered from lane to street, I couldn't escape the sight of it, nor the smell of heavy smoke. Like my own dreams, the heart of the city burned.

The veln had done nothing but toy with us the whole time. Couldn't get a good breath into my lungs. Couldn't stop thinking that I'd led Ieva right into the trap. Also couldn't stop thinking that if it'd played out just a hair different, my body would've been crushed and roasting in that fire right alongside hers.

As I walked in a daze, the afternoon deepened across the city of brick around me, making even the towering smoke rolling off the Everett take on a warmth as it broke apart over the river. My spirit broke apart with it. Hardship seemed like a stain on me— on all us Irish—and no amount of scrubbing and cleaning ever got rid of it. People streamed to the fire, and I walked against the current, strange feeling coming over me that I was a corpse, that I'd died and become a haunt. I paused at a dusty intersection a few streets off of Broadway.

I'd died.

Straightened up at the thought. The trap had been perfect. The veln or any of his slaves could see as much when night fell, still lit by the hellish light of the dying mill. And as far as he'd think, I was dead right alongside Ieva. He'd think he'd won. He'd think he wouldn't have to spare another moment of worry about us.

"Wrong," I said. My voice was thick from weeping.

I'D SEARCH the whole goddamned city, if I had to. Ran my mind through the various places where the veln might be holed up, the rides that Ieva and I had taken throughout the city: the old grist mill; the deserted shacks by the fens that bordered the Spicket; couple of burnt-out houses in the German neighborhood. As the list grew, I worked out a map, how I'd hit them all, searching until I found them.

I paused by the edge of the south canal where the railroad bridge crossed it. Smoke from the Everett blotted out the sun. I shaded my eyes.

"Admiring your handiwork?"

Jumped at the voice. I turned. In the heat, breathing hard, stood my admiring friend, Officer Glockner. He had a pistol in his hand, pointing it casually at my chest.

"Come on. It ain't that," I said.

"Oh, it ain't?"

He reached out for my shoulder, but I ducked his fat hand.

"And I suppose I didn't just see you race out the back door of that burning mill? Anything else you'd like to tell me ain't what it is?"

"You know what's really happening around here—that's what

I think," I said. "Maybe you don't know all of it, but you know enough to have your suspicions. And you know it ain't me."

I backed away, trying to keep a few yards between us. He smiled. Noticed a line of sweat tracing the dent of his temple.

"Low-life Irishman," he said. "Two words that no one will have a problem believing. You're not everyone's darling anymore, are you?"

I took another step. He raised the gun.

"That's it," he said. "You're done, Carey. Arson'll get you behind bars. Murder'll get you hung."

I held still. "That's what you're going to tell them, is it? And then what? What are you going to tell them when the next bunch of gals goes missing, when the next family is struck dead, the next boarding house? When it gets to the company housing—then what? I'll already be rotting in jail."

"We both know what people around here will believe, and what they need to hear. And right now the mayor needs a killer."

"Too bad I haven't killed anyone."

"Maybe not," he said, approaching me. "But everyone within a hundred miles is going to hear about how a thieving, Irish killer murdered a flophouse full of men. Killed the Winthrop family, motive clear as well water. Killed the Fitzgerald boys. Killed Father Flaherty over at St. Mary's, strung him up. Your trademark."

Shook my head. He came closer.

"Don't you know you're the biggest killer this city's ever seen? Hell, maybe even the state."

He grabbed me by my collar with his free hand.

"The corpses," I said. "The shadows stalking the streets at night. The voices. The devil that's hiding in the middle of the city. You know it, just like I do. You put me away, none of that will stop. Only going to get worse."

"Mayor wants a killer—not a devil."

"You put me away, that devil isn't going anywhere. It won't stop."

"Then I'll find the next Irish killer and he can rot in my jail until we string him up. And when his lifeless body finishes kicking, I'm going to pose right next to it, have a photograph taken. Just like I'm going to do with yours."

He gave me that odd smile of his and raised the gun to my head.

"We're done chatting. Hands in front of you," he said, his eyes as black as the open end of the gun barrel.

I exhaled as though everything he'd said had taken the wind right out of me, and then I whipped the bag of Ieva's up from where it hung by my knee with the same speed that my pa had taught me to use with an uppercut. Put everything I had into it, bruises, grief, and all. Sent the gun out of his hand, to the ground by the canal. Before he had time to see where it went, I swung the bag down again, catching him hard across his forehead. He staggered back, hands to his head.

I kicked him right in the gut and he tripped over the stones at the lip of the canal, pinwheeling his arms as he dropped into the silty green water six feet below. Kicked the gun in after him where it sunk out of his reach. His bald head broke the surface with a gasp.

"Well, the mayor's got a devil, whether he wants it or not," I shouted. "But don't worry. Got an Irishman right here who's going to care of it."

I gathered up Ieva's bag and sprinted off across the railroad bridge, through the steaming afternoon.

39

A DROWNING GIRL

Nell pulled hard against the ropes. In her head, she swore and cursed—but she kept it behind her lips. They were in a side room of the church, off of the main chapel. A door on the other side yawned open into a stairwell leading down. Nell used every bit of strength she had—but the ropes across her chest and arms were too tight, digging into her skin, through her dress. She sat back.

"Maggie," she whispered.

Maggie slumped in a chair back to back with her own, the same ropes looped across the both of them. Nell whispered her name again, louder this time. Nell craned her neck to see the door. Liam had gone down there not a minute before. Nell shifted. Tried to push the chair back with her legs, which were free. It didn't move. She leaned her head back. Nell pressed her lips together and swung her head back, hitting the chair, but also nudging Maggie's head. Maggie groaned.

"Wake up," Nell whispered. "He caught us. We got to get out."

She looked out the door that led to the chapel. The sunlight faded on the stained glass.

"Nell..." Maggie said.

Nell shushed her. "Quiet. Lean back, exhale. Might loosen the ropes for me."

"What? Where—"

Steps came up the stairs. Nell leaned back to whisper to Maggie.

"Close your eyes. Fake asleep."

The tread reached the top and paused.

"You're awake. Open your eyes." Liam's voice was a cruel scrape. He walked over and stopped in front of Nell. She opened her eyes and glared at him—even as she wanted to look away, look anywhere but that hollow face. He'd been her favorite brother. A cruel smile cut his unshaven face.

"He blew a breath over what you took, whelp," he said. "And like a hungry jackal drawn to the lion's kill, you crept closer, thinking you could just steal what belongs him. Time to pay the price."

Nell spit, hitting his stomach. He ignored it and squatted in front of her. His eyes were the worst. The whites had gone yellowed and bloodshot, and the gray-green color had darkened to the color of moldy bread.

"He's waiting for you." The smile on his face widened. He stepped closer to her, untied the ropes. He wrenched Maggie to her feet. She looked around, dazed. Blood caked the back of her head.

"And you. You already know what he will do to you." He leaned in closer, his face touching her hair. "Your visions. Your glimpses. You'll wish you'd been born blind to anything beyond the world."

"Finn can help. We can help you, Liam," Maggie whispered.

"Finn is dead. Walked into our other trap. Smashed him and the other one like a fly," he said. "Not even worthy of using."

"What?" Maggie said.

"Dead. Him and the vile false priest."

Maggie collapsed to the marble floor. Liam turned back to

Nell, tightened up the ropes once more. He brought his face to hers.

"And you're next, little one. I think the master knows just the right friend of his for you. You'll enjoy it."

Nell closed her eyes as though blocking it out, as though holding back tears. With one more hard yank of the rope, he turned away. He lifted Maggie's still form into his arms and carried her to the stairs. Without a look back, he descended into the shadows.

Nell listened to his tread fade, then she pulled hard on her left arm—the rope had loosened as he'd untied Maggie, and he hadn't noticed. Holding still—hard as it'd been—had kept his attention from it. She pulled and wriggled. The fiber of the rope scraped the top layer of her skin off at the wrist, but she kept at it. The chapel grew dim. Holding back a yell, she pulled her arm free. Dots of blood appeared where the rope had pulled away skin. She ignored it and used that hand to dig away at the knots on her side. Liam's cruel taunts to Maggie floated up from the church's basement. Nell hurried, muttering to herself—and then the ropes fell away. She stood up, careful not to make a sound. Parts of her arms went to pins and needles. She shook them and turned to the door to the stairs.

"All right, All right," she whispered. "Now what?"

Run? Get the police? Find a knife?

Fading light filled the chapel, the stained glass afire with it. Door. Stairs. Who could help her if she ran? Police only ever tried to shoo her off, or grab her by the collar and yank her around.

Then I'll fight. I'm a Carey, she thought. She turned back to the side room, hurrying. At the top of the stairs, she paused, looked into the darkness. Her knees trembled.

"Dirty sodder," she whispered.

Quiet as a draught, she told herself. Took each step slowly, one after another, sinking below the late afternoon light. At the bottom, she stopped. A horrid feeling filled the musty air. Dim light filtered in through an unseen window. She heard Liam's rotted voice murmuring and headed in that direction. She passed from the small antechamber through a storage room. Beyond that was a wide cellar with a furnace, a coal bin down to its last dregs, and walls of bare fieldstone.

Bodies filled the corners. In the dim light, they looked grotesque. Liam's back was to her. Maggie stretched out on a table before him, not moving. He cinched another rope across her throat. Beyond him, a narrow coffin stood upright in the far corner, ten feet tall, the shape of it enough to burn into her nightmares.

She looked around for something to clobber him with, to shank him in the kidneys with. There was nothing but a coal shovel. She started for it, quiet as possible. After just a step, a heat erupted on her chest—and she realized that it'd started as soon as she'd come down the stairs.

Then she remembered.

She pulled the front of her dress forward at the collar, reached in, and pulled out what she'd taken from the priest lady, just before Maggie pulled them out of the flophouse. On a worn leather tie, the medallion was smooth and heavy, a color somewhere lighter than copper. The metal seemed alive to her fingers. A light came off of it. From the corner, wooden knocking erupted inside the tall coffin.

Nell slipped the necklace over her head. Light washed over her hand and a pure energy ran along her arm. Liam stopped what he was doing. He turned—but Nell jumped forward and pressed the medallion against the back of his neck. It sizzled like a brand, sinking into his flesh. He howled and staggered into the table that held Maggie. He spun on her, still yelling. She shoved the medallion into his mouth, jamming her hand into his face. He jerked as though struck by lightning, limbs thrashing. Nell punched him in the crotch for good measure. He was too busy tearing at his own face to notice. A light poured from his mouth, making his cheeks glow. His head slammed back and forth and a gagging ripped from his throat. A scorching smell filled the room.

"Choke on it!" Nell yelled. She grabbed one of his legs below the knee and pulled. He slid to the floor and flopped. A spray of dark blood gushed from his nose and mouth, trails even dripping from his ears. Then he went still. Not a muscle stirred on him, his face stuck in a grimace. She stepped right onto him but he was as dead as a sandbag.

"Mags, hurry," she said. She slapped Maggie's face until her eyes fluttered open. Nell looked for the knots on the rope that held her to the table. "Got him good, but we got to run the hell out of here."

The shadows stirred. Nell looked up. In the corners, pale bodies trembled, limbs moving. Sighs filled the air in fell voices. Nell looked behind her as the faint light from the other room winked out. Maggie had her head turned, eyes fixed on the tall coffin. She whispered something.

"What?" Nell said.

"Run, Nell. Right now. Don't stop. Just go."

Strange light from the medallion poured out from Liam's mouth. The bodies opened their eyes and their gazes found her, full of infernal anger. Nell backed away. A pale figure rose in the corner, followed by another nearby. Something slid in the coffin, and a scratching sound began.

"I'm thankful you're here, child."

The voice came from the coffin. Nell's breath clamped. A malice found its way past the lid, through the slit of blackness that appeared along the length of it. Nell stepped back. Her heart fluttered. The words hung in the silence, rotted carcasses.

"I've worried that broken and meek and rotted souls are my only reward for my foraging. Imagine my delight when I wake to see your flame, a light so pure, a glimmering shaft of gold in the murk. And a thief after my own heart."

The coffin lid shifted, and the thrumming voice grew clearer.

"Come, child. Cheer my spirit—and there'll be no end to what we can steal. A push of door, a thought, an exhalation, and everything can be yours, forever. But, come. Come to me."

Quiet laughter—the worst sound Nell ever heard—filled the cellar.

"Run, Nell—run!" Maggie yelled. That snapped Nell out of the reverie she'd been sliding into.

"But—"

"Go!"

Bodies swarmed Maggie and more came at Nell.

"I'll kill you all!" Nell yelled. She darted forward again and grabbed the leather tie hanging from Liam's mouth. She snapped the medallion out from between his teeth, clenched it in her hand. The bodies recoiled at the glare.

"Nell!" Maggie barked, using the same tone she'd used a hundred times before when Nell wouldn't listen. The lid of the coffin slammed open. Terror swept over her. She looked at Maggie, who stared back at her with wide eyes. She nodded, desperate. A shadow stood in the corner, reaching the ceiling.

Nell turned and darted for the stairs, racing up them, reaching for the last light of day as a drowning girl reaching for the surface of the water. She skidded out the door at the top. The colors of the stained glass dimmed. As she ran down the aisle, Maggie's scream of terror echoed up from the cellar, flying around in the empty church.

40

THIS IS HER

As I raced to St. Mary's, I replayed the sequence in my mind: Fitzgerald at the Everett; the young lad at the sawmill. Each a lair.

Killed Father Flaherty over at St. Mary's, strung him up. Your trademark.

It had to be. I dodged past the Union soldiers and police who patrolled the curfew, sticking to alleyways and empty lots. As the night came on, the glow of the burning Everett rose into the sky, giving the city a strange and mournful glare. Bells still rang and water engines with their teams pounded down the streets, heavy with water taken from the canals.

But there was more than that in Lawrence, that night—all around, a new breed of devils, of veln, were rising at that moment, heading out into the darkness. Wondered how many nights until they doubled their numbers. How many nights until they were free, every last devil from the abyss? Until they enslaved the rest of the city? Until they reached Boston? Weeks? Pictured cities and countryside empty during the days, horribly alive under the stars.

How far could they go?

I ignored my protesting bruises and torn muscles, and hurried until St. Mary's rose in front of me, its slate roof and bricks articulated against the fading sky. An old moon rose over the city. I glanced over the church, trying to decide the best way in, how I might hold tight to surprise for as long as possible, when I spotted the wagon. It was just out in front of the church, empty. The reins dragged on the ground and the team stood listless in the humid evening.

He got them. Somehow, he got them.

Thought kept screaming in my head, getting louder each time. I was too late, by half. Too late. I shook my head, trying to make it go away. My mouth dried up. The last of my old self fell away as I stood there hopeless on the darkening street before that church, seeing the stars coming out behind the weathered bronze cross atop the steeple.

Gone. My family. My dreams.

If I couldn't do another thing on this tired world, I was killing that veln, avenging everyone he took from me—with my bare hands if I had to. The sun was down, it was his time. I moved my feet just the same, right up to the front steps. As I reached the bottom of the granite steps, I saw a small shape up at the top, off to the side. A shadow slinking to the nearest window. My heart leaped.

"Nell?"

She froze, turned toward me. I rushed up the steps and took her into my arms. She tried to push me away, but I pulled her in, felt her trembling, all over her body. She held a cross—looked like she'd torn it from the wall somewhere. Tears of anger and terror cut through the ashes on her face, rolled hot onto my neck.

"He's got her, and I ran, and then I couldn't," she said, her words tumbling out. "I killed Liam. He ain't moving, gone deader than a rock."

"Where are the others?"

"Theo's got Rose. Came up after us. I made him run off with her, get her somewhere safe, get help."

"What about Maggie?"

"Down past the altar. Stairs." She wrenched herself from my grip and spat out the next words. "I want to kill him. So bad."

I looked to the dark interior of the church. Grabbed Nell by the shoulder, spun her toward the street, and gave her a shove.

"Leave him to me," I said. "You run, fast as you can. Find soldiers, tell them anything—but stay with them, don't be alone."

"No, he's going to—"

I shoved her. "No more lip. Go."

She paused, then headed down the steps, slow-footing it.

"I said run," I said. That time, she heeded me.

Sunset had passed, and night filled the valley. Beyond the horizon, I knew, the world was still alight. I held that thought in mind as I climbed through the window into the poisoned blackness of St. Mary's. My shoes scuffed the window frame as I dropped inside. A terrible silence held the huge, empty room. A stench I knew well filled the air. Up at the front of the church, rotted moonlight angled in, illuminated beams starting where Christ's face and outstretched hands were missing in the stained glass.

Nothing moved.

I avoided the pews and stuck to the side, heading up to the altar, my pulse knocking, my eyes scanning the darkness for any movement, in front, above, behind. I spotted the black rectangle of the doorway that Nell mentioned. The evil seeped out of there, bringing with it the rank stench of the veln. I put my hand in Ieva's bag, not taking my eyes from the darkness before me.

A pale figure stepped out of the doorway. I stopped. Stared hard.

"Maggie?"

"I see two of you," she said. Her voice had gone husky, sultry.

"Are you All right?"

"Such dreams. Please hold me."

She opened her arms. The top of her dress hung loose and I saw her fair skin. Noises came from the murky dark behind her.

"We'll get you help," I said.

"It's as lovely as slipping into the soil of your own grave. You'll see."

My heart clenched. Her voice, her face—she had me frozen, crushed between love and fear, between grief and hope. She approached. Even then, my belly tightened at the sight of her lovely neck, at the curve of her shoulder.

"We owe him. We killed his best servant," she said. Her voice was deeper and held a promise of something beyond anything we'd done the night before. Her eyes shimmered as she got closer. "And we can help his brothers—help them find new homes."

"Maggie, let's go, I'll help you. Get you out of his grip," I said.

She leaped at me, slamming into me, knocking me onto the marble floor. I tried to wrestle her away, but she held on, her skin rubbing my own, her legs wrapping me with unbelievable strength. My head slammed, hard. She clawed at me, bit at me, breathed musky air into my face. I rolled her sideways and her head cracked against the corner of a pew. Scrambled free and skidded up to my feet.

Behind Maggie, devils stirred, coming out of the black doorway. Their eyes shone in their fiendish faces, watching me like a pack of wolves going in for the kill. Maggie stood.

"He wants you himself," she whispered, a cruel smile ruining her lovely face.

The other veln—a score of them, in various stages of deformation from the corpses they inhabited—parted. Something ancient and foul filled the space. Warm winds stirred, and I heard a low growl. The veln stepped through the doorway, ducking his ghastly head, horns curled and black. He shambled forward to the altar, and I saw his full form as he stepped into the moonlight.

Wisps of flame danced over his roasted body. Burnt, scorched, broken, destroyed. A devastating beauty, ruined. Damned.

He turned, tilted his head. Huge wings opened in back of him, blocking the stained glass.

"So you wriggled free of my surprise."

His voice didn't match his form, not one bit. Where I'd expected a gravelly, shredded sound, his words came out, sweet and sonorous poetry. As he spoke, a rank wind filled the room. The other devils filed out into the pews, a congregation of the damned. Maggie stood watching me, tilting her own head, running a finger along her lower lip, cocking her hip at a lurid angle.

"Perhaps I gave you too little credit," he said.

"He's beautiful," Maggie said.

The veln watched me.

"Wouldn't you like to join her?" he said. Something akin to a smile broke across his face, an eruption of flames dancing across his throat. "You can have each other every night as you serve me. Have each other like beasts."

Terrible as those words were, any resolve I'd entered that church with melted away. Seemed as fine an idea as I'd ever come across. I took a step toward Maggie. Her smile widened, and she opened her mouth.

The door behind me slammed opened. Theo stood in the open doorway, bringing in a spill of street lanterns with him.

"Got thirty angry Irishmen here, ready for a fight!" he shouted.

Then she did it. Nell. Somehow, she'd crept back into the church up near the altar—which she leapt off of, holding something in her hand that glowed like a chunk of the sun itself. I'd seen that before, and in a flash it clicked into place: she'd stolen it from Ieva, the medallion. She landed on the back of the veln, screaming out a string of curses at him, grabbing onto one of his wings. The veln sprawled forward, his wings flaring, the howl that burst from his animal mouth loud enough to shatter half the windows in St. Mary's. A flash of light exploded. The other devils jumped back, away from the glare.

I leapt over a pew and hurtled up the center aisle. As the veln struggled to fling Nell off his neck, I jumped, landing hard on his head, feeling his terrible horns pressing into my side. He twisted. I slammed the silver spike into his opening mouth, then brought the mallet down with every bit of rage I'd ever carried. The silver cried out, the blows clanging off the walls. The veln's eyes—black with golden slits—widened. Tongues of flame rose from his nostrils, his ears, shot along his back and limbs like lantern oil catching the blue of a match.

"Be clear about this," I said, hammering hard at the spike, gasping the words out. "This ain't me sending you back to Hell. It's Sister Ieva. Ieva Lazdin. This. Is. Her."

Slam. Slam. Slam.

I slammed the hammer one final time, then reached forward and yanked Nell off of him. Flames rose; a desert wind whipped through the space. The veln howled and thrashed, the same light of the medallion flaring from the spike. Smoke filled the air. I jumped off him, staggering back. His flesh moved faster than I could mark—and turned to cinders, some vital force pressing downward into the marble, into the ground. Into the abyss. A howling filled the air.

The other devils fled, running from the conflagration and light, bursting out of windows, through the doors. In another instant, all went still. Ashes floated down. A giant scorch mark darkened the floor before us. In the middle, the medallion glowed.

"You stole it," I said.

"I didn't mean to," Nell said. "I was just looking at it. And Maggie came by—I meant to put it back. You got to believe me."

Whether she was lying or not, I realized that if she hadn't swiped it, the medallion would be buried beneath the inferno that the Everett had become, lost along with Ieva and any chance we might have had to kill the veln. We wouldn't have had a hope.

"I believe you," I said.

Next to the medallion was the silver spike, and one more thing: the key, otherworldly, glinting. Ieva had called it the *Signum Profundum*. Key to the Abyss.

"Nell, don't even think about it," I said.

She kept looking at it. Light shot up through the floor, blinding beams of it. It mixed with shadows. The church shook. I pulled Nell forward, shoved her down the aisle to Theo, who stood gaping halfway to the door.

"Take her out," I said.

Nell caught herself, looked over at Maggie, lying on the floor, her body rocking with seizures, her eyes rolled up. I remembered what Ieva had said about the killing of a veln being fatal to a verg, the soul amputated, ripped from the body. Nothing but scraps remaining, worse than death. I knelt next to her. Nell tried coming over, but Theo took her arm.

"Fuckin' let me go," she said, trying to pull away.

"Theo, go," I said. I put my hand on Maggie's trembling shoulder. "Everyone out."

When I stepped outside a short time later, a crowd gathered. Irish and Yankee, soldiers trying to break it up, police shouting to clear the street. I found Theo and Nell, shaking off the hands of a policeman who tried to keep me back.

"Where's Rose?" I said.

"Safe," Theo said. "My sisters have her, just up the road."

Nell grabbed my hand and yanked. Her face was streaked with tears.

"Where is she?" she said. I took her into a hug.

"She's free," I whispered into her ear. "She's free, Liam's free. And we'll be All right, too. Don't forget it."

The moon hung between the chimneys across the river, and I held Nell tight.

41

THIS LONESOME, LOVELY WORLD

Autumn wind shook the rigging of the ship. I stood at the rail, watching the waves catching the fading daylight. Ireland lay behind, to the east in the oncoming night. America lay beneath the sunset to the west. The sails and masts creaked. In places, it was hard to tell where the sea met the sky.

It'd taken another two grim months before we got the last of them. Me and Theo. Barley and a few other men we trusted. They'd spread out into the countryside, onto farms, into the nearby towns and beyond, up into New Hampshire. Hard work, thankless—but each devil we sent back to the fiery pit was yet another victory for Ieva. I kept thinking of her, hoping to feel her presence. But I didn't. You don't. The work was her work though —and that's what mattered. I'm certain that's what she'd have told me, too.

Nell had wanted to come with us, each bloody time. Kept her away most times, though on occasion she followed us uninvited. Wondered who in the world would handle that in a wife. Better still, she kept insisting she and Theo were meant to be. Don't

know how he felt about that, but I could imagine. Now Barley—
well, he got fired from the paper. They thought he'd been hitting
the bottle. Couldn't sell his story to anyone, not with the war
raging, not with a state full of hard-headed folks working to
supply it and get ahead. Barley said Mayor Oliver was behind it,
and I thought that about right. Said he'd put it all in a book, if no
one would give him any inches of news column. Then he rolled
up his sleeves and joined us on our hunts.

I cupped a match and lit my pipe.

"The rolling of the sea ain't bad enough that you got to make
me green with that smoke?"

I turned. My ma shuffled up, holding to the rail, a cloak
wrapped around her, her hair blowing in strands. Most of the
passengers had gone back into the steerage to get out of the wind
and nightfall.

"You should be inside, Ma."

"As should you."

"I'll be along shortly. Have one of the sailors help you down."

She reached into her cloak and pulled something out.

"Take this," she said. She pressed it into my hand. String with
something metal. "Bit of luck for you, from your Aunt Nancy."

"Thoughtful."

"Promise you'll wear it. St. Peter."

"Is it, now?"

She closed my fingers around the trinket.

"Such luck we've had," she said. "I'm worried. There's a war.
It's not home. Praying don't ease my mind, neither."

"Don't worry, Ma. You'll love America."

I helped her back and got a sailor to help her on the stairs. I
had one more thing to do. Went to the stern. Reached into my
pocket, pulled out a leather sack. Inside, the heavy weight felt
wrong—as ever. Whatever it was made of, I wasn't familiar with
it, nor was Nagle. Think no one else would've been, neither.

I didn't take that cursed key out of the sack before I hurled it into the middle of the Atlantic. Hit the water with a faint splash that got lost in the wake of the ship.

"And there may you rot," I said.

The light of sunset behind me faded, as it does, leaving me in the starlit darkness. Course, by then I'd learned that some things don't fade at all: heartache and love both, staying as clear as the moment they happened. Seasons and years and dreams alike can slip into forgotten shadow. What's left burning marks the path of your time in the world. I used to think I could gather it up just so if I worked hard enough at it. Well, I couldn't.

Out of the west, a chill wind cut through the darkness, flapping the sails over my head, tugging at my coat. On a ship, again. Crossing over from Ireland, again. This time, though, I wasn't a boy, hiding on a ship he'd stolen onto. Was I any less determined than I'd ever been? I looked out over the dark ocean, looking for the spot now lost where I'd tossed the key, thinking of it still sinking into the black. Hell, no. The Irish ran too strong in me.

Knocked the embers out of my pipe, watched them glow for a moment as they fell. Before I turned to go down belowdecks, I took a good look up to the stars that hung over this lonesome, lovely world, scattered all across the sky.

~

KEEP up to date on my upcoming books, novellas, and exclusives by joining my private newsletter.

AS A WELCOME, I'll send you a free ebook of Sorcery of the Stony Heart *(the prequel novella to The Books of Conjury), along with* A Spark of Will: The Trans-Atlantic Diary of August Swaine, *an exclusive novelette you can't get anywhere else.*

. . .

I T'S EASY, *just sign up here:* **Join Newsletter**

ALSO BY KEVAN DALE

The Governor's Witch

Ghost at Dusk

The Magic of Unkindness

The Grave Raven

The Halls of Midnight

Sorcery of the Stony Heart

The Books of Conjury: The Complete Trilogy

Revolutionary Dead

Shades of the Grave: A Horror Collection

Find out more at www.kevandale.com